WHAT O

"Amazing - Bernheim is
"Inspirational, compelling, and extremely well written. This author will change people's lives. A rare find - a life changer. Read it twice." ★★★★★
LA Book Club Review "Los Angeles Book Club"

"WHAT A MAGNIFICANTLY TIMELY MESSAGE..." ★★★★★
"A novel that masterfully brings the story of Job to the 21st Century with a literary twist, *It is about the truth of the soul and deep spirituality that go beyond religious acts to a romance with God... Michael's Reward is again proof that God's eyes are upon the righteous and his ears are attentive to their prayers.*
Dr. Jesse Miranda
President and Founder of the Miranda Center
Chief Executive Officer – NHCLC

"THERE IS A GREAT ANNOINTING ON THIS BOOK." ★★★★★
"I read until 2:00 a.m. in the morning for two nights because I couldn't wait to see what was going to happen next even though I knew Job very well. This book not only speaks of the Lord's love and faithfulness, but also gives hope to anyone in any walk of life. *I highly recommend this book as someone who has many customers who have come in and said how much this book spoke to them.*"
Sandy Westad
New Beginnings Bible Bookstore, Owner
Anacortes, Washington

"A TRULY GRIPPING BOOK" ★★★★★
"I could not stop reading until I was done. It is not a re-telling or a re-imagining of the story of Job; it is as though the book had been written today and been named the Book of Michael. It is an inspired story with images and lessons of faith, hope, loss, powerlessness, and triumph. Even the format of the book makes it more readable - easy on the eyes, but food for thought and prayer."
Alberto Juan Negron, Pastor

"A REAL PAGE TURNER!" ★★★★★
"It's an amazing journey that will have you riveted. Moving, with great insight into human nature. **A compelling read you will not be able to put down**!"
Anna Cunningham
Author and Marketing Consultant

"VERY INSPIRING BOOK" ★★★★★
"This book captures a modern day realism that will hit you right between the eyes. Mario's ability to capture the passion and the faith of a conviction not seen is truly amazing, he is able to take a time honored story from a present day perspective. The reading is engaging and *I found myself not able to put it down until I was to the end... an entire afternoon well spent!* I bought several copies of this book to hand out to family and friends."
Chris Masten, Claremont, California

"Amazing story that will stay with you forever" ★★★★★
"Michael lost everything, but never his faith. That was the point that touched me the most. Never did he stop loving or believing in his heavenly Father. I have told this story to almost everyone I know. I have purchased the book to have in my coffee house and I encourage everyone to read it."
Cheryl Jose, Menomonee Falls, Wisconsin

Michael's Reward ©

A novel by

MARIO BERNHEIM

This book is dedicated to God,
Who knows what I'm going to do,
before I do.

www.michaelsreward.com

Cove Design by – Jennings Design/www.jenningsdesignonline.com
Author photo credit – Peter Duke
Copy editor – Martina Lewis
Cover Photo Credit - ©istockphoto/Marco Onofri
Cover Photo Credit - ©istockphoto/Renars Jurkovskis
Copyright © 2008 Mario Bernheim. All rights reserved.
First Edition – June, 2011
Library of Congress – TXu 1-596-886
ISBN – 978-0-578-00747-2
Published by Bernheim Press
Printed in the United States of America

DISTRIBUTED BY DELPHI DISTRIBUTION, INC.

WINNER 2012 INDIE EXCELLENCE AWARD RELIGOUS FICTION

Thank you

Mr. Bernheim would like to thank –
Sabrina Grace Rongstad, for being the first writer in the family,
Pam Smith, for being a lifelong river of inspiration,
Bette Olson, for making me believe I could do anything,
Brian Stein Shuster, living the walking definition of true friendship,

and my wife *Michelle*, whose love elevates this journey through life
and has always been there to catch me.

and special thanks to Marika Flatt, who was the first to believe.

God Bless,

Mario Bernheim

Table of Contents

FOREWORD

We live under the universally accepted principle that good things happen to good people and bad things happen when we're bad. And this equation that some call judgment and some call karma, ("what-so ever ye sow, so shall ye reap")* cannot be broken. We rely on the hope that the scales of judgment work magnificently best when it is blind and is immune to partiality. Looking at history, we see that we have always struggled with the deep causes of why bad and catastrophic events can violently shift our lives, when no wrong had occurred.

But what happens when this universal principle gets cast aside and disasters strike when there are no misdeeds, or wrongdoing? We search out for the *causes* of such misfortune and false accusations. All the while *knowing* that even God knows we are innocent.

This story of Michael is about a man who spreads so much love, faith and charity throughout his world and wherever he went that Satan himself noticed Michael's soul light shining brightly. And because Michael was a spiritual warrior, not even Satan could break his faith.

You will find yourself in Michael no matter your choice of religion, no matter your economic status, nor gender, nor race. It is written for a changing world at the epicenter of a great spiritual battle. It is designed to show how you are the pawn and perhaps player in this sometimes visible and invisible war. *And the best part is that you decide how you are going to engage the enemy of your happiness.* You ultimately decide how you're going to play your part through these incredible times, in this very real spiritual war, playing out on earth.

Mario Bernheim

*The Apostle Paul, Galatians 6:7

FOR JENNIFER -

Do not judge a book just by

chapter one,

and do not judge a life by just

one chapter.

Mario Bernheim

CHAPTER ONE

HEAVEN

I've always been captivated by the horizon line out on the ocean because that is where heaven and earth come face to face. And you can never touch that beauty because the line is perpetually moving away from you. Is untouchable beauty to be found under the definition of heaven? I believed there is a heaven after we die. But I also believed that heaven can exist on earth. And my heaven on earth was far more than I could have ever imagined. I lived in a five thousand square foot home with a four-car garage on two acres in the upper hills of Santa Barbara, California in a neighborhood called Montecito.

In the hills above Montecito and its many mansions is a place called the *Tea Gardens*. Behind a fence and up a quarter mile at the end of a paved road you'll find a terrace with three arches. With fifteen foot tall columns connected by arches and benches that face the ocean, one can sit for hours. The trestle extending from the arches to the railing is thick with purple irises and an enormous purple bougainvillea. There is no house, just a slab of cement with one magnificent view of the town, the ocean, and the distant Channel Islands. Montecito folklore has it that a wealthy woman, in memory of her deceased husband, erected this isolated gem. She was driven there every afternoon to have tea and spend time longing for her lost beloved. This fairytale spot is a reflection of what heaven might be like.

From down in Santa Barbara, I could look up and find the arches. Even at the bottom of State Street, or the Pacific Coast Highway, I can sometimes make out the arches sitting completely alone, faraway on the mountain slope.

Daily, from my backyard patio I watched heaven itself radiating beautiful sunsets out over the ocean and across the Santa Ynez

Mountains right behind us. It's such a stroke of God's artistry, that one could forget to breathe, taking in so much beauty.

One Saturday afternoon, a week before Christmas, as we tore across the blue ocean waters off the coast at the helm of my 58-foot yacht, the *Oh Happy Day*, I had flashes of heaven on earth. The shining sun radiated particles of gold across the blue waters. From a well of gratitude I shouted an explosive "Thank You" through my huge smile as my arms reached for the blue sky for all He's given me: my family, my career, and my perfect health (nothing more than a cold and I'm forty-two). I believed that part of this, or I should say *all of this,* was because God allowed me to have it. And I never forgot it is He who gave me this caviar life.

I never allowed any room for guilt in my mind for having all of these gifts. The gatekeeper that keeps guilt a safe distance away is tithing. I remembered God's law for tithing. Tithing is good. It takes just ten percent and that makes you a part of God's universal flow of good will. Personally, I've watched tithing pay dividends in more good deeds over decades of time. My attitude was, if you hang close enough to the big laws, the big laws will protect you. I'm guessing that in most major religions in the world, God desires ten percent. So there's no way of getting around it, wherever we live or however way we worship Him. I believe I was living the life God fully intended me to live.

In the early seventies, deep in the gospel world of Charleston, South Carolina I was the lone six-year-old white boy in my neighborhood who would walk himself to the all African-American church a block away every Sunday morning and sometimes evening. At this impressionable age I watched grown-ups praise God with their soul. And the congregation didn't seem to mind my six-year-old restlessness as I moved from pew to pew to pew to pew to pew.

While attending Cal Tech in Los Angeles, I met my future wife Joanne on a church winter-camp retreat for young adults in Lake Arrowhead, about ninety miles northeast of the city. The moment I laid eyes on her, I was struck. No one ever told me that love at first sight is like getting sideswiped by a speeding bulldozer. It is an obsession floating in euphoria. But beware! There's definitely a concussion.

We dated two years before we married, when we were both twenty-four years old. And for the first three years of our marriage she helped me get my Masters of Science in Mechanical Engineering at Cal Tech. I've known her longer than anyone else in my life.

Joanne has spent the last four months redesigning the cabin and galley of our new 58′ cruiser.

Passing the Channel Islands to our south at twenty-five knots, under the sun, all I felt were waves of happiness.

We stole quality time with the kids out on the *Oh Happy Day*, where friends couldn't drop by and cell phone range was miles behind us.

When Joanne appeared at the top of the stairs with lunch, I was again, appreciative. Rachel, my fifteen-year-old daughter, followed her mom with drinks as I traded the steering wheel for my sandwich. Joanne at the helm was unpredictable. She liked to make the letter "s" across the waters. She's a born show-off and today was no exception. As I bit into the sandwich, she swung the wheel abruptly and caused me to smear the sandwich halfway across my face. We laughed, but Rachel laughed the loudest. I never knew I could get so much satisfaction just hearing Rachel laugh at the silliest things. I took it to mean a sign of innocence. And I'm convinced that innocence, at any age, keeps us young.

I got part of the sandwich in my mouth, but I was finished with her antics and headed down to the galley to hang with my two sons.

I slid into the booth next to my sixteen-year-old John, and across from him sat his thirteen-year-old brother Edwin. Edwin's toughest issue in life was that he lived in the shadow of John. They were watching the end of a football game on television. And why did I put a TV onboard the ship?

John asked, "Can I go rock climbing with Ray and some friends?" I consented to let him go because he was always safety conscious.

Edwin could always be relied on to ask the same question: "Can I go?"

I explained to him, "Edwin, it's not my place to invite you to go on an outing with your brother and his friends. If they want you to go, they'll invite you. Otherwise, there are ten other things we can do."

Edwin asked suspiciously, "Together?"

"Not necessarily," I told him, letting him off the hook. The boys got up from the table. Through a mouthful of food I asked, "Where are you going?"

John answered, "To the fly bridge."

"I came down to finish lunch with you and now you're leaving me," I protested.

"Dad, we're not leaving you. How can we leave you when we're out in the middle of the ocean?" Edwin retorted. But sometimes Edwin's remarks were just a little too cute. He tested the edge of sarcasm but rarely crossed it.

"Sure, go ahead, I'll be all right," I said, whining some more. I liked whining at times. Sometimes I actually got what I wanted. But this was not one of those. They left me with commercials on the TV. I channel surfed until I stumbled onto the Travel channel showing an image of the blue ocean, identical to the ocean outside the starboard window. I chuckled at the coincidence and then turned it off. I didn't come all the way out here to watch the ocean on TV.

I looked around at the sleek stainless steel galley Joanne had remodeled. On the port wall I saw a new photo she had recently hung. It's of the entire family up on the fly bridge taken a couple weeks earlier. I remember the moment Ralph, my best friend and attorney, took this photo of us. We were all smiling from a place of genuine happiness. We hugged each other as Ralph froze our happiness in Technicolor as proof to the world that paramount joy filled our family. It was the perfect photo.

As much as I wanted to shut out the real world, I kept thinking about business. I forced myself to think about something else and climbed my way back up to the skipper's chair.

A couple hours later, back at the dock, I slid the *Oh Happy Day* in her slip at the yacht club. I logged our hours and noticed it was only 3:30 p.m. I liked that there was still half an afternoon left to do things.

A jeep full of teenage boys pulled up to the wharf gate. They came to pick John up to go rock climbing. Joanne went to greet them and talk a bit. Shortly after, she walked back to me while I secured the boat.

"See what I just did?" she asked.

It's a trick question. I could smell one a mile away and hesitantly asked, "What did you just do?"

"I walked over there and I got close enough to look at them, listen to them, and smell them. I got in their face, just to let them know I'm not above getting up close to smell out any bad behavior."

I looked at her and said, "Wow, I'm suddenly afraid of you."

When we got home, Joanne and Rachel decided to go Christmas shopping. Edwin got on the phone and found a better offer than spending it with his dad. This meant I was left alone to get some work done. In my office I opened up the Pentagon bid on my computer. Was I was doing this out of habit? All the while I knew the bid was in the top drawer at my company office ready to fly in a FedEx envelope. Even the cover letter was already written and just waiting for my signature. It was all done and prepared before we left for Christmas vacation, so out of habit I opened it on my computer, again.

I found an envelope with receipts from a trip to DC a couple weeks earlier. I recall the initial presentations we had at the Pentagon with several high ranking military officers who are going to ultimately decide whether or not our company, BriMar Industries, will get the new Blackhawk fuselage contract. Charles McGraw, the company president, went to help pitch the sale by bonding with the brass. He left it up to me to pitch the numbers and specifications.

As senior vice-president for BriMar, it was up to me to make sure those deals come to us. So far, I had an impressive ratio of wins over losses and that's why they kept me around at my gigantic salary.

I delivered enormous profits for the company, and they showed their recognition with super-sized bonuses. And the board did show their appreciation this bonus season with a check for half a million dollars.

I figured Charles had another five years left as president and perhaps one day that office would be mine. But until then, I had nothing to complain about. He was my boss and I valued his impressive leadership skills. He had a keen eye for looking ahead at the long-term business landscape, and he never panics.

Charles was warm and friendly outside an office environment. Joanne and I have had him and his wife Charlotte over for dinner too many times to count.

I reviewed the bid presentation we planned on sending just after the first of the new year. With all the required signatures showing that my executive peers signed off on this ever-important bid, I'll sign the cover letter and ship it out the day we return after the first of the New Year. I'd been so consumed by this bid for the past eight months, I've watched many other projects fall by the wayside. Yet the potential profit was a staggering one hundred and twenty million dollars.

I lost two hours in the details of the numbers and surfaced in a small panic. It didn't matter, I reminded myself. It was only Saturday.

Sunday morning arrived, streaming with sunlight piercing our dark master bedroom. I reached over to find that Joanne had already gotten out of bed. Slowly I made my way downstairs and to the veranda to pour myself a cup of coffee. I went looking for her and followed her distant voice to the gift-wrapping room. I heard her murmuring on her cell phone, and as I approached she quickly ended her conversation. I'd say it was almost suspicious.

Every morning of our lives we greeted each other with a hug and a kiss. I looked at the gifts she'd bought and asked, "Who is this one for?"

"Samantha, Rachel's gymnastics coach," she answered. I left her to her wrapping and went back to the veranda and my coffee, and the Sunday paper, and the view. It's always about the view.

Looking out across my backyard lawn I could see for miles up and down the coast. The visibility in December can be infinite. The Channel Islands looked so close, I could see details in the landscape. Although the marina and yacht club are miles away, I could make out the docks, and through the telescope I could actually make out the *Oh Happy Day.*

I savored the perfection of the moment and started thanking Him for this day. But alas, any quiet perfect morning can be ruined by a pack of groggy teenagers. And just like every other Sunday morning, we rustled them into their clothes and got them in the car by 9:40.

As I drove down a main neighborhood street in Montecito, we passed a colossal mansion. It is a soft white French chateau with three floors and scattered majestic architectural touches. With huge deep purple canopies protecting the windows, it's strikingly beautiful. The four Greek Corinthian columns guard the nineteen-foot high front doors. The long driveway ends in a circular path around an elaborate water fountain, making it all look very regal. It is set back from the street with a half-acre of nothing but a green carpet of lawn, giving the chateau huge vistas. Every time we drive by, it calls out for our glance and attention. Its size and beauty are so pronounced, it's become a local landmark. And that speaks volumes when your address is on mansion row.

John asked, "Dad, how much do you think that mansion's worth?"

"Guessing, I'm figuring around sixteen million dollars," I said, shrugging my shoulders. John shook his head.

"John, you're just jealous because that's not our house," Rachel said accusingly.

Joanne remarked, "Yes, they have a splendid mansion, but are they really happy? They probably argue and have family squabbles over money all the time. How could they be happy? They're probably not even going to church."

That morning, Pastor Ryan preached on the subject of "Bargaining with God." From the pulpit he sermonized, "There is no bargaining with the Almighty, also known as the Omnipotent. What possible bargaining position can you claim when approaching the Maker of everything you see, everything you hold? What could you bring to the table that would make Him stretch His arm on your behalf? What possible bargaining chip could you offer Him who *is* everything?"

Pastor Ryan went on: "Besides, you try to bargain with God not knowing what the future may hold. When you make promises to God, you set a condition of your love for Him, because a promise usually entails something for something. When was the last time you promised God anything without asking for anything? The Creator does not have to bargain with you. He'll have His own way every time, like it or not. There is no getting your way without Him allowing you to have it. Rest assured that His overriding *will* comes to pass every time. All you can bring is an open heart and a prayer. And if it doesn't show results, then believe that it is not in your best soul interest. He knows the future and the past, and that's why He withholds things from us."

Occasionally, I noticed a few friends and co-workers sitting with their families. I smiled, realizing how blessed I was to have so many good friends here.

Focusing back on Pastor, he said, "Our blessings come from the fact and truth that God is infinite love. God's love is the most powerful force permeating the farthest reaches of the known and unknown universe."

I noticed Claire, my assistant and friend, was sitting alone, again. I spent more awake time with her than I did my own kids. And it was a real gift to see her coming to church. What that did was set a level of respect for how we should conduct ourselves towards each other. She's just young enough to do anything she wants, but old enough to have old-fashioned good manners. I'm surprised no man has married her, but I can only imagine that she has such high expectations.

When the sermon was over, we stood in line with the congregation on our way out the front door. As we approached Pastor Ryan, I shook his hand and told him how much I appreciated the message in his sermon.

I said, "Thank you, Pastor, we'll see you next Sunday." I said those very words to him every Sunday as a matter of ritual.

Stepping into the sunlight, it was another beautiful Sunday afternoon. As we walked across the parking lot to the Range Rover, in my peripheral vision I saw a homeless man standing in the distant corner of the parking lot. He was looking at the exiting crowd with a look that spoke desperation. I felt as if I had to do something. I said to the family, "I'll meet you at the car, just go on." I tossed the keys to John and walked away towards the corner of the lot near the street.

When I got closer to the homeless man, I motioned for him to follow me around a van where we could not be seen by the other members of the church. Handing him a hundred and fifty dollars made me feel like lecturing him, as I did not want him to waste it. I suggested that he spend it wisely. Who was I to tell this poor man how to spend what was now his money? I wouldn't want anyone telling me how to spend my money, so I could only suggest with a tone of voice that showed some level of compassion and direction. Sensing his appreciation, I hoped he was not going to misuse it.

When I got to the car, Edwin asked, "Where did you go, Dad?"

I replied, "Just helping out someone who needed some help." On our way home, I swung south to Yanonali Street to the Santa Barbara Men's Shelter to drop off some shoes, clothes, and overused designer jackets.

When we arrived, John and I jumped out and took armfuls of jackets and bags of clothes inside the lobby. We handed the items to a staff member in the main room. The guests were scattered about the large open room. Some were talking and laughing. Some were reading, some looked sad, and others just stared.

Driving back to the house, I looked forward to napping on the veranda and eating some lunch. But I knew that sometime that afternoon I would have to sneak out and buy some Christmas gifts.

As we pulled into our garage, Joanne said, "I'll start making some lunch for everybody." As we walked away from the car, I headed to the back kitchen door. Whereas, Joanne and the kids headed towards the front door.

I stepped through the back kitchen door and into the kitchen. As I turned the corner to the living room, I was startled to see people silently crouched down behind furniture looking at the front door. I froze. The nearest body to me was Claire about five feet from me, looking at the front door. If I were coming through the front door, she'd be hiding behind a pillar. She turned and looked right at me. And then she screamed.

Everyone turned around and through their utter shock and laughter, managed to scream, "Surprise!"

I yelled back at them, "Haa, surprise!"

And then an angry Joanne ran up behind me, frantically yelling, "I thought you were right behind me! You were supposed to be right behind me!" The whole room was laughing. And they did surprise me.

Pastor Ryan stepped out of the crowd with a blown-up check that was the exact duplicate of the check I gave him a couple weeks earlier in the privacy of his office. I looked at him, not believing he was doing this to me. I had been ambushed by my friends and bushwhacked by my pastor.

He stood beside me with one arm around my shoulders and the other holding the two feet by three feet half a million dollar check with my signature made payable to the church.

Deep inside, I just wanted to disappear. I screamed inside my head, "I can't believe this is going on!" But my outer shell, still in shock, smiled and laughed as the crowd sang "For He's a Jolly Good Fellow." I prayed, "Dear Lord, would you just take me now, kill me now before they finish the song?" When it was over, it got worse.

A couple fellows from the church Youth Group rolled in a table on wheels with an architectural display model of the new youth center with miniature shrubbery, etc. Wow, I was lost for words, and then when I read the lettering on the building model, I wanted to jump out of my skin. It read, "The Joanne Whiley Youth Center." I looked at Joanne, now giggling like a nine-year-old school girl pointing out her name to a girlfriend.

I kept smiling as my laughter turned to silence. And then back to laughter. Internally, I just wanted to kill someone, maybe start with myself? Pastor? Joanne? Too many choices. So, I shook Pastor Ryan's hand and stood at attention while someone took a photo of us holding the check.

Ralph shouted, "Say something, Michael."

I searched for words in my head. "I just want to say that what I did was what anyone else would have done---and thanks for ambushing me. The Whiley family is now taking donations. You can drop your money by the front on your way out the door. Thank you, now go home." Everyone broke into laughter.

Joanne shouted, "Lunch is served on the veranda."

I turned to Claire and said, "Nobody listens to me."

Claire smirked, "I do, but only at the office." And then she turned and walked away.

I turned to Joanne. "When you said you were going to make lunch for everybody, I didn't think you meant *everybody*. How long have you been planning this?"

Joanne boasted, "Since Pastor Ryan called me the very afternoon you gave him the check. We've been planning this little shin-dig ever since."

Jokingly, in my head I thought, "If only that check had bounced, I would have saved myself all of this." I took a deep breath.

I turned to Pastor Ryan privately and as the crowd disbursed, I whispered, "Can I see you in my office?" Pastor Ryan followed me to my office and I made sure to close the door. I thought to myself that I didn't want to sit behind my desk and appear disrespectful to a man with his connections. With a sigh of disbelief, I slumped into the sofa next to him. I started, "Pastor, do you remember when I gave you that check?"

I recalled a couple weeks ago signing the cashier's check at my desk at BriMar. I slid it into an envelope and then into my jacket pocket. I drove to the church and entered the office door. Wendy Schmidt, Pastor Ryan's secretary, was at the church that Monday afternoon. I stepped into Pastor Ryan's office as he greeted me with his warmth and openness. He walked me to the chair across from his desk. As he took his chair, I reached for the envelope. I pulled it out and said (not knowing the day would come when I would regret saying these words), "Pastor Ryan, for some time now I've been feeling God speaking to me about giving a donation to the church, and, although I give weekly, I just thought this might be of use for the youth center that I know you're trying to build."

Pastor Ryan opened the envelope and took out a check made out to the First Calvary United Church in the amount of $500,000. He sat with his dropped jaw and his mouth opened for a while. When he snapped out of it he said, "I don't know what to say."

I replied, "You don't have to say anything."

Pastor Ryan found his posture again and looked at me with sincere appreciation in his tone. "Michael, thank you so much for being such an inspiring man. You have made the youth center possible. Up to now, it was just a dream, but now, with your contribution we're going to help so many young people stay out of trouble and find a place where they'll feel like they're among true friends. WOW."

Holding the check in his hand, he walked around the desk and gave me a hug. Naturally, I returned the hug as I felt his relief flow right out of him. Apparently, he'd been stressed out over how the promised youth center was ever going to become a reality. He shook my hand and looked me in the eyes. "God is going to bless you, Michael, you can rest assured."

Inside I felt good, a bit elated too, thinking that maybe I had an extra chip lying on God's table in this game of my life.

He continued, "I believe this is a sign from God that our ministry is to go full tilt ahead."

In that instant an alarm went off in my head. I alerted him that I did not want my name on the youth center. "So just do me a huge favor, please do not put my name on it. You have to promise me that," I insisted.

Pastor Ryan replied, "But don't you think that people should know that there are still good and generous people out there? You're an excellent example to all our church members and many who aren't."

I didn't care where he was going with this; I just didn't want my name on it. "Please Pastor, promise you won't put my name on it," I pleaded. I continued explaining my motivation. "Pastor, I'm trying to practice the scripture passage 'Don't let your left hand know what your right hand is doing.' "

"Of course, if you don't want your name on it, we can call it something else. I'll respect your wishes," he promised.

―――――――――――――

Now, back in my home office he quipped, "But I didn't put your name on it."

I shook my head and reminded him, "That cute little miniature model with Joanne's last name on it is the one I gave her. What do you think Whiley is?"

His face turned to one of concern about my feelings. He offered, "You're with friends, Michael. These people here today all love you, and isn't that enough to know that you can relax among people who care about you?"

I realized it didn't really matter in the long run. So what if people know I gave the church that much money. Since the cat was out of the bag, it didn't matter or not if I cared. I decided not to fight the issue that was already lost. I was going to drop the subject and go with the flow of the moment. "Okay, let's go get some lunch," I said to him.

When we stepped outside to the backyard, I found our kids, friends of our kids, and kids of our friends running around the huge lawn.

The center piece of our backyard decorations was the Nativity stable that was nearly life size. And this set didn't spare any barnyard animals: cows, roosters, sheep, mule, and somehow a reindeer got thrown in for the atmosphere of it all. The baby Jesus slept in a bed of real hay and a real wooden trough. The wise men, Mary, and Joseph all leaned in towards the sleeping Child of God. It looked good in the daytime, and even better lit up at night.

And then I noticed my friends at a table by the Nativity. Pastor Ryan and I walked over to them. They were all there: Ralph, Adam,

Larry, and Terry. Ralph was the most sensible of all of us; being my lawyer, he should be.

One of my production executives, Adam, was working at Boeing Aircraft until I made him an offer. But it wasn't the money that sold him, it was the weather. He was still single and that's probably because his other life was ministering to teenage kids, or to inmates at the county prison.

My friend, Larry, also worked with me at BriMar. I've never regretted signing Larry to a contract that gave him fifty thousand dollars more a year to get him to leave Lockheed and move to Montecito. Larry bought himself a nice home here for his two daughters and beautiful wife. BriMar had a huge gap and he had to fill it.

Even though Adam and Larry worked for me, we were friends, and never did one world poison the other. I've regarded these friends beyond any employment arrangement, and would forever have been their friends even if there were no BriMar.

The odd man out would be Terry, who was a successful real estate agent in town. He attended our church with his family before hitting the road on busy Sunday afternoons checking on his many units. But he took this Sunday afternoon off.

Adam couldn't resist the opportunity to skewer me. "I'm just blessed to be without the burden of having so much money like you, Michael."

I turned to Pastor Ryan, shrugged, and said, "I told you so. This is why I didn't want anyone to know." They all burst out laughing.

Terry chastised Adam. "Oh jeez, Adam, it's Sunday, give the man a rest."

Since we were all close friends, we tended to know each other's business. Larry, Adam, and I talked openly of BriMar in our tight circle.

Larry brought up the Pentagon bid we were about to submit. Concerned, he said, "I talked to accounting, and the word is that we may have to cut back personnel next year if that contract doesn't come through."

I told them, "I know the odds are in our favor, but you can never be overconfident. I do feel this bid is right on target because I know what the brass is looking for. This is in their budget and we're the most reliable."

Adam pitched in his two cents. "I can't see how they could give it to anyone else. We've delivered too many big projects on budget and always beyond their expectations."

With a nod I confirmed Adam's hope and tried to fill the air with optimism.

Larry's confidence sprang a leak when he retorted, "But what if it doesn't come through?"

At that point I went back to the tried and proved, "Have faith, Larry."

Adam asked, "But what if...?"

"Stop with this negativity, so close to the Nativity. You can't say that too often," I injected. We chuckled our worries away.

CHAPTER TWO

THE DEAL

High above the earth at 70,000 feet, God's Gulf Stream G650 flew pilotless as it pierced the upper stratosphere. When God was the passenger, you didn't need a body in the pilot seat. And God just happened to be the only permanent passenger on this ultra luxurious aircraft. Everyone else came and went. And flying high above the earth, God was taking requests. In the main cabin, He sat in a plush captain's chair on the copilot side.

He was taking a meeting with His archangel, Rafael. Rafael, looking strikingly charismatic in an electric blue silk suit by Versace, remained on one knee while delivering the news to God. Rafael, even with all his strength and courage, was moved when he reported to God that two hundred thousand lives were lost when the Yangtze River over-flooded in China.

When Rafael felt God was finished with him, he stood. God dismissed him with an order to send in the next angel.

Gabriel walked down the aisle towards God and knelt before the Almighty. When he stood, he wore a steel gray Versace three-piece suit. Gabriel began, "Master of All, I come asking Your blessing on a small island in the Caribbean called Jamaica."

God replied, "Gabriel, I know Jamaica is in the Caribbean. I put it there. Why do you give me so much information?"

Gabriel answered, "I figure the more information I give You the better in the little time You give me."

God scratched his white hair and looked back at Gabriel, "I give you so little time because you give me too much information. What is happening in Jamaica?"

Gabriel replied, "A hurricane is on a direct course for that island, but there's still time to save their humble world."

God asked Gabriel, "What would you like Me to do?"

Gabriel answered, "I need winds. If the winds could come from…"

God cut him off. "Don't give me the details. I'll always know which way the winds should blow."

Gabriel, ever confident in his relationship with the Omnipotent, ventured deeper in his request. "And Sir, I know You don't like to be told *when*, but right *now* would be good."

God heard the urgency in his tone. "Running late, are we?" God just sat there with His eyes closed and took a moment to Himself.

He came back to Gabriel and said, "Thus, have I heard their prayers. If there's nothing else, Gabriel, go save Jamaica, the one in the Caribbean."

Gabriel took this to mean he needed to be present in Jamaica in order to save it, and that everything was going to be all right. "Thank You," Gabriel said appreciatively. He headed down the aisle to the door in the rear compartment from where all angels come and go. As he approached the door, Lucifer entered and walked past him on his way up the aisle. Gabriel was so taken aback by the sight of Lucifer that he stopped to witness this interaction.

Lucifer found God napping.

But obviously God knew through His closed eyes that Lucifer stood before Him. Lucifer knew that God knew that he was there, yet He acted like He was asleep. Lucifer looked at Gabriel with a shrug that asked, "What's up?"

Gabriel pointed at his knees and then to the floor. Lucifer resented having to kneel before the Almighty. He realized that God wouldn't open the store until he first knelt before Perfect Love sitting before him. With resentment on his face, Lucifer dropped to one knee and then quickly stood up.

God, feeling Godly, opened His eyes and acted like He was surprised to see Lucifer. "Lucifer, what brings you? What is it that is so irking you that you would approach the Peace that passes all understanding?"

Lucifer casually strolled over to a window and looked down at the earth. He looked back at God and claimed, "I've been all over this earth. Around and around, from pole to pole and back again, and frankly, I don't see much worth saving, do You?"

In His infinite love, God tried to reach into Lucifer. So He occasionally took him up on his petty challenges. And sure, He'd let Lucifer win some, but those that fall will eventually make their way here. Because God has the advantage. And with that, God confidently reassured Lucifer: "I have plans that don't include you."

Lucifer feigned hurt feelings and challenged God with "The truth is, I'm hard pressed to find even one, just one righteous man. So how are You going to fulfill any 'plans'?"

God wasn't amused by Lucifer's assumption that he knew everything there was to know. He pressed Lucifer's doubt by telling him "Oh, they are out there, yes indeed. And you want me to give you their names so you can use them for entertainment? No, it's not your business."

Lucifer knew how to play the game, as his negotiating skills were still sharp from the days of the Cold War. He knew that if he gave something, he might get something bigger in return. He offered God, "Well, there is one man I know of who believes he's a righteous man. His name is Michael Whiley and although he's amassed a small fortune, he's probably on a very short list of righteous men."

God asked curiously, "What makes you think Michael is a righteous man?"

Lucifer remembered he had tried to involve Michael previously in a business deal that would have personally made Michael millions. But Michael walked away from the deal, feeling uneasy about the brokers and the metallurgical integrity of the product. And above all, he didn't want to jeopardize BriMar's reputation.

God, the All Knowing, remembered this too and lectured Lucifer, "You can't always get what you want, and you can never ever underestimate the depth of one man's love for his God."

Lucifer knew people were weak for the material world, and their never-ending thirst for more things made them slave-like addicts. And he was proud of his efforts to create a sense of "materialism frenzy." Through television, Lucifer massaged the egos of the masses and propped up a false sense of happiness. Lucifer found Michael to be an interesting target for the amount of wealth and fortune he'd garnered while still practicing more than just the fundamental laws.

But Lucifer didn't have much patience for this lecture. He didn't risk shedding some of his evil in the presence of God, just to be lectured. He came to bargain and entrap one more soul into hell with him.

Lucifer, ever the genius, thought best to change his tactics and not to act like he knew everything. "Maybe Michael Whiley is a righteous man, and maybe he isn't. Sure, it's easy being righteous when you live off millions and have all the luxury and comforts anyone could ever want. It's easy loving You when you're living high off the land and high above the rest of the real world that suffers day to day."

God saw the irony in his words and rebuked him. "You are wrong, Lucifer. It is the man in *need* who calls out My name. But Michael has enough for many lifetimes, yet he still calls out for Me. Michael doesn't love Me because he *has* to, or needs to, but because he *wants* to. He's earned his wealth."

Christmas morning arrived with an explosion of excitement and smiles. After breakfast, the family was enraptured by the opening of one gift after another while happy Christmas songs filled the house. Beautifully wrapped gifts got tossed around the room, and torn and mangled wrapping covered the floor.

John tore open another box revealing a nice Hawaiian shirt from Mom. He hugged her with an appreciative kiss on her cheek.

Rachel squealed when she opened a jewelry box with her first silver charm bracelet. She loved horses, so I made sure her first charm was a silver horse. I put it on her wrist and locked the clasp tight. "Merry Christmas, honey," I said with a hug.

She promised, "Daddy, I love it so much, I'm never going to take this off."

Edwin ripped through the wrapping of a box containing a new baseball glove. He played third base in Little League, and I'm hoping he'll want to keep his sports interests as he moves into preteen.

"Merry Christmas, Edwin," I said, gently tossing a new baseball into his new glove.

He smiled and tossed me a gift. "Merry Christmas, Dad," he shouted above the joyous chaos and noise.

"Thanks, Edwin," I said. I opened it to find a black Greek-like Captain's hat with the name of the yacht, *Oh Happy Day,* embroidered across the front of it. I put it on to a perfect fit. I gave Edwin a bear hug because I knew he actually had to think about this gift. I liked it so much, I doubt I'd ever take it off.

Joanne handed me a beautifully gift-wrapped box. I opened it to find a money clip with a sparkling gem adorning the gold plated metal. It was impressive and I knew I could put it to good use. "Thank you, honey," I said with kiss and a hug.

I reached for Joanne's gift and with a kiss I said, "Merry Christmas, darling." Joanne knew I held something really special, and she acted very excited. All the kids stopped to watch me hand Joanne the iconic Tiffany's baby-blue box with that girly white ribbon.

———

Lucifer continued to challenge God. "How can a man be so wealthy, and yet be on that short list of righteous men?" He sensed someone wasn't telling the truth and it wasn't God. He suspected Michael was lying. He asked himself out loud: "With his yacht and gold-spoon-fed lifestyle, how could he make a sincere effort? I don't understand. What would be the point of calling out for God if he didn't need anything?" He was perplexed. He reinforced his disbelief in the power of God's love by doubting Michael's faith.

Lucifer finally articulated the core of his proposition to God. Lucifer claimed, "I propose to You that Michael does not love the Giver of the gifts, as much as he loves the gifts themselves."

God smiled confidently. He contradicted Lucifer, saying, "I have searched his heart, and I have no doubt that Michael indeed loves the Giver of the gifts more than the gifts themselves. He'd love Me whether or not he lived in this abundant manner or any other way for that matter."

"Then show me," Lucifer requested.

"I don't have to show you," God replied.

"As far as You know, he'll be cursing Your name within a week of his troubles," Lucifer claimed.

"Not Michael," replied God.

"He'll be spitting the ground at the mention of Your name within a week of his woes," Lucifer insisted.

"Not Michael!" God said louder.

"You don't know until it happens!" Lucifer shouted.

"Not Michael!" God shouted back.

Lucifer knew he couldn't win with words. "Then show me. Am I asking too much?" he begged of God.

God considered Lucifer's words. "Leave Me until I call you," God said to him.

Lucifer walked back down the aisle to stand near Gabriel by the back door. Gabriel stared at him with suspicion.

God gazed out the window and closed His eyes. He saw Christmas morning in the family den. He saw the three kids, Joanne, and the room with all the celebrating, and then He looked at Michael. God asked Himself, "Can you do it, Michael? Will you remember Me when times get bad? Will you still love Me when all this is gone? Will you love Me when your world is upside down? I want to believe you will. I have so much faith in you, Michael."

God opened His eyes and waved His arm indicating Lucifer to return. God leaned into him and said, "He can do it."

"I don't believe You will ever really know until it happens," argued Lucifer.

God replied, "Very well, everything he has I put under your control."

"Everything?" Lucifer asked. Even Lucifer was surprised at God's generosity.

"Everything, but you cannot take his life," God stipulated.

Lucifer saw that he had just won a huge victory and knew that he wouldn't have to kill Michael in order to destroy him, and most importantly, destroy his relationship with God. Lucifer beamed at his own genius, and through his sarcastic laughter assured God, "Take his life? I won't have to take his life!"

But beneath his fake yearning to understand Man's love for God, Lucifer was motivated by his need to be entertained. And you can only entertain the devil by destroying something, or someone. So Lucifer asked God, "How long do I have with Michael?"

God looked at Lucifer and telepathically reminded him that He is still in control of the situation.

God answered, "When I AM that I AM is satisfied."

Knowing when he was ahead, Lucifer took a step back and nodded. Because Lucifer knew that even he exists at the whim of the Omnipotent.

God said, "Now you can leave."

Lucifer turned and walked back down the aisle, passing Gabriel, who was still standing there. While passing him, Lucifer turned to Gabriel and asked, "Aren't you forgetting something?"

Gabriel quickly remembered and whispered, "Oh God, I have to save Jamaica."

From the far side of the cabin God heard Gabriel's whisper and commanded, "And you'd better hurry."

It was a beautiful, sunny Christmas day, full of nice gifts and a wonderful meal as we sat out on the veranda enjoying our banter and food. I loved Christmas Day afternoons because they were the best. As tradition had its way in our home every year, a local catering company delivered a full turkey dinner with all the trimmings.

That evening found Joanne and me curled on the couch in the family room in front of a blazing fireplace. Our beautifully lit Christmas tree showered the room in a rainbow of colors. The kids were doing their thing somewhere in the house. As we channel surfed the TV, we stopped on a news report showing Hurricane Cindy moving away from Jamaica. Yet another Christmas miracle, I thought to myself.

Much later that night and across town, Charles turned over and over in bed because he couldn't fall asleep. He was too hot. Then he was too cold. He was agitated. Every little sound pulled him back from the shores of sleep. The finances in the new Pentagon bid prodded him like a hot poker of a worrisome thought.

Charles didn't see Lucifer walk into his bedroom through the open door. Nor did he feel the mattress slump when Lucifer sat on the bed next to him. Lucifer watched Charles squirming and turning over.

Lucifer peered into Charles's thoughts. He saw a man who was always in want of more. In fact, Charles had such an insatiable appetite for more things that he could never ever be satisfied. And he had a strong ego that Lucifer could work with. Lucifer smiled.

Lucifer saw the bid as it passed through the projection screen in Charles's head. Using Charles's weakness for money, Lucifer quickly saw his angle. Whispering into Charles's mind, he pressed how the bid amounts are too low and he could make so much more money by increasing the numbers just a little bit. A tiny bit here, another tiny bit there, and that would satisfy Charles's economic neurosis.

Charles sighed. Finally, he found an answer. He would just increase the particulars in unnoticeable amounts. But how would he do an end run around Michael?

Lucifer used his evil genius, and Charles quickly picked up the telepathic message.

Charles thought, "I'll have to get to the office tomorrow and send that package myself." He sighed again, feeling a great weight lifted from his shoulders, having found a way to put several more millions of dollars into his pocket and with little resistance. He would work out the specifics later on the computer at the office, but for now he smiled at his own brilliance and fell asleep.

On the following morning, Friday, December 26, Charles used his key to enter the very secure administration wing of BriMar Industries.

He turned off the alarm and went to his office where he found a copy of the bid in his drawer. He turned on his computer. With a pen, a pad of paper, a calculator, and the bid on the computer, along with his hard copy to work from, Charles went to work on the numbers with exacting mathematical precision.

At every step, he stopped and scrutinized the repercussions down the factory line if he were to adjust certain numbers upwardly, or even downwardly. He also had to recreate the factors in the equations throughout the 230-page presentation bid.

His revised calculations now stood to generate an additional forty-seven million dollars profit for the company and over four million for himself, personally. He was meticulous and detailed, always noting which pages were altered. He made two copies of each of the revised pages and copied the file onto a CD. He then walked to Michael's office.

He searched through Michael's desk and found the actual hard-copy bid that was being sent to the Pentagon by FedEx. And he knew this because it had an unsigned cover letter from Michael attached to the front. Charles looked around Michael's desk for his signature. Looking in Michael's drawers for any letter he might have signed, he found a file of letters with his signature on every page. On a blank piece of paper, Charles took a couple practice shots at Michael's signature and forged it on the cover letter. He then inserted his revised pages into the bid and prepared the whole thing for flight.

Charles cleaned up after himself and even double-checked everywhere he went. With the FedEx package in hand, he walked to the door, turned on the alarm, and stepped outside. When he got in his car, he turned on his navigation system to locate the nearest FedEx drop-off spot. When he was done inserting the data, the computer told him how to get there on the dash monitor. Charles smirked at having seen it on his way home. "Could this have been any easier?" he said out loud to himself. The whole process took him six and a half hours.

When Charles handed the package over to the FedEx agent, he felt a wave of confidence that what he had done was best for the company. Charles was certain his friends at the Dept. of Defense would choose BriMar over anyone else's bid because it was the best, and the boys at the Pentagon were his friends. After all, Charles reassured himself, "We're all in the same club."

Who would not agree that the happiest time of the year is the week between Christmas and New Years Day? Through this vacation week, I made sure we all had a good time together and included our friends. From horseback riding above Goleta, to climbing up the waterfalls in the hills behind Montecito, to taking the *Oh Happy Day* out to sea, we played loose and laughed hard. On one outing on the yacht, I counted nine friends the kids brought with them. I didn't mind, we all had a good time. One day melted into the next and before you could sneeze, it was New Years Eve.

During the week, I thought about a New Year's resolution. I pondered the thought and asked myself, like every other person in the world, "What should my resolution be?" And from outside of me, out of the blue, the thought "infinite forgiveness" came to mind. I thought about it and how much strength and goodness can come from forgiveness. So I smiled, knowing that my resolution wasn't going to evaporate in a matter of days due to the lack of attention. No, this was a big resolution that was going to take a conscious effort and one I was going to have to nurture every day. But I felt a little pride that I picked a profound and meaningful resolution, instead of some lame goal that I would end up resenting in a matter of days.

On New Year's Eve, Joanne and I traditionally went to a gala party put on by the Santa Barbara Yacht Club. Black tie, enforced. And that's why we like to go. We enjoy the world of ritual and protocol. Besides, many of our neighbors and friends were always there. The event was held at an elegant mansion high above Santa Barbara. We always had a good time, as no one ever egged us on to drink more.

I rarely ever drank alcohol, except that night, when I'd likely have a couple glasses of champagne. Besides, I didn't need alcohol to enhance the flavor of fine catered delicacies and out-of-this-world dessert. And I certainly didn't need alcohol to enjoy the fifteen-piece orchestra with an eight-man brass section. And I never needed alcohol to enhance the pleasure of dancing with the most beautiful woman in the room, my wife.

Finally, the time came to get ready to go to the ball. I had an occasion to wear my new white dinner jacket I picked up at Bergdorf Goodman in New York last summer. As I looked at myself in a full-length mirror, I realized there's something about being in a white jacket that lights up a room.

I finished getting into my formal attire long before Joanne was finished dressing, so I meandered to the large window overlooking the backyard. I looked down at the Nativity scene and I lost myself in its significance. It took me back to the time I was in Bethlehem.

For one semester in college, I enrolled in a foreign travel program. It had nothing to do with my engineering major, but it seemed like a good way to see Europe. The two professors who led us through the great museums and landmarks of Europe and the Middle East showed us the shadowed drama behind the history of western civilization. To learn history, it's best to stand where history was made.

I'll forever remember the time in Israel when we stood on a rustic hillside overlooking Bethlehem at sunset. A professor pulled out a music box and started playing "Hallelujah Chorus" from Handel's *Messiah*. Hearing the explosive opening of the song made me burst out laughing as it hit me like a soundtrack. What other song would you play over-looking the little town of Bethlehem, I thought? I was quickly taken by the profoundness of the moment and froze the memory of it in my soul: the little town before us, the setting sunlight behind us, and the breeze coming off the Mediterranean Ocean. The music will forever live in me. Those few moments take up a whole chapter all by itself in my conscious library of impressions that make up who I am.

As I looked at the colorful Nativity scene sprawled across my backyard, I knew it wasn't anything like the way it really was. Back then, that stable was dark, smelly, dreary, and full of anxiety. Joseph was told by an angel in a dream to flee for safety in Egypt. Why couldn't I see an angel in my dreams?

I went downstairs to the family room to hang out with the kids and give them their marching orders for the night. Rachel was on the phone with her friend Sara, Ralph's daughter.

Rachel asked me, "Dad, is it all right if Sara comes over and spends the night?"

I replied, "Sure, but how is she going to get here?"

John piped in, "I'll go get her." Of course, what is more obvious than a teenager eager to drive anywhere at any time. With a warning and strict orders, I gave my permission for John to pick up Sara and come straight home. No stopping anywhere, no excuses. Sara was part of our extended family, so I saw no harm. Rachel spoke back into the phone and they worked out the details.

From the second floor, Joanne yelled, "Okay, I'm ready!" That was our cue for the whole family to proceed to the foyer to watch Mom come down the stairs. She made her appearance at the top of the stairs as we oohed, wowed, and aahed her way down. She smiled that rich, diva smile in her dazzling blue shimmering designer gown. She flaunted the moment for us. The fifty thousand dollar diamond necklace from Winston's topped off the whole….what's the word….event.

But it didn't stop her from barking at the kids. Sternly, Joanne warned them to "Keep the house clean and don't leave the kitchen in a mess!" Not the words I expected to come out of this sparkling jewel of my life, but whatever. My wife, I loved her because she could yell at our kids with equal fervor wearing a million dollars or wearing flip-flops.

I updated her with the news that Sara was spending the night. She smiled and said, "Let's go." In the foyer, we hugged and kissed every one of the kids as we wished each other a Happy New Year and told the kids we loved them.

We stepped out and closed the door behind us. "Haa! Freedom!" I shouted at Joanne.

Joanne twirled and asked, "How do I look?"

"You look breathless, like a movie star," I told her. And all I could do was take her in my arms, lift her off the ground, and spin her around while kissing her. She giggled like a teenager and I felt like I truly was the luckiest man in the world. With the sparkling Christmas decorations lighting up the atmosphere, I spun her in my arms as I whispered in her ear, "Happy New Year, my darling, I love you so much."

She replied in kind and we sealed our bond with a kiss. It was ladies choice as far as which vehicle we'd take. She picked the fastest Mercedes. So at $120,000 we were going to fly across town at an average top speed of just thirty miles an hour.

Research shows that the happiest time people experience in their lives are the few minutes just before they go inside a theater to see a movie. When I was in the fifth grade, I lived on a military base, and every Saturday afternoon the base theater would show a double feature matinee, with cartoons, all for just a quarter. And not only that, with military precision, the U.S. Government would actually send an ugly gray bus around the neighborhood to pick up the kids every Saturday at 12:15 p.m. The absolute happiest moments of my life were when I'd see that military gray bus pull around the curve on Armstrong Street. My endorphins exploded across the daylight sky. It was so impressionable that after all these years I remember the name of the street.

As we drove through Santa Barbara, lit up with festive Christmas decorations, that same euphoria came ricocheting through my insides.

When we arrived at the mansion it was sparkling like a castle. The valet took the car as we beamed with excitement. Approaching the doors, I looked up and saw a dark cloud right above us. As I stepped inside, I reached out to test the rainfall when a couple of heavy drops hit the palm of my hand. As I entered, I looked down at the water in my hand and reached for my handkerchief. I dried my hand as I beamed at the lavish and festive atmosphere abuzz with people having lots of fun and laughter.

It wasn't long before we bumped into Ralph and his wife Bette. She's a pretty woman with stronger than normal bonds with her family, meaning she's a little overly protective. Bette and Joanne had their own friendship.

When the ladies turned the conversation to their dresses, I turned to Ralph and said, "I'm assuming you know Sara is spending the night at our house, or are you the last to know?"

Ralph retorted, "Hey, I resemble that remark." He continued, "I told Sara that she was not to go anywhere but your house and that's it."

In her bedroom, Sara stuffed her backpack with her overnight things and checked the time. It was 7:45 p.m. She came out of her bedroom, dropped her backpack by the front door, looked out the window, and saw gusts of wind carrying the heavy rain horizontally. Then she lost an hour, absorbed in watching her favorite TV shows.

Sara called Rachel, but there was no answer. She picked another favorite show and lost herself laughing at Earl.

In the banquet hall, under a canopy of decorated lights strung over the sixty formally dressed couples celebrating the evening, Joanne and I enjoyed the fine five-course dinner along with a small mountain of desserts. Lit candelabras adorned the white linen tables, and calla lilies served as our name cards. The delicious dinner part of the night lingered for more than an hour.

Sara called Rachel again on her cell phone and even tried her a couple times on her home line. She expected them an hour ago. She repeated the phone call process for another half hour during which time she often checked the driveway for any signs of them. She started an internal debate of whether or not she should call her father. Another half hour flew by. Finally, she did.

Ralph's cell phone vibrated in his jacket pocket while he danced with Bette. He answered it and walked off the floor to take the call. Bette followed him. Sara told her dad that John and Rachel were two hours late and she couldn't get anyone on their phones. Ralph reassured Sara to stay calm and to call him when they did show up. And then they hung up. But Ralph knew that he couldn't keep this to himself.

As Joanne and I were dancing to "Summer Wind," I smiled at the perfection of the moment until I watched Ralph walk towards us with anything but a happy look on his face. He walked up to us and pointed to follow him off the dance floor. I took Joanne's hand and we followed Ralph into another room. Ralph repeated to us what had Sara told him.

Annoyed, I reached for my cell phone inside my jacket. I told the phone to "Call home." The home phone line just rang and rang; after six rings the answering machine picked up. I turned to Joanne. "I'm sure if they hear my voice, they'll pick up. Maybe they have the music so loud, they can't hear it." Finally, the beep came on, "Hey! Are you kids home? Pick up the phone, it's Dad. Pick up the PHONE! Whoever gets this message better call me at once, hello?" Nothing.

I hung up, turned to Joanne and said, "I remember specifically telling John that he was only to go pick up Sara and then come home. Do you remember me saying that?"

Joanne spoke into her cell phone, "Call Rachel." Rachel's voice mail finally came on, letting Joanne leave a message.

I tried John on his cell. It didn't even ring, going straight to voice mail. I recorded, "John, it's your dad, where are you? You are to call me the minute, the second you get this message. Your mom and I are very disappointed that we're not able to reach you. Bye." I asked Joanne, "What do you think? Should we go home?"

Joanne's happy mood dropped as she asked, "You mean, like go and never come back?"

I looked at my watch. It was 11:15 p.m., so I replied, "No, like go home, and then come right back."

She beamed at realizing her party was not over. "Sure, we could be back here by 11:45."

We both walked briskly to the car and we were on the road in seconds. Joanne didn't want to ruin the evening shouting at the kids. I countered her leniency with the importance of teaching them that we deserved our time together without drama. She made me promise that after five minutes of yelling at the kids I would have to put my party face back on, race back here, and ring in the new year with a smile. I promised.

When we pulled into the garage, we immediately noticed that the Escalade was gone. We walked into the house and started yelling,

"John, Rachel, Edwin!" Nobody came. We walked to different rooms calling out their names. It seemed like no one was home.

I wondered out loud, "What if they just went to Rusty's Pizza and they forgot their phones?" I dialed Rachel's cell phone again. Her phone rang in her bedroom upstairs, startling me at first. I walked upstairs and found it on her bed. I dialed John's cell again. It went straight to voice mail. I looked in Edwin's bedroom to see if he might be sleeping, but he wasn't. I noticed all the lights and TV were on in the house, as if they just got up and left, not intending to be gone long. And that would make sense.

I found Joanne in the back part of the house on the first floor, still yelling, "Edwin, John, Rachel! They're not here."

I called Rusty's Pizza to see if they were there. They weren't. I called Sara to ask if they had showed up. They hadn't. A half hour went by with no answers and no leads.

We walked to the family room where the clock happened to strike midnight. I turned to her, the most wonderful woman in the world, and confessed, "I feel bad that we couldn't have shared this moment back at the party. Happy New Year, darling." I hugged her and sealed it with a kiss.

She replied, "Happy New Year, my love."

But here we were, entangled in a drama with good kids gone bad.

We heard the sounds of a car pulling up the driveway. "Finally, they're home," I said angrily. Outside the car pulled up and came to a stop.

We walked to the foyer. I could see Joanne was fuming. In the foyer, I held Joanne back from going to open the door and said, "Let them walk in here and be shocked when they see us standing here. I'm grounding John's license for three weeks. Forget it, the whole month of January he's not driving one car, not even one mile!" I was ready to let them have the brunt of my anger. Joanne stood stoically, holding back her steam.

Then an odd thing happened that startled us both. The doorbell rang. We were not expecting the doorbell to ring. We were just expecting the kids to just come walking through it.

I walked to the door, opened it, and found a policeman standing there with his hat in his hand. I was both alarmed and curious. I spoke first. "Yes, can I help you?"

He replied, "Can I come in, pardon the late hour." Of course I let him in.

"I'm Officer Marcus, maybe you should sit down," he said.

Joanne took a step closer to me. But rather than do as he said, I asked, "What is this about?"

Officer Marcus insisted we sit on the nearby bench. So, we sat down as I took Joanne's hand in mine.

He asked, "Do you own a Cadillac Escalade?"

I replied, "Yes. Where is it? Was it towed? Did you find the kids?"

Then he asked us how many kids we have.

Joanne answered, "Three. Where are they?"

I could see something in his face. He said, "Well, maybe you should know, there's no proof yet, so don't rush to.....well, there was an accident involving a black Escalade, and we don't know anything yet, but there were three victims."

"Were they children?" I asked.

"I don't know," he answered.

He lowered his head and revealed his lying side when he said, "Don't rush to any conclusions, that's why I'm here. I've come to escort you to possibly identify the passengers."

"Oh my God!" Joanne shouted as she stood up.

I asked him, "Where are you escorting us to?"

He couldn't even look me in the eye to answer, "The morgue."

I heard his words but I couldn't make sense of them. My outer layer jumped right out of my skin and my inner world suddenly turned deaf.

What brought me out of this daze was Joanne screaming, "Oh my God!" I pulled myself back and took a hold of her in my arms. I held her tight and said, "We can't assume. Don't make any assumptions until we have proof. Don't let it get away from us. We don't know for sure." Joanne just nodded her head.

And then I heard Officer Marcus offer to drive us.

Sitting in the back seat of the police cruiser, we held hands and prayed silently. I looked out the window and I could not imagine an empty life before me without my three children. I thought, "Be strong, and don't rush to conclusions. Don't let your mind wonder into a never-ending, never satisfying scenario that may not have anything to do with reality."

The red-flashing light from the top of the car bouncing off everything created a very surreal, ominous effect that exasperated the blender that was now in my mind. Thankfully, he left the siren off.

I prayed, and I prayed with the deepest sincerity. I prayed silently, and with my inner voice I shouted at the top of my lungs as if from a mountaintop and across a valley below. From my deepest particle, I mustered the micro charge of my soul to come begging to God. "Oh, Lord, if these are my children, grant me the peace to endure all things. For You are the infinite well of love from where all peace comes. And if they are not mine, then I pray for the parents of those children. May You grant them infinite compassion and peace in their hearts."

Suddenly, Officer Marcus slammed the brakes to avoid killing a dog and then turned into the parking lot behind the Santa Barbara Municipal Facilities. And before we knew it, we had arrived.

I opened the car door and helped Joanne out of the back seat. We had not said a word to each other. I didn't know if that was good or bad. We followed Officer Marcus through the doors and down the corridor.

He passed us off to the coroner on duty, who said, "This way." The first thing I noticed was the cold, and the second was the smell. As we made a left turn down a long corridor, I could see the doors at the far end. Thinking that Joanne should probably be spared the horror of seeing our children like this, I pondered if I should go in alone. She had the right, but why should she if she didn't have to. Why inflict more pain on the wounded? Twenty feet before the doors, I turned to her and said, "Joanne, you don't have to do this. I can do it, just let me go in there alone."

"No, I have to see them," she insisted.

"Joanne, you don't want to see them like this, please don't," I repeated. The scars would last a life time if she saw her children in the worst condition imaginable. "Please, stop, Joanne," I pleaded. Why should she suffer the sight of our children looking like that? "Please, stop, Joanne," I begged. I had to stop her. My compassion for her overrode everything else so I shouted, "Joanne, stop!"

She stopped, but continued arguing. I took her arm and pulled her close to me because I wanted her to look into my eyes as I said to her, "I don't want you to go in there. Please, don't do this. Just let me go alone." I gave her a deep hug just before walking her to a bench along the wall. I said, "Please, wait here. I'll be back." She sat down and I followed the coroner.

CHAPTER THREE

THE EXECUTION

Hours earlier, and not too long after Michael and Joanne had left for their New Year's Eve party, John, Rachel, and Edwin all piled into the Cadillac Escalade to go pick up Sara. Rachel always sat shotgun whenever John drove, except of course if they were with Mom or Dad. When John started the car, they all heard the gas warning audio reminder go on.

John pulled the vehicle up to the gas pump just outside the garage door. He filled up the tank because Dad told him it was best to do it that way. As he returned the nozzle to its cradle, he felt a few drops of rain hit him. By the time he got settled into the driver's seat, the windshield wipers went on automatically. John looked up at the sky and asked, "When did they say it was going to rain?"

Rachel gave him a look and said, "It always rains in December, idiot."

John was taken aback by the tone in her voice and reminded her, "Mother told you not to talk to me like that." John turned back to Edwin and asked, "And you're not going to be a show-off and do anything really stupid to impress Sara, are you?"

Edwin looked embarrassed and replied, "Maybe."

John headed north to the hills above Summerland. He continued up the dark winding curves alongside the hills against the howling wind. He drove cautiously through the wall of rain. At Olive Street, he was surprised to encounter some traffic; but after all, it was New Year's Eve.

He crossed the boulevard and made his way higher up along the hillside with the ocean and cliff-side to his right. He made out the intermittent guardrail defining the road boundary. The windshield wipers knocking back and forth wildly caused the oncoming headlights to appear out of focus. Through the sheets of flying water drops, distance was difficult to measure. John told Rachel, "Why don't you call Sara and tell her we'll be there in ten minutes."

Rachel shrugged him off. "I left my cell at the house."

About a half a mile ahead, coming in the opposite direction, an old man slowly drove his old car through the pouring rain. But the old man was slowing down the fast Porsche behind him. The expensive German machine passed on his left and if it hadn't been for the buckets of rain, the driver would have been able to see the no-passing lines painted down the middle of the road.

John pulled his cell phone out of his pocket, but it fell and slid behind him on the floor of the backseat. Edwin unbuckled his seat belt and reached for the cell on the floor. As John made a left bank curve on the wet road, he saw both oncoming cars taking up both lanes.

The Porsche driver also saw John's oncoming lights and floored the accelerator. He shot past the slow car. But that put both oncoming cars at a combined speed of 120 miles an hour. John saw the lights coming at him faster. He blasted his horn.

Being inexperienced, John hit the brakes too hard as he turned the steering wheel sharply to avoid the Porsche. The SUV skidded out of control across the pavement towards the guardrail. Nothing John did could correct the SUV, now hydroplaning across the wet cement. Rachel screamed. John screamed. They slid at an angle until the right rear fender hit the guardrail. The momentum tilted the SUV over the guardrail and gravity pulled it down over the cliff.

As the vehicle bounced down the cliff rocks, Edwin slammed against the roof repeatedly. John and Rachel faced the oncoming canyon floor with horror. John tried to grab Edwin, but the chaos would not let that happen. The kids screamed in panic and terror as they slid uncontrollably down the cliff rocks.

At the bottom of a steep drop the SUV slammed into the ground upside down.

In an instant, the sounds of honking horn, crashing metal, and screams climaxed to a haunting silence. Inside, John and Rachel, still in their seatbelts, were dead. Edwin's lifeless and broken body landed a few feet away from the wreckage.

Up on the highway, the Porsche driver stopped and dialed 911 on his cell phone. As he got out in the vicious rain, he raced to the twisted guard rail and in a panic he summoned help from the operator.

The old man in the slower car pulled over and came out with a flashlight. He ran to the railing. The old man pointed his light down the canyon and found the wrecked SUV. Both men saw that it was upside down. The Porsche driver impulsively started to go down the cliff when the old man stopped him, shouting, "It's too dangerous!" They both saw the angle of the canyon wall was far too steep for anyone to climb down. He knew the old man was right. The Porsche driver pulled himself away from the old man and stepped back to the shoulder of the road. He looked up into the rain and repeatedly screamed, "Oh, God!" at the top of his lungs, realizing what he had caused. He crumbled where he stood.

At the morgue, I slowly pulled back the first sheet and I could see that it was Rachel. The air rushed right out of me. I reached for her hand. And that's when I saw what I was looking for: the charm bracelet I put on her wrist a week ago on Christmas morning. The words she spoke when I put it on her came back to slug me in my heart: "Daddy, I'm never going take this off." I covered my eyes with my hands, not wanting to see what was before me. Tears flooded my eyes as I realized the moment.

I moved to the second body and pulled the sheet back and found Edwin. I noticed his little shoulders and spine were bent out of shape.

"What monster did this to my son?"

As I walked to the third, I realized John was under that sheet. And that was when an endless procession of tears started falling down my face. His handsome face was broken and bruised as was most of his body. I leaned over him, wrapped my arms around him, pulled him up to my chest, and said to myself, "So much promise, so much denied." Gingerly, I laid him back down, took a deep breath and realized my assignment. I took another deep breath as I walked towards the doors. But by the time I reached them my ashen face could not hide my grief and shock.

When I stepped through the door, Joanne stood up. She could see my face and she screamed, "Oh God, no!" I went to hold her and moved her back down on the bench. We sat down because the weight of the horror was too great to bear standing up. Joanne buried her head into my chest and sobbed. We both wept freely and openly, expelling our horror. Our wailing echoed up and down the hallways. I felt so many things at once: sadness, anger, despair, shock, and more than anything, a bewilderment why God would allow this to happen to us.

She bellowed, "I want to see them!" But as she bolted for the door, I stopped her.

It took a lot of strength to hold her back. "Don't Joanne, please don't!" I held her tightly. The coroner returned and walked us to the entrance. He handed us off to Officer Marcus, who walked us back to his cruiser.

As we were driven home, Joanne buried her head in my chest. I held her close. I called Ralph on my cell and without explanation told him to go to our house as quickly as possible, and then I hung up. I felt myself falling down a black hole, all the while asking: Why? I wanted to scream at the top of my lungs and put my fist through the back door window, but this wasn't the time. Joanne's sobbing continued all the way to the house.

When we arrived, Ralph and Bette pulled up at the same time. As we got out, Bette came rushing over to help Joanne.

Ralph asked, "What happened?" I waited to answer until Bette walked Joanne out of earshot. And with the fewest of words possible I told Ralph what had happened.

Officer Marcus came over to me to offer his condolences and then left.

I turned and stared at the front door. I stood frozen. I had to walk through our front door knowing my children would never be there again.

My whole being felt as if a huge vacuum in the sky had just sucked the very life, air, and soul out of me. I had to consciously inhale. Feeling and looking like I could fall over any second, Ralph came up beside me and put his arm around my back. He walked me to the front door and into the foyer. Immeasurable sadness had overcome my home this day.

We heard Joanne's sobbing coming from upstairs, so that's where we went. As I rounded the top of the stairs, I noticed the kids' rooms. Someday I'll go in each of their rooms and have a moment with them, I thought to myself. It's inevitable, but not tonight. I had to get to Joanne.

Joanne lay on top of the bed as Bette comforted her. I looked at Bette and nodded towards Ralph. She took my cue and walked over to him. They went downstairs. I went to sit by Joanne and I held her. I kept my grief at bay, as I had to think of her first. We didn't speak. Our pain went beyond words.

Downstairs, Ralph led Bette to a chair in the kitchen and told her what I had told him. Her complexion turned pale as she cried into her hands. Ralph held her as they both wept. They sat together crying over the loss of children they watched grow up from the time the kids were toddlers.

Breaking away from our embrace, Joanne looked at me and through her sobbing asked, "Why?" Shaking my head in disbelief, my only answer would be more questions.

Ralph and Bette returned to our bedroom with water and tissues for Joanne. As Bette touched my shoulder in tenderness, I looked up and saw her tears. We traded places.

Ralph and I went downstairs and sat in the living room. We just sat in silence. There were many things to talk about, but I couldn't articulate, as my mind exploded with what ifs, whys, and why nots.

Bette gave Joanne a painkiller and helped her change out of her formal dress and into her sleeping gown. After Bette tucked Joanne back into bed, she came downstairs to join us.

I didn't want to leave Joanne alone. I should be with her. Ralph and Bette let themselves out with a promise to return early next morning.

Climbing the stairs, I felt the jabs of quantum questions demanding quantum answers. I asked, "Who am I weeping for? The kids are in heaven, so how can I weep for them who are with God?

No, I must be weeping for myself and my own loss. Who could expect any man to bear the agony of losing all three children at once? Can it be done? Can it be done without going insane, vindictive, or bitter?" This event was one that will forever change the foundation blocks of who I am.

Joanne was still crying when I snuggled up against her and wrapped my arms around her. She squeezed my arm tightly as she wailed her pain openly. Suddenly, she flew out of bed and screamed, "Why would God do this to us? Why?" She slumped onto the bed.

I took her in my arms and I held her tight. We climbed back in bed together as I tried to soothe her to sleep. I knew that the pill she took should kick in any minute and give her peace from this madness.

And as she was quieting down, I realized that I was still in my tuxedo. I got up to change clothes. The glamorous party clothes denied the truth of the moment. In my walk-in closet, the process of getting into my pajamas was a start-and-stop operation that lasted a half hour. I thought about the accident and then I had to sit down in a chair, hold onto myself tight and let out a burst of sorrow. I prayed, "Oh, Lord, what did I do...what did we do...to deserve this? I don't understand."

Finally, I got in bed and stared at the far wall. Joanne had fallen asleep. Eventually, I too fell asleep.

At about four o'clock in the morning, I vaguely noticed that Joanne got out of bed. I Expected that she would walk to the bathroom, but she walked out of the room instead. I pulled myself out of my subconscious to make sure she was okay. She walked down the hallway, turning on every light. I had to follow her to keep an eye on her, but I kept my distance. She went from one kid's room to another, turning on the lights and telling the kids to "Wake up." She repeated, "Wake up!" and got louder. She threw herself on John's bed, crying, yelling, "Come back!" I knew I had to get to her.

Abruptly, she walked past me and headed downstairs. I figured she'd gone for some water, so from a distance, I followed. But she didn't go to the kitchen. Rather she went through the sliding-glass door into the backyard. I watched her cross the lawn. She walked straight up to the large-size Nativity, held out her arms, looked to the stars, and prayed. I knew I should go out and pray with her. So I stepped into the cold late night air.

I didn't get ten feet before she grabbed a wise man and threw him across the lawn. She karate kicked the large cow so hard, it knocked over a few other animals when it went down. Sheep were not immune as she threw one like a discus, landing it in the pool. The second and third wise men were taken by their heads and shot put into the pool and across the grass. With her arms swinging, she knocked over Joseph and Mary. And then with all her might, she picked up the fake stable covering and pushed it over, turning it upside down, exposing the baby Jesus. She looked down, and then looked up. At the top of her lungs, she yelled at God, "Why would You do this to me?" I ran to her as she slipped on the wet grass and fell to the ground.

I held her tight. "We'll get through this, I promise," I said to her.

I took her back into the house and back upstairs to bed.

Again, I stared at the same far wall. I closed my eyes, and then images and smells from the morgue came haunting me.

I got out of bed and knelt on the floor at the foot of the bed and prayed some more. But moments later, I keeled over and fell asleep in a fetal position on the carpet.

I dreamt I was playing tag with the kids when they were smaller, as we did hundreds of times at the jungle gym in the park. In my dream, I ran as fast as I could, but I could not catch them. Edwin, John, Rachel, they were all faster than I was. They all taunted me with "You can't catch me." We all laughed hard. And then I turned to look at Rachel. I shouted, "Rachel!"

Suddenly, the sound of a ringing cell phone woke me. I recognized it was Rachel's ringing tone. Mumbling, I said out loud, "Rachel, answer your phone." I thought, why doesn't Rachel answer her phone? And then I discovered myself on the floor. What was I doing on the floor? In the distance, Rachel's cell phone kept ringing. And then I remembered the nightmare my life fell into last night.

Slowly, I stood and saw Joanne was also stirring. I staggered to Rachel's room and turned the phone off.

Returning to the bedroom, I saw Joanne sitting up. I went to hug her. She looked at me and asked, "Did it really happen? Or was it bad dream?" I didn't have to say anything, as my face showed my sadness. The front doorbell rang. I got my robe and went to answer it.

Ralph was knocking. I let him in and we made our way to the kitchen. He asked a few questions and offered to handle all the arrangements. I totally appreciated his support and readily took him up on his offers. As the day progressed, news of the tragedy spread quickly across town. Around noon, friends and neighbors began to stop by. My four best friends and their families came over to show their love and support and to share our grief.

Ralph handled the funeral arrangements from my home office. I sat nearby, trying to keep myself together.

My sister-in-law, Mary Ruth, lives in Bel Air and would have been here, except she was in Ohio. She's Joanne's only sister. When Joanne finally got her on the phone, Joanne broke down again. Just speaking the words and hearing the words come out of your mouth made you want to cry. Joanne dropped the phone on her lap. I heard Mary Ruth sobbing on the other end. She loved the kids profoundly and they loved her back.

Ralph took over the conversation and organized her travel plans.

I was told the accident made the newspaper. And a neighbor told me that local TV news mentioned it that morning. I didn't see any of it, nor did I want to.

By mid-afternoon impromptu well-wishers swelled through the day as the news continued to spread. I kept asking, "Where would we be without friends?"

Over the next couple days, I noticed my grief would come and go in waves. One minute I'd be okay, but a minute later it would overtake me and I would have to find an isolated spot away from everyone. Whether it was a bathroom or upstairs, I just had to be alone. I noticed that lapses of time disappeared and then I would find myself here, or there.

Before I knew it, three days had passed and all I vaguely remembered was people coming and going. Folks brought food and flowers in a blur of activity and grieving. The flowers that came by the vanloads covered the entire downstairs.

Alone at night, we noticed the nights were harder to take than the days.

When I walked through downstairs at night, I could almost hear the distant chatter and rumbling of activity. But I knew it was not real. It was that replay button just on the other side of my audio subconscious, forever there to remind of what I once had.

Four days after the accident, the most dreaded time in all my life arrived. We buried our children.

Pastor Ryan took care of all the details in organizing a church service. At the service, it was standing room only as the sanctuary was packed with classmates, schoolteachers, church members, business associates, friends from the yacht club, and many people we didn't know, but they all had a connection to our kids. The crowd also filled the foyer.

At the altar, the three caskets were lined end to end. We sat in the front row. Joanne sat to my right, and Mary Ruth sat on her other side. They both wore dark veils to mask their grief. Although I was in the front row, I couldn't hear a word the pastor was saying over the screeching pain in my heart and mind. But later, I heard he gave a beautiful sermon on how God loves us and watches over our ultimate well-being. From the bitter cold Arctic of my soul I thought, "Well, what else would he have talked about?"

The kids' friends and teachers told stories about them for about a half hour. And so quickly, we were standing up to lead the caskets out of the church. Mary Ruth took Joanne's other arm and we all walked together.

It took eighteen pallbearers to carry the caskets down the aisle and through the foyer. At the church entrance, we stood aside as each casket was carried out to the procession of cars. We fell in behind the last one and walked to our limo.

After we got in, I closed my eyes to shut out the world. Inside my head, I kept asking, "How could this be happening to me, to us?" I asked this all the way to the Santa Barbara Cemetery. We sat in the quiet hollow of our disbelief that this could have happened to us. The funeral procession of cars and limousines stretched a mile.

Ten minutes later, as we drove through the gates of the cemetery, I had flashbacks of entering these very gates when I buried my mother and father. Years ago, when Mom and Dad passed away, I bought this family plot so we could all be together. But in my head, it was always the kids burying us, not the other way around.

Two blocks from the family plot, I noticed a large crowd already there waiting for us. This wasn't the crowd that was at the church. They were all behind us. This crowd was a mixture of more friends, neighbors, classmates, and strangers. Who knew I had such fantastic children? I was sincerely moved. It moved me because it showed my children touched so many lives in a positive way. It's a true testament to their loving and kind disposition.

They were good kids, but I was continuously realizing that my children were gone. The car stopped and I led Joanne and Mary Ruth up the knoll to the plot. When the caskets arrived, they were set above their open graves.

I didn't understand why God would bring me to this point of my life. To give me so much and then take it all away so suddenly made no sense to me. It wasn't fair. We listened to Pastor Ryan speak his words, but I didn't hear any of it.

Our closest friends stood directly behind us. They were all there with their wives and children, along with Claire and Charles, who closed the company for the entire day out of respect.

Pastor Ryan walked over to me and nodded. That was our cue to tenderly place the roses we held on the caskets. I took Joanne's elbow and guided us to John first, since he was our oldest. I took a moment to remember when we first brought him home. Joanne and I were so nervous holding and taking care of this human so small, we were certain that we were going to break him or even accidentally kill the poor infant. I remember the sparks of magic he brought into our lives. I was sure that God had blessed me with a son among sons.

We moved to Rachel's coffin. We laid our hands on it. Our princess was gone and she took her laughter with her. Why did she have to be taken out of our lives so wickedly?

And then we moved to Edwin and thanked him for having come here and having been a part of our lives. He shared his playful demeanor and enormous curiosity with everyone he met.

It was hard to realize that two weeks ago we had the perfect day on the *Oh Happy Day*. The great benefit from parenting is the unconditional love demanded by any circumstances. But right now, flashes of anger wanted to explode out of me, but I didn't let them. Not now. And besides, I wouldn't know what to do with my anger.

As soon as I saw them lowering the caskets, I dropped my head into my hands. This blow went to the very core of me, forever branding its bitter memory on the front pages of my soul. Somehow, I felt this was entirely my fault.

When Pastor Ryan finished speaking, the graveyard crew went to work. The large crowd turned and slowly dispersed back to their cars. A few came up to us to give us a hug or a few words of assurance.

Charles came over to give me a hug and offered, "Michael, if there's anything I can do, you just have to ask. And take as much time as you need, really." And within a few minutes, they were all gone.

We stayed to watch the grounds keepers complete the burial process. When they unrolled the pre-cut grass over the dirt, my heart turned numb, as I now knew more than ever that the kids are not ever coming back. But this moment keeps repeating itself and I never expected this would be part of the process.

I had to spend a moment with my parents, so I went over to their graves and had a few words with them. I said, "Hi, Mom and Dad. I know this is a bit of a shock, but I want you to take care of John, Rachel, and Edwin. You're going to have to watch over them for us now." A part of me wanted to say more, but I couldn't articulate the words.

Joanne, Mary Ruth, and I sat for a long while before it was time to leave.

On the way home, inside the limo Joanne laid her head against my shoulder and for a minute I felt strong, that we were going to survive this calamity. We were both going to need counseling after this, and soon. Are we supposed to start a new family? Is that what this was about? Did we so screw up raising our kids that God had to take them away from us so that we could try again and maybe do it right the next time? No, I didn't screw up. Don't trip, I told myself.

The sun was setting as the limo dropped us off at our front door. The driver let us out and then left. I held Joanne's hand to the door, until I had to unlock it. Inside the foyer, subtly we both stopped and listened for the sounds of a lively house. That's what parents do when they get home. They listen for the sounds of life, love, and laughter. And from whatever room it may be coming, they search it out in hopes of finding a hug, a kiss, or a smile.

But alas, there was none of that today. Nor would there be any of it any other day. Joanne and Mary Ruth walked into the family room. I stood alone, frozen in the foyer. I was immobilized by the void of silence coming from inside my home. From my gut came a surge of despair and confusion. It turned into a cauldron of anger. I begged out loud, "I just want to know why. Can't You tell me that much?" I yanked off my shoes and threw them as hard as I could against the wall. I slammed one shoe into a painting, and to my pleasure the whole thing fell off the wall and crashed to the floor. I targeted a lamp with my other shoe and it also went crashing to the floor.

I walked straight to the backyard and up to the grill. I lit it. I took off my socks and threw them into the fire. The black jacket followed, as did every piece of clothes. I had to burn every piece of clothing that witnessed the burial of my children. And when I was done throwing it all on the fire, I stood naked and watched it turn to smoke and ashes. My head fell into my hands and I sobbed from a bottomless place of loneliness I had never felt before. When did God ever think I had the strength to go through this?

Well, He was wrong this time. Then I reminded myself that all children belong to God. They all belong to Him. They never belonged to me at any time, and from the moment they were born they were always His. "Oh God, I need You to get me through this. Why would You do this to me? Oh, God, give me wisdom. I need wisdom! You are the essence of all wisdom that permeates the whole universe. Would You please pity me with an ounce of it? Just a drop of it! Why me?

They were Yours to begin with. You had the right to take them, but why? Just let me know why!" I demanded.

Joanne walked up behind me and wrapped me in a blanket. She embraced me, and in the comfort of her arms I said, "We need wisdom. Let's pray, Joanne."

She replied, "Pray for us both, Michael." And then we cried in each other's arms. We were consumed by our pain, sitting near the flames and ashes.

I thought about my resolution of forgiveness. And who was I going to forgive? What could I do to the driver of the Porsche? I could kill him. No, I couldn't do that. That's not me. That's not what I'm about. I could stalk him for a few days or maybe weeks, but what would be the point? That's not who I am. But didn't he cause the accident? That creep killed my family. Yes, he's to blame. No, he's not. I couldn't blame him. As if my three children could be killed and God not know about it until the eleven o'clock evening news? No, that's not the way it works. If He knows when the sparrow falls, then He surely knew when He was going to take John, Rachel, and Edwin. I know He knew it before it happened. I just know He did. So why would He do this to me? I never saw it coming.

God is more mysterious than all the mysteries ever combined. He hides when He wants to and shows His face when it fancies Him. I begged Him to touch me with a drop of His healing powers as my sadness yearned to know what life could be like never seeing my children again. The love they radiated throughout our lives will never shine again. I will say this, God sure did send me three wonderful children and for the time I had them, it was real joy. And now He took them away. Is He laughing at me? Could He find pleasure in our pain and horror? Is that who He is?

Sometime through the haze of the night, Joanne and I found ourselves walking to our bedroom. As I climbed into bed, I failed to find what used to be the happiest moment of the day: climbing into bed, knowing everything was all right with the world. But tonight it felt hollow. Lying here, I hoped to dream of a life I had, that I may escape from the reality of this one. Sensing the open distance in bed between Joanne and me, we're going to counseling. Maybe we'll ask Pastor Ryan? Maybe we should seek out a professional? Maybe someone who handles trauma cases? And I'd be okay with that. She would too, but this isn't the right time to bring it up. We both sighed in synchronicity and fell asleep.

Sometime the next morning, Joanne told me she would like to spend some time with Mary Ruth at her house. Without hesitation, I encouraged her to get away for a while. I would miss her, but I understood that she wanted to get away.

Throughout the morning, I spent time in my office reading scripture. Earlier, I had closed the doors to the kids' rooms. I didn't know when, but the day will come when I can walk through those doors to take care of business. Perhaps find a little closure. Maybe I'd get around to it next week, or maybe next year.

The afternoon arrived too fast as Joanne and Mary Ruth were ready to leave. I told Joanne that whenever and at whatever time of the day or night she wanted me to come and get her, she should just call. We kissed and hugged before she got into the front seat. Mary Ruth came around to give me a hug. I surely welcomed her love and support.

I watched them as they drove down the driveway to the street. I didn't know what I was supposed to do now. The thought of spending the night alone in this house did not appeal to me.

At around four o'clock I decided to spend the night on the yacht. I could be out the door in a few minutes, and why not? I locked down the house and grabbed a few belongings and some leftovers from the kitchen. Instantly, I felt a little relief just knowing I was going to spend the night on the *Oh Happy Day*. I called Joanne and told her of my plans.

Lucifer found the Oh Happy Day *with no problem. He came looking to destroy the yacht, and what better time to get some entertainment than when Michael was actually on it and out at sea. Invisibly sitting in the captain's chair, Lucifer waited patiently for him.*

As I stepped onto the wharf, I noticed some beautiful clouds that should make for an impressive sunset. I unzipped the various canvas panels, climbed inside, and prepped the boat for sea while putting my personal items and food away. After executing the routine checklist, I pulled away from the dock in minutes. I didn't know what I wanted to find out there on the ocean, maybe just a different environment. I felt some satisfaction just knowing I was going away. Maybe I'd wake up early before dawn, have a bagel and cappuccino, and watch the sunrise from the fly bridge.

As the yacht raced for the open ocean chasing the sunset, the silhouettes of two men could be seen against the big bright red clouds that reached all the way down to touch the horizon. The captain was at the steering wheel high up on the fly bridge, and the other was downstairs reclining his feet up on the port wall. The two silhouettes were made of complete opposite polar fabrics.

I headed due west and throttled up some more. I turned wide to watch the town recede in the background, leaving nothing between that and me except time and a lot of space. And then I asked, "How can I leave behind me that which is an integral part me: my children?"

I throttled up more and lifted the twin engines to full speed and sizzled over the water like a skipping stone. The onslaught of the rushing air made me work at keeping my face facing forward. But I didn't care. I was at full throttle with two full tanks, and I just held on. The remnants of a majestic sunset surrendered to the big electric blue sky bringing on the night. Lonely planets edged out their places in the darkening blue. I turned around to find land was scarcely visible.

I screamed out loud. I screamed for God to hear me. I shouted His name at the top of my lungs, repeating my screams like a mantra. "God! God! God! How could You not hear me? I know You're listening!" I bellowed my questions at Him at the top of my lungs. "Was it my fault? Is it Your fault?"

After an hour of ranting and relentless appeals for God's attention, I pulled the throttle back down to neutral and coasted awhile. Maybe I wanted something to eat?

I dropped anchor, although it wouldn't do much good this far out to sea, and made my way to the galley. Pulling my Bible and some other inspirational books out of my bag, I put them on the table. After

I warmed up dinner and settled into the leather booth, I stopped to give grace.

However shallow my gratitude may have seemed, I gave it with the minimal amount of anything I had left in me. I folded my hands in prayer. "Father, I just want to ask that you bless this meal, and I pray for my three children. I ask that you bless Joanne…"

Invisibly, Lucifer made his way down to the engine room. He looked around at the possibilities of creating some entertainment. He turned this knob and that knob, and a lever here and a lever there. Finally, with the power of evil, he pressed his foot against a bolt and broke off the fuel injectors. Gasoline squirted out between the metal threads and onto the floor, quickly forming a puddle. It seeped down onto the engine and causes a chemical reaction.

I continued praying "…And Father, I pray for Your peace"…and when I said the "c" in "peace," a loud boom rocked the boat left and right. My heart pounded as I got out of the booth. I ran down another half-flight of stairs to the engine room where a small fire had broken out.

I ran up to the main level for the fire extinguisher. When I got there, I pulled the fire extinguisher from its cradle and raced back downstairs to the engine room. At the galley, I missed a step and because my hands were holding the extinguisher, I went face first onto the floor. "Ough," I yelled. I got up and continued to the engine room. When I got there, I was stunned to see how quickly the fire had spread. I opened the extinguisher and sprayed it at the bottom of the flames.

As I was putting out one corner of the fire, I noticed a spray of fire right on the engine block. The gas leak near the injectors was spraying gas, but as soon as it came into contact with oxygen, it turned into flame. It was like a fan of fire and nothing I've ever seen before. I pointed the hose at it and was about to hit it with foam, but thought I'd better not.

I took off my shirt to pound the air out of the flames. But when I ran my shirt over the engine, the squirting fuel splashed it with gas and in a mini-second turned it into one ball of fire in my hand.

Immediately, I ran to the fly bridge, and at the controls I turned off the gas valves and bolted back down the stairs.

In the engine room I saw that the spraying gasoline was out, thank God. But the fire was now burning up the ceiling and the forward wall. I hit it with the extinguisher. I ran it across the ceiling and at the wall. I could see I was making progress. With half the fire out I was feeling hopeful.

But a minute later, the extinguisher went belly up on me. It sputtered to empty. I shook it and sprayed again, but only a little trickled out. I shook it again and sprayed. But even less came out. I had a fire onboard with no way to put it out. The smoke was thickening up through all the levels and cabins. Instinctively, I knew I had to get an S.O.S. message out.

I ran up to the navigation table and reached for the radio handset and shouted, "May Day! May Day! This is the *Oh Happy Day.* May Day! May Day! Anyone hear this transmission? May Day! May Day!"

I looked back at the black smoke and realized I had to abandon ship.

I ran past the column of smoke coming up the stairs and outside to the bench against the stern wall. I lifted the leather bench for the inflatable raft. I hauled it out and hit the inflate button. No! Too soon! And before I knew it, a ten-man raft exploded to full size right on top of me. I grabbed onto it. I had to get a rope for it. I reached back into the box, and I put my hand on top of a thirty-foot rope with clipped ends; exactly what I wanted. I clipped one end of the rope to the raft and the other to my belt loop. I threw the raft overboard into the dark waters. To my surprise, a built-in strobe lit up. I forgot about that feature and thanked God I had it. I ran to get back to the navigation table and the radio.

I looked at the flames coming up the stairs that in a couple minutes could potentially cut me off from the stern. But I had to try calling out again. When I reached the radio I shouted, "May Day! May Day! This is the *Oh Happy Day* at 34 by 26 at 50 degrees west."

I repeated it half a dozen times before I had to make my escape while I could. Then I remembered the photo. Should I try to save the family photo hanging in the galley? Was it worth it?

Outside, along the narrow walkway, I rushed to the forward, opened a hatch above the master cabin, and climbed down. I grabbed a blanket, covered myself, and ran through the smoke on my way to the galley. I yanked the photo off the wall and turned back to make my escape.

I climbed up onto the deck and looked at the stern. It was spewing six-foot flames coming up from the stairwell. I stood with the photo in one hand and the rope to a raft in the other.

Before I threw myself into the dark open waters, I tugged on the rope, bringing the raft closer to me. I pulled it up out of the water and close enough so I could slip the photo into a pocket below the flap bench seat. I let go of the raft and dropped it back into the dark water. The only thing left to do was to throw myself overboard.

I stole only a couple seconds and took in the destruction of our family boat now engulfed in flames. Then I remembered there were still 200 gallons of gas. I should get as far from there as quickly as possible.

I didn't want to throw myself into the raft, as I could tear it as I landed in it. The smallest rip could be disastrous. I took a deep breath and threw myself overboard. I landed about ten feet from the raft. As I swam towards it, a current kept me in place. So I just tugged on the rope to get the raft to me.

But the current was so strong, I started moving backwards. The raft came towards me, but the current was strange, and as the raft got closer, it suddenly passed by to my left. With rope in hand, the raft pulled me, and then I was following it. I looked at the boat in flames and saw that it was drawn into the same current. I didn't understand any of this. I kept yanking on the rope, as I had to get in the raft.

The flames on the boat were lighting up the ocean, and I could see that I was captured by one big whirlpool.

The whirlpool pushed everything in a circle. I watched a funnel at the bottom of the whirlpool grow larger and larger. And worse, with every spin around, I was coming closer to slamming into my flaming boat.

Knowing I'm a good swimmer, I let go of the rope and watched the raft move to my right behind me. I started swimming to get out of the whirlpool but I got nowhere. I didn't even remember to put on a life jacket. How stupid was I. That should have been the first thing I did.

I saw the raft coming back around. The whirlpool got stronger and deeper. It was now just a large drain. I was being pulled counter-clockwise along a curve wall of water. As the raft got to the closest point, I reached up to grab it. But the current pulled me to the left, and gravity pulled me down.

I fell through several feet of air before dunking under the water at the center of the vortex. My face surfaced just long enough to take a big gulp of air and then I was under again. I could feel water itself taking me down, pushing me deeper into the ocean.

The rope tied to the raft on the surface stopped me from sinking farther. I grabbed the rope and started pulling on it. I was able to crawl my way up the rope. I looked up and I saw the boat crashing into the funnel above me. The whirlpool current spun the boat around and around underwater. But now it was between me and the surface. It was sinking fast and it was all I could do to get out of the way. It passed within a foot of me. As the stern glided by on its way to the ocean floor, a dagger of mockery cut me as the words *Oh Happy Day* floated in front of me. I continued pulling on the rope tied to the raft.

I finally reached air and took the longest breath of my life. Air, sweet air filled my lungs. "Oh, God, please don't leave me now! Help me," I pleaded. Instantly, I felt the cold water and the cold air. I swam to the raft. I had to get in the raft as quickly as possible.

I climbed in. Shirtless and completely soaked, I curled into a ball to try to stay warm. I hoped the strobe light would get someone's attention. I snuggled up against the side of the raft to keep the cold wind from hitting me.

I tried to remember the little nuances of what transpired just before I heard that bang. What did happen? I never smelled gasoline, yet there was a gas leak. I was vexed. And why didn't I have a second fire extinguisher? I was so careless. But who would have thought that I would ever need even one extinguisher, much less two? Oh, my God, what happened to me? Is God punishing me? Did I do something wrong? If I screwed up, will He ever tell me?

I shivered, half-naked and exhausted, huddled in the raft. My hands and feet were freezing. I tried to keep warm by burying my hands under my arms and rubbing my feet together. I felt insignificant as I prayed to survive, with only the stars bearing witness to my struggle.

If I lived, would it matter? By all definition and purpose, my life had come to an end. I stared at the stars and wondered where my three children had gone. Are they out there dancing through the Milky Way? Where did they go? Are they out there visiting Orion? I wanted to know. Because if they were, I was ready to walk away from all of this so I could be with them again.

So, God, if there were ever a time that You would take me, this was it. "What do You want from me?" I screamed at the top of my lungs. I screamed so loud the stars could feel my anger. "What do You want from me?" I begged of Him. My anger kept me warm.

I thought, "I'll drift for days and slowly starve and dehydrate to death. No matter, I'll see my kids in just a few days time from now. However this turns out, I'm totally fine with it." I looked at the stars and shouted to God, "Kill me, or let me live. It's a question You, oh Lord, hold in Your hands every day. Every day You decide if You want me today. Is it today, oh Lord? Is it today? Because I'm right here! I'm right here!"

And with that, I felt that if I died out there right then, I would be okay with it. I was ready. But, what would happen to Joanne? And then I passed out.

I woke up feeling a change in the level of light of the open sky. I opened my eyes and saw the predawn light. It turned into a colorful sunrise. But look at me. I was supposed to be having my cappuccino and bagel on the fly bridge. But look, Oh, Lord, this is where You find me this morning: half naked, floating aimlessly out in the middle of the Pacific Ocean. I tried standing up and almost tipped overboard. I sat down. That was stupid, I thought. Perhaps I should go back to sleep. Or, should I continue my rant and rave at God, now that He can see me in the sunlight?

Was anyone looking for me? Did anyone hear my message? Too bad daylight arrived. I had a better shot at getting seen at night with this strobe light than I did in the daylight. I was just a dot on the ocean. I was nothing more than just a dot. I lay back down and fell asleep.

Sometime later, I heard a roar. It scared the sleep out of me as I saw it was a helicopter hovering above me. I saw the helicopter crew lowering a basket. When it reached me, I grabbed the photo and climbed into the basket. As I was lifted off the raft, I looked at the huge open sea. The basket spun a few times, giving me a 360-degree view of the seascape. It's a natural wonder so large, so inviting, so mesmerizing, and yet so dangerous. My eyes were transfixed on the horizon line, that great divide between heaven and earth.

So that day, God spared my life. As I was lifted skywards under the belly of this Coast Guard angel, I thanked God from the bottom of my heart. I thanked Him repeatedly and most sincerely for not leaving me to die out in the open ocean. And then I remembered my lost children and instantly my happy heart sank at the memory of reality.

When the basket reached the bay of the helicopter, a couple guys in helmets reached out to me. They pulled me to safety and out of the basket. I stood up, handed one of them the photo, and tried to find my balance. And for a second, I was all right. But my legs didn't do what I wanted and I think someone caught me on the way down to the floor. Because no matter how hard I fought it, I passed out.

In the white, overstuffed booth onboard God's Gulf Stream G650, John, Rachel, and Edwin sat opposite each other with their eyes closed. Beautiful music slowly woke them up. John looked out the window and marveled at the view.

Rachel looked out the window, too, and invited Edwin to share the vista of the earth from 70,000 feet. They wondered, like everyone else wonders, how they got here. "Can you smell that perfume?" she asked them. The cabin was filled with the sweetest fragrance they had ever smelled.

John wondered out loud, "Where are we?" Edwin looked up the aisle and saw God walking towards them. He sat down next to John as they smiled at His arrival. He seemed very familiar to them.

"Welcome, my children," He exclaimed. His countenance was filled with bliss.

Rachel asked, "Why aren't we with Mom and Dad?"

"Because you are with Me now," He answered.

Edwin piped in, "What happened?"

God heard the question and wanted to answer truthfully, but considered the consequences. So God, being God, smiled and answered Edwin with, "That is not important right now. What is important is what is about to happen. I called you home for a very special purpose."

Rachel asked Him, "Did we do something wrong?"

God reached His arm around her and assured her, "Absolutely not. I'm so proud of you in every way. You always showed a love for Me, respect for your parents, good manners, you never swore, and *mostly* you were respectful of others." God glanced at Edwin.

John asked, "What's going to happen?"

God explained to them, "Your father on earth is in a spiritual battle of strength over failure, of living faith over doubt, and a testament to one man's love for Me. If your daddy succeeds, there will be a great wave of love and kindness reverberating throughout the world. He will be a testament across the cosmos to the spiritual fortitude of mankind."

Rachel asked, "But why couldn't we stay and help?"

God smiled and told her, "You are helping."

John tried to understand but had to ask, "Is that why we had to leave?"

God answered, "Yes."

Edwin wanted to know, "Where will we go?"

God laughed and answered, "You're here. Well, not here *here*, this is just a stopover but you're here. Isn't it nice?" God gestured around at the luxury, hoping for their approval. The kids murmur how nice it was but there was only one thing on the kids' minds.

Rachel asked, "Will we ever see our parents again?"

God looked her straight in the eye and said, "Yes, in time."

John smiled and made an observation about himself. He glanced out the window, took a deep breath, and confessed, "I feel really different."

Edwin, feeling his first glimpse of bliss, smiled at John and offered, "John, I feel so much love, it's sort of neat."

God looked at each of them and etched these words in their hearts: "That's because love never dies."

CHAPTER FOUR

WHERE DID IT ALL GO?

I felt my tongue against the roof of my mouth. That's what it was, my tongue touching my teeth. And I discovered I had hands and feet, and a body to go with it all. I inhaled deeply and before I knew it, I was opening my eyes. But where was I? I looked around trying to recognize the room, but I didn't.

I turned my head and saw a woman in the chair next to me. I looked at her. She turned to look at me and stood. Her smile radiated through my memory bank and I smiled back at Joanne.

Joanne asked, "How are you?"

I took her question to heart and did a brief analysis of my body. I was not in pain. I felt my feet and rubbed my toes against one another. I made a fist with my hands and I said, "I guess I'm okay."

I looked about the room and I could see I was in a hospital. And then I remembered the freezing cold night I passed, nearly dying in the raft. Oh, wow, I remembered struggling under water. And then I remembered this life apart from my children. I survived all that, to wake up to this, again. How was I supposed to survive with this canyon of woe in my heart and in my mind?

Overcome with emotion, Joanne leaned over and hugged me. She started crying on my chest, "I was afraid I was going to lose you, too. Don't ever leave again. I'm the one who's supposed to die first and don't forget it."

Slowly, my arms reached up to hold her. It was good to feel her hug. I was happy to be alive, I guess. I asked, "How long have I been here?"

She said, "You were rescued nine days ago."

"Nine days?" I asked in disbelief. How could nine days have passed? Nine days passed on the earth, and I wasn't even a part of it. "Where am I?" I asked her.

"Cottage Hospital. Thank God you're all right. What happened?"

I took a deep breath and remembered. The more I remembered, the crueler it appeared from every angle. An involuntary "Ugh" came from my gut as I remembered the high points of my seaward journey into hell. I stuttered, trying to speak. "I was in the galley, there was a fire, a loud explosion sound, a gas leak, I switched the fuel off, a gas leak caught the engine room on fire, and it got out of control."

My parched throat made it difficult to speak. I pointed at the water, and Joanne poured me a glass. After a swig, I continued, "And then there was a whirlpool. I was caught in a whirlpool that spun me around and around. And it nearly knocked me into the burning boat. Then I fell into the whirlpool and got sucked under water. The boat sank. I got to the surface. I got in the raft and drifted...until I passed out. The next thing I knew it was sunrise, and then awhile later they picked me up. I remember the helicopter."

Joanne held her hands in prayer, and gave a genuine "thank you" to God for bringing me back.

"Was I in a coma?" I asked.

She said, "Two days ago you woke up and then went right back out. Do you remember that? The doctors said you are experiencing a breakdown from exhaustion. I believe those are the words they used."

I became more cognizant of the room and the flower arrangements from one end of the room to the other. I thought to myself, we've been getting too many flowers lately.

Joanne said, "I think I should find a doctor and let the nurses know you're awake." As she turned to leave, Larry walked in. It was good to see him, and apparently he'd been by to see me every day since I got there. Joanne left the room.

I asked, "What's the date?"

Larry answered, "It's January 19th."

In no time, Larry told me the bad news. Just the day before, he had heard that BriMar did not get the Pentagon contract. He heard it from Charles, as Charles was the one to get the call in my absence. Larry said apologetically, "Maybe it was not my place to tell you, Michael. But I thought you should know."

"You did right, Larry, thanks. Please hand me my pants," I said.

Larry looked at me and said, "I don't think you should get out of bed, Michael."

"Larry, get me my pants or I'll get them myself," I demanded. He handed me a nearby pair.

I sat up and turned out to put my feet into my pant legs. It all seemed fine and painless. I untied the hospital garb and dropped it on the bed. "Where's my shirt? I must have a shirt here somewhere. No, I didn't show up with a shirt, that's right, I have no shirt. I can't go anywhere without a shirt, can I?" I asked Larry. Larry shook his head no. But as I was asking, I started opening drawers. And lo and behold, Joanne had brought a couple shirts and some clothes for me from home. I smiled at her consideration while putting them on.

Joanne walked back in and barked, "What are you doing?"

"I have to get to the office. Something has gone terribly wrong," I explained to her.

"Michael, get back in bed, the doctor is on his way," she said, reaching for my arm.

"Joanne, I have to go. I'll call you in a little while, please don't try and stop me." I continued out the door.

Larry drove us to the office. On the way there, he told me the contract went to an aggressive and relatively new upstart competitor, Rabill, Inc. out in Phoenix. They took our contract by undercutting us by a margin that wasn't even close. When we arrived, I surprised everybody. People were genuinely happy to see me. I didn't want to say much to anyone. I just wanted to find Charles.

I walked past my office and surprised Claire. But I continued to Charles's office. I asked his secretary Eveleen if he had anyone in his office. She replied, "No."

So I walked in, taking him by complete surprise. "What happened?"

After Charles caught his breath, he asked, "And how are you, Michael?"

I repeated, "What happened?"

Charles started into the bad news. "Well, it's like this, the bid that you submitted was over-inflated and it crashed and burned. I've been taking calls around the clock from every board member and have done nothing but damage control in the past couple days. They're all very upset and are calling for *change*. They want to shake things up and I can't blame them. They want to fire somebody and I can't blame them. Losing this bid will set this company back years."

I stood my ground. "Nobody knows that better than I do. I'm the guy who steered this ship all the way to get listed on the stock exchange!"

"Of course, that's what I told them," Charles said. But he turned a different shade of flesh. In an instant, I was yanked out of my security and knew I was really, completely alone. Charles was always my champion to the board, but if they overrode him, it could be bad. Charles stood up, looked me in the eye, and said, "Several board members called for your resignation, but I couldn't fight them. I tried, but they didn't see any other choice."

The president of the board of directors was Mr. Henry Beck, who was in his sixties and still active in a variety of businesses. BriMar was successful because Mr. Beck insisted on an atmosphere of listening to those in the field, and on that day he apparently wasn't listening to Charles.

"I've done all that I could. They let you go," he stammered.

"What do you mean?"

"They fired you," he said to me.

I asked, "How can they do that? I helped build this company. They can't fire me, not over this! We can make a comeback, we always do. And why didn't we get that contract?"

Coldly, almost accusingly, Charles fired back, "Because your numbers were too high!"

"You approved those numbers," I reminded him.

"There's nothing I could do!"

Sadly, I watched Charles turn into someone I had never seen before.

So, without much to lose, I threatened his bottom line with a prediction: "BriMar will be lost without me."

Charles found his vanity, and with a jerk of his head and a heap of sarcasm said, "Ask me in a year and I'll let you know. Personally, I think we'll be just fine. I'm sorry it had to end this way."

"This is not over yet," I said as I turned and left.

I got to my office and motioned for Claire to follow. I told her, "Close the door. Charles just fired me, and I'm going to get out of here now. Would you please find a box so I can put my things in it? And call for a town car to drive me home. I want to get out of here soon." By the look on Claire's face, I realized the callousness of my delivering such shocking news to her, my greatest supporter and loyal friend. I went to hug her and said, "I'm sorry, Claire."

"How could they do this to you?" she griped. "This place will fall apart without you. Don't they know that? I'm just an assistant but I can see that!"

I shook my head. "You were never just an assistant, Claire."

When she returned with a couple of boxes, we started packing all my personal things. Luckily, the town car arrived in fifteen minutes and then I was gone.

I sank into the seat and looked out at the passing neighborhood. I was stupefied by the events over the last month. I didn't understand any of it. My life was in free fall and my parachute, God, was letting it happen. Otherwise, it wouldn't be happening. If, after dedicating my life to Him, this nightmare could happen to me, then He had to have known about it. He had to know. And since He knew, why was He letting this happen?

Joanne was not going to take this well. I was already worried about her before. Maybe I should worry about me? I didn't know what I was going to do. I didn't care. We had enough paper and tangible assets that we could dispose of to carry us a few years. But, down in my gut, I didn't think Joanne was going to take it very well. It was one more bad news day for us.

When the car pulled up to the house, I felt emptiness in my heart just looking at it. Memories had taken on a force that I couldn't shake. And maybe I shouldn't try. It was okay to remember. I got out and asked the driver to drop the boxes around the side entrance. I didn't want Joanne seeing them and asking, "What's up with the boxes?" I'd tell her when the time was right, definitely that day. But just not immediately.

In the foyer, I yelled, "Hello?"

"I'm in the kitchen," Joanne answered back. When she appeared, she scolded me. "You're supposed to be in the hospital!" Instead of replying, I hugged her. And in our embrace I just wanted to believe that we were going to get through this.

She kissed me and said, "I love you. Thank you for coming back to me."

I meant it deeply when I replied, "I love you, too."

We took a moment in silence and held each other. The moment didn't need words. And then I realized how much my body hurt and how tired I felt. "I'm going to go lie down," I said while sliding away from her arms.

She said, "Dinner will be ready in half an hour. Would you like me to bring it up to you?"

"No thank you, I'll be back down in twenty minutes," I replied.

I walked upstairs and passed the kids' rooms with a deep sigh. They were no longer there, I thought bitterly to myself. When I got to the bedroom, I walked into my closet, pulled off my shoes, and changed into my home clothes. For some odd reason it seemed like it had been a long time since I was here last. I was devoid of sentimental value as I looked inside my closet filled with extravagant clothes and expensive shoes. Nothing had the same color it used to have. I would do without all of it if it meant one more hour with my children. And without warning, my eyes filled with tears and in no time they rolled down my face. I just had to allow it. I'd been through shock after shock, and I wasn't going to judge myself. Apparently, God was doing a lot of that on His own.

I sat on the bed, humbly broken. In my pursuit of living right, I tried to practice a motto I once came up with: "Find humility before it finds you." Right now, my humility had no bounds. I prayed, "Oh, Lord, if Your hand is in this, I pray that You give me the strength to see my way to wisdom. You did say to pray for those who offend us. Is this the part where I'm supposed to be practicing 'infinite forgiveness'?" What was I thinking? But regardless, "Your wisdom shall override my ignorance and doubt, so I pray for Charles, oh Lord. I pray that You rain blessings and love on him; shower him in Your love, drown him in Your love, and bless his family. And God, I ask that you bless Henry Beck, overflow his life with Your love, and to all the other board members that wanted me out...I'm just at a loss for words. If this is what You want, this is how it's going to be. I don't know what else to say...I pray for Your strength as I tell Joanne more bad news."

A half hour later, over dinner, her questions inevitably led to why I had to rush out of the hospital to get to the office in a panic.

I knew that I had to tell her the truth right then. I swallowed, placed my fork down, and looked at her. I took her hand in mine and said, "Honey, there's something I have to tell you. When I got to the office today I was told by Charles that since we didn't get the pentagon contract, I was let go by the board of directors."

I worked at putting my best spin on it and reassured her that we had plenty of money to get through to my next career opportunity. And even if that takes years, we still had enough.

Joanne quickly inhaled as she pulled her hand back. "I don't understand how you can take this so lightly, Michael. Without your income, how long do you think this will last?" she asked, waving her arms everywhere.

"Charles told me that he did the best he could to talk them out of it, but they took a vote."

She put her hand to her lips and squeezed her fingers into a fist. Her anger and confusion throbbed in her hands when she admitted, "I don't understand."

"Darling, I can't explain it, because there's no explanation for it," I told her.

"There has to be, Michael, you just don't know it yet. But I want to know why all this is happening to us. I want answers to why God is punishing us."

I stuttered and failed to form a complete sentence that had any resemblance of reason.

"What is going on, Michael?" she asked, demanding an answer.

"I don't know, Joanne, I don't know why this is happening."

"Oh, my God, what are we going to live on? What are we going to do?" she asked, panicking.

I could see she was cementing her faith in doubt. I reached for her hand and held it in both of my hands. I assured her, "I've got a few ideas. We have plenty of paper money we can unload. Our total assets are worth several million dollars."

"And how long do you think that will last us?" she yelled.

"It should last us a few years, maybe five if we cut back here and there," I answered her. I really did not want her to go crazy over this. Jobs come and go, that's life. There was nothing I could do but to let go of my attachment to the job.

She rested her head in her other hand, and with a tone in her voice that I had not heard in years asked me, "What if you pissed off God and you don't even know it?"

There came that other woman who lived in Joanne. She used that snobbery tone that came from growing up in snooty South Pasadena. On the snob scale, Beverly Hills has nothing on South Pasadena.

I asked, "What do you mean? How could I piss off God? And if I did, then I asked for His forgiveness. Don't you think I have gone to Him and asked Him if I've upset Him? Of course I have. I haven't stopped begging to know why."

She looked at me sideways, and with a face I have never seen she declared, "You must have done something. Why would He take our children and almost kill you too. But you survived only to get fired? What does it all mean? Since our lives have been turned upside down, maybe we can go to Pastor Ryan and ask him for some of that half million dollars back that we gave him."

"I would never consider such a suggestion. It was money we gave to God, not Pastor Ryan," I reminded her.

At the pinnacle of her arrogance she replied, "I'm not asking for all of it back, maybe just half. Can't he live with that?"

"He who? Pastor Ryan, or God?" I asked sarcastically.

"Either one."

Since when did she become so cynical? I replied, "Don't be ridiculous, you can't give something to God and take it back when it was His in the first place!"

In a razor-sharp tone she bellowed, "Well then maybe He won't notice it's missing! Have you stopped to think that God has it in for us, Michael? Do you see a pattern? I mean, doesn't three make a pattern? And we're in a pattern!"

I was not subscribing to her doubt and negative slants, so I questioned her pattern theory. I asked, "Pattern of what? Tragedies happen every day! Yes, children die in car accidents. Yes, people are killed in boating accidents in the ocean. And yes, right or wrong, people are fired every day for things beyond their control. What else do you want me to say?"

"I want you to say it's just not all a coincidence, that's all," she answered.

"I can't say that until I know what's causing all this," I confessed.

With one hand on her hip, she pointed the other hand at me and waved it around the air to proclaim, "This is not all one big coincidence."

I took a deep breath and said, "We're both in shock and in need of counseling. Would you like to get counseling?"

"That's not the point," she answered. She continued her open hostility throughout the night until it was time to go to bed.

Climbing into bed she said, "I want you to say that maybe your faith isn't what you think it is."

"What does that mean?"

"I want you to consider that maybe God isn't impressed with the half million dollars you donated," she said.

"How can you talk to me like that?" I asked.

In her open anger she berated God when she said, "Because, darling, what kind of God would let so many bad things happen to good people like us?"

Her words were like bullets ricocheting through my analytical mind. "I don't know. That's what I've been asking myself. I want to know the same things you do, Joanne, but I haven't found any answers yet," I said with a tone that pleaded for her to stop arguing.

She turned off her lamp, and before turning over she said, "You'd better figure it out soon, although I can't imagine what else could happen." She rolled over and gave me her back. I knew she had checked out. She was cold and not at all like herself.

I thought I'd just let it go because she was under a lot of stress. Just drop it and go to sleep. I turned off my lamp. I remembered I should get up and pray. But I was exhausted and I'd probably prayed enough that day anyway.

Hours later, at 4:45 in the morning, any creatures of the dark outside near my pool would have noticed the water sloshing back and forth over the lip.

Inside the house, the distant rumbling of moving earth rose. I woke up feeling the bed vibrate ever so slightly. The vibration grew stronger. The rumbling sounds grew and grew. The closet doors rattled and the bed shook. Joanne turned to me, but I pushed her back. She slid herself off her side of the bed. I turned over and fell next to the bed, hoping a lamp didn't fall on me. The right place to be in an earthquake isn't on the bed. Living in Southern California, we learned the best place to survive an earthquake in the bedroom is actually on the floor right next to the bed. In case the roof collapses, the bed will create a pocket and that's where people survive earthquakes. Doorways are not pockets. The whole house shook as the rumbling pitched like that of a passing train.

As the pictures pounded against the walls, most of the stuff on top of our dressers went bouncing to the floor. The sound of crushing wood and bending metal was loud and terrifying. I turned my face towards Joanne. We could see each other across the open space under the bed. From the other side, I found her looking at me and screaming. And then the electricity went out. And suddenly it all went very dark, as the house continued to shake.

The quake suddenly turned into vertical hammering. Lying on the floor, I could feel the forces of earth coming up to pound the surface. Joanne continued screaming through it all.

I remembered the flashlight I had in the bottom drawer of my night table. I pulled it out, turned it on, and pointed it at Joanne. I could see her looking my way, crying and screaming, "Oh God!"

I turned the light on myself so she could see me across the bed. "I'm here Joanne, it's okay!"

As the earsplitting roar shook the floor, the walls, the bed, and my bones, it sent my adrenaline into hyper-mode. I heard crashing sounds coming from throughout the house. Water pipes broke in the bathroom. We felt like we were being bombed from above and below. I could hear Joanne still screaming. It seemed to last an eternity, what was in reality 45 to 50 seconds. When the shaking stopped, the first thing I did was put on my shoes, because I had heard glass shatter everywhere.

With my flashlight pointed at Joanne, I ran around the bed to hug her tightly. I said, "We got to get out of here, get your slippers on." We bolted upright and headed for the door. She clung to me like a frightened child.

At the bedroom doorway we stopped for a second as I shined my flashlight down the hall to see its condition. I waved the flashlight around the hall and saw large cracks moving horizontally along the middle of the wall. A dozen photographs and framed art had crashed to the floor. I said, "Be careful where you step." That's when I looked up and saw a large four-inch-wide crack in the ceiling, running from one end of the hall to the other.

As we passed the kids' rooms, I wondered how they would have taken to this earth-shattering event. But there was no time for that line of thinking.

I pointed the light down the staircase.

"Is it safe?" she asked.

I answered with doubt and no options, "It looks okay."

Holding onto each other we started down the staircase. We steered close to the wall and away from the drop. What surprised me was all the dust. When we were halfway down, an aftershock rumbled the house with a frightful terror. Joanne screamed, "Tell it to stop! Make it stop!" I held her tightly, and then it stopped.

We hurried down the remaining steps to the door and when I opened it, we discovered that the house had fallen off the foundation. At some point during the first impact, the house fell three feet, and I wasn't even cognizant of exactly when it happened. That's how intense and long the first quake was. I lifted Joanne up onto the ground level, as now the foyer floor was three feet below the pavement level.

As I lifted myself up and out, the electricity came back on. Quickly, I needed to get a visual on the cars in the garage. I grabbed Joanne's hand and hustled her to the keypad near the garage. I punched in the code, and when all the doors opened I could see that all three cars were undamaged. "Thank God!" I blurted out.

But in that second another aftershock rumbled everything, even the trees. It swayed us back and forth, and then once again we felt it turn to punching from the earth below. The electricity went out again. We staggered backwards away from the garage. After ten seconds of continuous pounding and jolting, the point of attachment between the garage roof and the house broke apart. The garage roof fell down on top of all the cars. We both gasped in shock as we shouted, "Oh, my God!" We watched the whole thing go down right in front of us. The aftershock finally stopped. A cloud of dust wafted upward from the garage.

We stood, silently dumbfounded and with all the vulnerability of shaken children.

It was cold, and we were only in our pajamas. I looked out in the distance and beyond the trees. Everything looked normal. I didn't see any plumes of smoke when I looked across the vista.

I turned to Joanne and said, "Let's go to Tom's house." Tom was our nearest neighbor, who lived about half a football-field length away.

We pounded on his door. I held Joanne close as we waited for what seemed like forever before he opened the door.

"Everything okay?" he asked, startled.

Both Joanne and I started talking at once. I asked, "Did you feel the earthquake?"

Tom said, "Yes, I thought I felt something."

Joanne exclaimed, "Something? It knocked our house off the foundation!"

Tom asked, "Really? Are you all right?"

"We need to use your phone," I told him.

Inside, Tom turned on some lights, and I was a bit puzzled that he had electricity and we didn't. When the 911 operator came on, I said, "We've had serious damage caused by this earthquake. The house fell off the foundation. I'm calling from a neighbor's phone. My address is 970 Santa Ynez Road, Montecito."

She asked, "Are there any injuries?"

"Negative," I answered.

Then I got the standard response: "Units are on their way."

Tom offered us coffee, and Joanne replied, "Oh, please."

But I was concerned about the gas line. I told them, "I didn't turn off the gas valve. I should go back up to the house and turn it off. You wait here and catch your breath."

Joanne nodded and said, "I'll be right behind you."

I asked Tom, "Do you have extra flashlights and maybe a couple jackets?"

"Oh sure," he said. He retrieved coats and flashlights from the closet.

I hurried back to the house to shut off the gas valve. Halfway there, I looked up at my house to see if the electricity had come back on. It had not, which was good. I didn't need electricity mixing with gas fumes. And in the far distance I heard sirens. I figured they were off to some other quake-related crisis.

My flashlight led me around to the eastern side of the house where I opened the lid to the gas valve. With the attached wrench, I turned the valve off and heaved a sigh of relief.

I went to check the gas tank next to the garage. The gas tank was buried under the driveway, and I was concerned it might have cracked and could be leaking. Maybe I could measure the amount of gallons over time, to see whether or not it survived. As I hurried to the gas pump I could see Joanne coming up the street, her flashlight bouncing around in the dark. The sirens were getting louder. I shined the light on the gas pump, but without electricity I was going to have to measure it the old-fashioned way. I went to the tool shed and got the twelve-foot long measuring stick for the gas tank.

When I got back to the gas tank and opened the ground insert valve, I dropped the stick into it. I pulled it out to see that we had 190 gallons of gas. I thought it was about 5:00 a.m.

I saw Joanne approaching the driveway from the street. At the corner near Tom's house, the sirens made their appearance. A fire truck and a police car came barreling up the street and turned into our driveway, passing Joanne.

When the fire truck stopped in front of the house, six guys poured out of the truck and went for their gear.

The chief fireman came up to me and asked, "Is there a fire anywhere?"

"No. I just turned off the gas valve," I told him.

"What happened?" he asked.

"We had an earthquake."

"An earthquake? We are going to have a look around," he said.

The cop walked up to me at the same time as Joanne did. She handed me the cup of coffee as I turned to the cop and another fireman to tell them about my gas tank. They should know that all that explosive liquid was a factor in the equation.

The cop asked, "We heard from dispatch that you said something about an earthquake?"

"Yes, the earthquake knocked our house off the foundation."

He stepped towards the house to get a good look at it. He put his hands on his hips and shook his head, saying, "Okay, I have to call this in." He walked to his car and got on his radio.

I joined the firemen at the front door to take a look inside. Their flashlights darted throughout the foyer and up to the ceiling. I noticed the dust had settled. Looking through the house to the backyard, I could see flashlights checking out the rear of the house. That's good because I had not even been back there yet for a visual appraisal of the damage.

From the front doorway, the firemen just looked at the inside. They didn't even want to go in the house until the county surveyor had a chance to inspect it. So the fire chief made a call to have one come out. They estimated it would take him forty minutes to show up. I figured we had about another hour of darkness left.

Forty minutes went by as we walked around and around. The sunrise could be seen starting its ascent into day when the county-issued sedan pulled into our driveway. The man got out of the car, and we went up to him to introduce ourselves.

"I'm Sam Goldstein. Are you the owner of the house?" he asked.

I introduced Joanne and me as the owners. Joanne told Sam, "The earthquake knocked us out of bed and we ran out of the house."

Sam looked at the fallen house in amazement. He walked up to it and got a closer look. "I'm stunned at this level of damage. This morning at 4:45 my pager went off telling me that an earthquake registered in this area with a 4.2 on the Richter scale. But I didn't hear of it from any other source. So I thought they were screwy. But by golly they were right."

The firemen placed a stepladder inside the foyer at the front door. Sam got his flashlight and took four steps down to the floor of the foyer. I started to follow him, but he ordered: "Stay put." He took a few steps inside and went left towards the kitchen and then towards the living room.

We were left standing at the front door waiting for him. We watched him move up the stairs, but he didn't go up but a few steps.

"Is everything okay?" I yelled out.

"Yeah, I'm coming back now." He appeared at the front door with the ground level at his waist. He climbed up the steps and out the door. He dusted himself off. He looked at us and said, "I'm sorry, Michael and Joanne, but I'm going to have to red tag your house."

Joanne asked, "What does that mean?"

Shaking his head he said, "It means that no one can live in it or even go in it until it's repaired. You have serious structural damage."

"But it's ridiculous that you're not going to let us live in it while we repair it," Joanne said, getting excited.

I couldn't believe it either. But actually I knew it when Sam climbed down those steps into my foyer. I knew it was bad and that's why, unlike Joanne, I didn't argue with him. And when the firemen didn't want to go inside, that also was not a good sign.

"No ma'am, I'm sorry," replied Sam. The consequences ran through my mind like a spinning accident out of control. I had to hug Joanne, gently removing her away from Sam. As we slowly walked away from him, he said, "Now if you want to go in there and take out your most valuable possessions, I'll let you go in for ten minutes."

"Only ten minutes?" we both exclaimed in unison and shock.

As we made our way down the ladder to the floor, Sam's last words were, "Ten minutes. It's not safe." We each took a flashlight and stepped down into the living room. In my gut, it didn't feel safe. The fire chief gave us each a couple of burlap bags to collect whatever we could gather.

I turned to Joanne. "Honey, we'll do the upstairs first, and then come downstairs. I have to get stuff out of the office, too." We started up the stairs; I went first, staying close to the wall.

When we got to the bedroom, we were shocked by the level of destruction. It seemed as if the aftershock was as destructive as the initial quake. The 36-inch Sony TV crash landed right in the spot where I had been lying against the bed. Yes, I would have been slammed in my safe pocket by 40 pounds of Sony plasma. Every lamp crashed to the floor. There was nothing left on the walls.

Joanne went straight for the jewelry boxes. She shoved numerous specialty-crafted velvet boxes into the burlap.

I went to the hall closet, pulled out the family photo albums, and started filling a bag. I didn't care about the clothes; I wanted the irreplaceable family memorabilia and heirlooms. "My wallet, I have to find my wallet!" I said, searching under the debris on the floor. I remembered I had put it on the dresser the night before, so it had to be on the floor. "Here it is," I exclaimed with great relief. "Don't forget your purse," I reminded Joanne, who was working through her closet across the room.

"Oh my God, my purse," she said, dropping more valuables into her bags. She found her purse and threw it in, too.

She went to another closet, grabbed huge armfuls of expensive garments, and threw them out the window. These were her eight to ten thousand dollar designer gowns, along with her designer shoes, coats, purses, and armfuls of her blouses. I thought that was really smart of her to save them like that. But then I realized she must have just thrown a couple hundred thousand dollars out that window!

From downstairs, we heard Sam shout, "Five minutes!"

As we walked cautiously down the hallway, we passed the kids' rooms. I thought to myself, I never had that moment in their rooms that I thought would help my closure. I'd been cheated even of that. As we carefully got down the staircase, I thought to myself how blessed we were to be getting out alive and without getting hurt.

Joanne and I emptied our burlap bags at the front door, where Sam and a fireman moved the stuff off to the side. As we hurried back into the house to my office, I realized we just entrusted strangers with several hundred thousand dollars worth of jewelry and private stuff.

When we got to the office, I started dropping handfuls of important documents on the desk into the bags. "Joanne, empty the safe," I said to her. She pressed the secret panel that opened to expose our Pinkerton safe. Joanne cranked the dials until it opened and she started removing bonds, jewels, deeds, financial certificates, and other key family items.

I opened my file drawers and started stacking files on top of one another. When I got a hefty amount, I ran to the front door and dropped it on the ground, which was at about my waist level.

When I returned, I saw Joanne had opened a jewelry box that exposed a sparkling ruby necklace. She sighed as she closed it and dropped it into the bag.

"I just have to get a few more files," I said. I took the wastebasket and turned it upside down to empty it, and then used it to collect stuff from around the office. I threw in some more valuables.

Just then I heard Sam yell, "Come on, folks, it's time." I looked around some more but didn't find anything else worthwhile.

"Come on, Joanne, and don't let go of that bag," I said leading her to the front door.

At the front door Joanne climbed up, stepped onto the ground level, and then outside. I climbed the few steps and turned back to take one last look at our house from the inside. I took it in and frowned. "What was meant to be will never be," I lamented silently inside myself.

After I got outside with my arms full of stuff, the firemen pulled their ladder up and out of the house. I got back to the front door to pick up my files off the ground. Sam took a roll of red tape and stretched it across the door several times.

I couldn't watch him. I looked away and walked towards Joanne, standing alone in the driveway. She looked so vulnerable standing by her bags. "Joanne, why don't you call a car rental company and have one brought over?" I asked her. Suddenly I remembered that I forgot to find my cell phone!

"Oh, no! How could you have forgotten your cell phone?" Joanne asked in disbelief. Lucky for her, hers happened to be in her purse.

Sam opened his trunk and pulled out a wooden stake and a two-by-three-foot red sign that read "Danger! Do not enter." He walked near the front door and hammered the sign into the ground.

The firemen got back in their truck, and when the driver turned on that mammoth diesel engine, it startled us both. The fire truck pulled away.

Sam closed his trunk and walked over to us. He handed me his business card and said, "When your insurance company starts the paperwork on the repairs and the settlement, call me so I can accelerate the permits. And after a few work-in-progress inspections, we'll change the status to under restoration. And after that I'll have to come out here again and certify it to be safe." He extended his hand to shake mine and said, "Good luck." He returned to his sedan and drove off.

As Joanne walked away towards the backyard, she said, "I'm going to pick up the things I threw out the window."

Michael's Reward

At the street entrance to our driveway, Sam stopped to hammer a condemned warning sign at the entrance of our driveway.

Suddenly, it was all very quiet again as I was left alone with my dream home broken, our vehicles ruined, and the property worthless. The eerie silence belied the ongoing screaming in my head. I didn't want to leave. What had I fallen into? And when does this falling and falling ever stop? I wanted to know. Was this a test? Yes, it was all a test that God was putting me through. I could see it. I knew He was behind all of this and He was watching me.

The early morning sun felt like a slap in the face amongst all this ruin. Everywhere I went, disaster. Everyone I loved, disaster. I begged out loud to God, "What are You doing to me? How much further must I fall to be worthy of Your love? You want everything, take it. You want it all, it's all Yours to take! What do You want from me? If I haven't given enough, I'll give more. Just why are You doing this to me?"

From the fathoms of my sincerity I asked God, "What did I do? What did I *not* do? You can take it all. I don't care about anything anymore. I can't, it's not worth it. What can I do to make You stop this? How am I failing You?"

Joanne walked up behind me. "Honey, calm down," she said gently. "It's going to be all right. Really. We'll have the insurance people rebuild, and the house will be even bigger. And who knows, we might even come into some cash."

But she'd forgotten that our policy didn't cover earthquakes. "We are built on landfill," I reminded her. "Do you remember putting your initials on the paragraph that acknowledged our awareness that this is landfill? When we bought the property, we saw that the geological survey maps showed the earth beneath us was put here in the forties. There is no earthquake insurance." I sat down on the grass. "There is no earthquake insurance," I repeated.

"How can that be?" she yelled.

I answered, "Don't you remember accepting the terms for the house without the ability to secure earthquake insurance? It was one of those points they made us initial. It's one of those points they're supposed to by law talk about, and we discussed this, Joanne. And we consciously decided to go ahead and buy the house."

Joanne was so taken aback, she didn't say a word.

Concerned, I said, "Come here and sit down."

She plopped down on the grass next to me. She cried, "We've lost everything. Do you realize that?"

"Honey, we have enough in that bag to build something really nice," I assured her. "Just don't go far from that bag," I said, trying to be light. "We have enough in those bags that could build this all over again," I chuckled.

"Michael, how can you be so cavalier?" she asked.

"Joanne, let's be honest. We took a million dollar hit today, but our paper assets are worth millions more. This hit us hard, but it's nothing we can't replace," I said, trying to alleviate her worry.

Joanne's tone of voice became demeaning. She turned on a dime from whimpering child to evil football coach. She gutted me clean when she asked, "Michael, did you piss off God? Did you think you could buy your way into heaven?"

"No! I wasn't trying to do that at all. You know that," I said defensively.

"I don't know anything anymore."

I stopped her in her tracks. "Don't let the demon of doubt come through the doorway of your mind, Joanne. God has a purpose and a reason for all this to happen. It's not a coincidence, I can tell you that."

"So why is He letting all these bad things happen to us? Why is He letting all these bad things happen to good people like us? What did you do, Michael, to upset Him? Were you unfaithful to me, Michael?"

"No, I was never unfaithful to you."

"I never suspected you were," she replied. Then she looked away and asked, "Do you realize that within the past four weeks our children were taken from us, you almost died, you lost your job, and we lost our house. So what are we supposed to do now? Start everything over again? Why? What did we do wrong?"

I searched myself in that brief second and could not find an answer worthy of her honor, because there was no apparent answer.

Two cars pulled up the street and into our driveway. This must be our rental; there's a sedan and a compact. When the drivers got out, they came with the paperwork. "I take it you're leaving the gold sedan?" I asked one of them.

"Oh no, sir, there's a reservation for that car back at the office. The only one available today is that compact."

I signed the papers. He handed me the keys, and they drove off. I looked at this tin can that couldn't be more than ten feet long and three feet wide.

Joanne sat on the grass this whole time, watching. "Couldn't they have left the bigger car?" she asked.

"No, this is the only thing we could get this morning."

"You can't be serious," she said indignantly.

"Honey, it's just temporary. We can get a bigger car later this afternoon or tomorrow," I said, hoping to calm her edge.

We stuffed the car with our bags, files, clothes, shoes, and photos. It was packed like a sardine can. I thought perhaps we should go to Ralph's house. Maybe stay around there longer. But what would be the point of that?

I asked, "Joanne, do you think we should go over to Ralph's? Or do you have any thoughts about what you want to do?"

"Let's get a hotel room."

We got in the car and coasted down the driveway. At the street, I stopped as usual, but I had to turn back to look at the house one more time. It was a mess, an absolute disaster. I was in a total state of disbelief. Believing it would overtake my sense of control and all reason, I had to continue in a vague haze of denial. It was the only way I could get through these minutes. I looked left and right, and pulled into the street, driving away from all that I once knew and loved.

I'd never go back, because I suspected it wouldn't be there to come back to. And not knowing where we were going only exacerbated my confusion.

CHAPTER FIVE

TO NOWHERE

We drove down Carrillo Boulevard along the ocean. I asked Joanne if she had a preference for hotels. "I don't care," she replied. So I pulled into the Hacienda Hotel.

After we got into our room and brought in all of our valuables, she went back to harping on the same subject. She stirred up our confusion by raising the same questions, to which I still had no answers. Then she asked, "Were you trying to kill yourself on the boat?"

Baffled, I asked her pointedly, "Knowing God disapproves of suicides, how could I ever think of taking my life? Why would I intentionally abandon the woman I love by killing myself? I never considered such a thought. It implies failure, and if I have you, I know I'm not a failure. I believe together we can make a comeback."

Joanne hugged me and confessed, "I'm scared, Michael. Who knows what could happen next?"

I assured her, "There's enough money and assets to reconstruct our lives. This won't last forever, please believe me."

"You just told me you didn't know anything!" she yelled, jabbing at my resolve. Joanne started to pace. "I'm scared, Michael," she said again.

I got up close to her, looked her square in the eyes, and said, "If I know just *one thing* in this world, it's that this too shall pass."

"You don't know that, Michael," she said, cutting a swath of doubt.

And deep down in my heart, having gone through hell, I knew that she was right, I didn't know *anything*. I hugged her and said, "Don't be scared, this is going to work out. We need to pray and come into agreement that we'll get through this together."

"I'm out of prayers, Michael," she said with a bite.

But I was not going to play into her doubt. I told her, "We can start another family, I'll get another job. We still have the property value of the land and our stocks to fall back on. Let's just have a little more faith."

"Faith?" she said mocking me. "Did faith keep our children alive? Did faith almost kill you in the middle of the ocean and then take away your job? Did faith almost kill us in the middle of the night while destroying our home?" she demanded.

"Faith kept me alive in that raft," I replied.

"Well, from here it looks more like the Coast Guard kept you alive. Besides, you thought you were going to die out there," she said coldly.

Her double jabs hit me hard. I asked, "How could you say such a spiteful thing to me?"

"Oh, I've heard worse come from you, so don't act like the perfect husband," she said, indicting me on false charges.

"This won't last forever," I kept telling her, hoping to convince both of us.

"Michael, why don't you go back to Pastor Ryan and get some of that half million donation back?" she asked me.

"I can't believe you want me to ask God to give back some of the money I gave Him for the poor, the ministry!"

"Maybe not all of it, but maybe some of it," she countered.

I reassured her, "Joanne, we're not broke. I've made sure of that. You don't have to worry about money, darling." I went to hug her to ease her anxiety, but she tensed up.

I looked at the clock; it was 8:30 a.m. "We should get some breakfast. I'm going to call Ralph," I said to her. Using the hotel phone to call Ralph only reminded me that I had lost my most vital source of communication, my cell phone.

While I gave Ralph more bad news of what just happened, Joanne lay down on top of the bed. Before I hung up with Ralph I let him know that we would be coming over shortly. I turned to her and said, "Come on, it might help you to be around others."

"You go. I just want to lie down for a while," she said. She was tired and I believed her. We'd been up since four o'clock that morning.

I suggested she order room service for breakfast, but I still needed to consult with Ralph on what I should do next. Closing the drapes to keep out the sunlight, I laid a blanket over her. I kissed her with a promise to return shortly. Closing the hotel room door behind me, I jiggled the doorknob to make sure it was locked.

By the time I got to Ralph's house, Bette had already put out breakfast pastries and coffee. I started telling them the whole episode. They were amazed and shocked. Ralph and Bette invited us to stay in their home, but I couldn't impose on anyone to that degree.

In the dark hotel room, Joanne lay there succumbing to the chaos and escalating turmoil in her life. Her exhaustion, physical and emotional, from the past several weeks exacerbated her fears and doubts. She cried, feeling the weight of the world coming down around and on top of her. All alone, and in her self-pity, she felt abandoned by God and by Michael. Her many unanswered questions had been laid on God's deaf ears. Her unanswered prayers scrambled her faith into question. Feeling victimized, she wiped the tears from her face and stared at the ceiling. And above all else, she missed her children's love.

She could not hear the knock on the door because it was a muted knock. But there was someone knocking. On the other side of the door, Lucifer stood knocking on Room 315. He was knocking to please his wit, because he just walked right through the door. He saw Joanne lying on the bed, so he walked to the second bed and sat down on it. Stopping for a second to analyze her, he put thoughts in her mind. Lucifer whispered fear and anger in her spirit.

She was so lost in her pain, she screamed, "Why would God do this to a good Christian woman like me?" Her weeping continued as she felt the weight of so many family crises. She recounted her series of misfortunes. Finally, her sobbing subsided.

Lucifer sat there speaking aloud in her own voice and in her head. Hearing her own voice, she took for granted that these were her own thoughts: "Oh, my three kids are dead and Michael almost dies, am I next? I've lost everything, but why? Who knows what could happen next? Everything around me is being destroyed. Why should I live like this? Living in fear of what might come next? Look at me, my life is falling apart, and I can't stop it from crashing into one more disaster."

After breakfast, Ralph and I went to his home office to talk about my finances. We needed to initiate insurance claims, such as the children's life insurance, the boat insurance, and the car insurance. I knew I had to be patient for these monies to come through, but we had enough cash on hand to buy ourselves a two or three bedroom house.

Ralph offered to contact the city and county with respect to the property tax. I suspected they were going to have to demolish the whole house, and I would to have to start over again. I didn't need to wait to hear it from a county engineer. But after losing the children, a change of house might be good. And that's why I was willing to bulldoze the whole thing and start anew. Or maybe make the identical house over again. Maybe we could make a different house, even larger. Ralph argued that we should sell the land and walk away. Why invite disaster twice? Sometimes he was right. And that's why I was a hundred thousand dollar a year client. I sometimes listened.

Back in the darkness of the hotel room, Joanne continued analyzing her suddenly warped universe. In her own voice Lucifer asked, "How could God take away my three children and call Himself the supreme love of the universe? What kind of God is He that could do something like this to such a God-loving Christian woman like me?"

He kept sweeping the air with his thoughts of fear, such as "I better get out while I can," "I don't deserve this," and "Michael brought this on." Lucifer knew that he could cut her down in any number of ways, but his analysis found her to be a valuable tool for further mayhem and destruction.

Thinking these were her thoughts, Joanne heard, "You're living in a hotel until who knows how long. Michael says, 'Everything is going to work out for the good.' For the good of what? What good could possibly come from any of this? We passed that miles ago. How can God reward good people with this hell we've fallen into? What's the point? What's the point of being a good Christian woman if all roads lead to this misery?"

Lucifer interjected, "I don't need to take anymore of this curse that follows him." And the great deceiver added, "He's not worth dying for. Besides, there's no future with him. He's ruined. I don't need to be with a man who found his peak and it's only downhill from here on. It's all gone. There's just what's in these bags and the insurance claims, and that's it. I'm so done with all these never-ending catastrophes. I'm just done with it."

Joanne sat up and wiped the tears from her eyes. She pulled out her cell phone out of her purse. She made two calls and then she started organizing the contents of their shattered lives in the burlap bags. She emptied the burlap bags carefully, removing anything that belonged to Michael, personally. And she took a few minutes to put make-up on her face.

There was a knock at her door. She answered it. Room service was delivering her bagel, butter croissants, fruit bowl, and a large café latte, to go.

Minutes later, a limousine glided through the driveway at the Hacienda Hotel.

Another knock was heard at the door. She went to the door and told the driver, "Put everything in the back with me." They carried several loads of the expensive belongings into the car. She laid her lavish gowns across the leather bench on the side. The two burlap bags were put on the floor right in front of her. "Close the door and lock it, I'll be right back," she told the driver.

Back inside Room 315, she looked around for anything else worthwhile. She saw the perfect photo taken on the fly bridge and picked it up. She walked around and around, making sure she had everything she wanted. She took a pad and pen to write a note.

Finally, she went for the door, but she stopped and decided to leave Michael the photo and tossed it on the bed. And with that, she closed the door behind her, making sure it was locked.

She got in the back seat, and the driver closed the door for her. She delved into her breakfast. When the driver took his seat she told him *"Bel Air"* and then pushed the button to raise the partition for total privacy.

At Ralph's house, he and I came up with a plan that would get us into a three bedroom house right away and continue meeting our payments on the old one. He suggested that I have the post office transfer my mail to his business address. I thought that would be a good idea. On my way back to the hotel I stopped at a bakery to pick up something to eat for Joanne, just in case she was hungry.

I let myself into the room quietly, as she was likely still asleep. But when I got in, I found she was not there. And for some reason, my next thought was to look for the burlap bags. They were gone, too. Where did she go? I reached for the hotel phone on the desk. I dialed her cell phone. I guessed she may have gone for something to eat at a nearby restaurant, but where were the burlap bags? And that's when I saw the note on the desk. Her cell phone started ringing in my ear, as I picked up the note and started to read it.

In her limousine cruising down the Pacific Coast Highway with the ocean out her window, Joanne was slumped in the black, overstuffed leather. Wrapped in luxury, she suited the limo well, along with her thousand-yard stare. She had finished her breakfast when her cell phone rang in her purse, startling her. She took it out and saw the display was "restricted ID."

I read: "Dear Michael, I never ever wanted our lives to come to this, but I have to get away for a while. Away from you, from Montecito, from everything..."

In her limousine, Joanne shifted uncomfortably and frowned as she held her ringing cell phone. She knew it was Michael who was calling. And she knew she did not want to answer it.

I continued reading: "...Please understand, I didn't want to wait around to find out what could happen next."

I thought to myself, "It just did. It just did."

I continued reading: "I don't know how long. I'll be in touch. Love, Joanne."

In her limousine, Joanne shifted again, agitated by her cell phone that just kept ringing. She found the orange juice in the ice box and the vodka on the bar and made a screwdriver. She absolved herself of her sin by claiming out loud, "After the morning I've had, HAA!" And she took a healthy swig. After getting another aftershock, this time of Stolichnaya at 9:30 a.m., she looked down pitifully at her continuously ringing phone. And then mixed herself another screwdriver.

How was I to know she was so scared? I figured she knew it was me calling, and that's why she was not picking up. The venomous missive continued on the reverse side of her note: "I'm too afraid to be near you right now. I'm taking everything to protect it."

Protect it? I stared at the note and re-read the few cutting words.

Why did she take everything? If she didn't answer her phone, I promised I'd go find her and confront her, face to face. That's what I'd do. If she didn't answer my calls, I'd drive down to Bel Air and have a word with her. I was certain she went to Mary Ruth's in Bel Air. That would be her first choice. After about thirty-five rings, I realized she was not going to answer, and I had to hang up.

In the limousine, Joanne's annoying cell phone stopped ringing. "Finally," she said to herself. But the alcohol buzz wouldn't take away the pain of a lost life she adored. She called her sister Mary Ruth and poured herself another.

I looked around the room and saw that she'd left the business files and my things. I looked at the photo on the bed and I thought to myself, "What's the photo doing on the bed?" She must have taken it out of the bag, and then left it for me as a crumb. She had better answer her phone today.

I called Mary Ruth. She didn't answer, but at least I got her voice mail. I left a message and then hung up. What should I do? What can I do? I should call Ralph. This was not good. I called Ralph and told him what happened. He told me to come back to his house, which I did.

When I got back to Ralph's office I showed him the note she left me. He read it and shook his head. He read both sides and then asked me, "How much was in the bags?"

"Off the top of my head, I don't know, but it's in the millions," I said.

"You have to have an account for whatever is in there and how much it's worth," he advised me.

Everything instinctively told me that she went to her sister Mary Ruth's house. I just knew that's where she was going.

Ralph offered, "I can't tell you what to do, but if I were in your shoes, I'd go get her. Show her how much you love her, and follow your instincts. You should make her tell you to your face that she wants out of your marriage."

Annoyed, I said, "Ralph, whoa, nobody said anything about getting out of the marriage. She just needs some space."

Ralph tilted his head and asked, "Is that why she took everything?"

"I don't want her to want to get out of our marriage, I just want her back. I want to forget the note, forget what it said, and forget she ever wrote it. I just want her back. She is suffering from trauma fatigue and we haven't gotten the counseling we need yet. That's why she is freaking out like this."

Ralph tried to see my point of view, but the lawyer in him asked, "If she had such honorable motives, then why take everything?"

Defending her I said, "She's panicking. If I could hold her, look at her, kiss her, I know she'd come back to me. I know it."

"I believe you," he said, reassuring me.

"What should I do?"

"You should sit down and write down everything you remember that was in those bags," he answered.

He was right. But I wondered out loud, "Or should I just get up and drive down to Bel Air and talk to her in person."

Ralph smiled. "You should do both. But right now, you need to cool your temper and sit calmly to remember what was in those bags and jewelry boxes. And then drive down to Bel-Air to talk with her." He got up, walked to the door, and said, "I'll leave you alone to write your list."

I walked over to the sofa and flopped into the leather. I knew that when I got to Mary Ruth's I could take an inventory, no matter if she refused to give them up. I was still going to get an accurate account of whatever there was of my hard work in those bags. And I was even going to take photographs of it too. Wait a minute. The insurance company may have photographs already. All the jewelry was insured. But it wasn't like it was missing or stolen, either. So there was no claim to be made.

I could not believe she had it in her to do this to me. Stop thinking about what just happened and focus on those bags, I thought. Right now, I had to go back to the time when we were in the bedroom gathering our things after the earthquake. And remember the few times I looked at her, what was she throwing into the bags?

As I slowly started remembering the contents of the jewelry boxes, I had flashing memories of when we got those jewels. Remembering to list her ruby and diamond necklace, I had memories walking down Worth Avenue in Palm Beach, Florida with her on my arm. It was a sunny Saturday afternoon when we happened upon Cartier and walked out with a ruby necklace with encrusted diamonds that I got priced down to $94,000.

And for thirty minutes of living memories, I recalled the many thousands spent on earrings, a $20,000 pearl necklace we bought in Thailand, the $10,000 cameo from Naples, and the list went on.

I felt a wave of pain coming up from my gut to my heart. An emotional attack filled with confusion and self-pity hit me. Oh, no, please, I had to think. Don't go there, I said to myself. I needed to be clear-headed, and I couldn't afford to be emotional. I filled four legal-sized pages of what I remembered was in those boxes and bags, including all the very important financial matters as well. I made a copy on Ralph's scanner and printed him a copy.

I got on the road at about noon and headed south. Sara was kind enough to let me borrow her cell phone. Passing Carpinteria I called Joanne's cell phone again. But there was still no answer. I was not surprised. But she would be when I was standing at the front door. She'd be really surprised. How could she think I wouldn't come after her? Especially when she took everything? None of it made sense. I was just failing at answers.

A couple hours later on the 405 South, I exited at Skirball and made my way to Mulholland Drive. It was easy to remember how to get to Mary Ruth's house. Just keep going uphill until you can't go any higher and that's Strathmore, a street that runs along the very top of

Bel Air. I drove up to the house and parked. I walked to the front door and rang the bell. I stood there a bit before I rang again. There was no answer, but through the doors I heard it chiming, so I knew it worked. Could they know I was here and refuse to answer the door? No, I couldn't believe they'd treat me like that. I kept ringing for ten minutes, but my patience was wearing thin. Maybe they went out. Knowing them, they were probably on Rodeo Drive by now anyway.

I sat in the car and waited. I got into the passenger seat and tried to make myself comfortable. I sat back and waited. How long should I wait? I could wait for hours. I didn't care. I drove this far, I was not leaving anytime soon. I'd go get dinner somewhere and come back and wait some more if I had to.

I waited for more than an hour. Beautiful rich people strolled by, walking their manicured dogs. In all likelihood, they wondered about the stranger sitting in the little cheap car. Now that I thought about it, I must have looked disheveled and completely out of place. Alas, I had been going since 4:30 that morning. I needed to stretch my legs. I got out of the car and leaned against it for awhile. Then I went up and rang the bell again. No one answered, so I got back in the car.

Another hour went by. I could see that it was close to five o'clock. As I looked back over that day's events, I sat numb and lethargic. I could not believe that in one day a man could lose his house, his wife, all his cars, and his entire fortune (well, I didn't lose my fortune, it was just being protected from me). And the fact that that man was me made me question the fundamental nature of my relationship with God. Or, was I speeding towards the inevitable: insanity.

An old woman from across the street came out of her front door and walked up to me. She smiled pleasantly and asked, "Are you waiting for Mary Ruth? I notice you've been sitting here for a long time."

"Yes, I'm her brother-in-law, and my wife came down to visit, but I guess maybe they went out shopping or something," I said, explaining myself.

"Oh, because Mary Ruth isn't living here now," she said.

"No?" I replied in a mild shock.

The lady continued, "She's having the house remodeled and is renting a house somewhere in Pasadena."

"Pasadena?" I asked dumbfounded. Then I thought to ask, "Do you have a phone number? I have her number in my cell phone, but I lost it this morning."

The old lady was sweet, but she shrugged her shoulders and answered, "No, I don't. She moved everything out a few weeks ago so the construction could start." I thanked her and went on my way.

I couldn't believe that Joanne wasn't there. And I couldn't believe I didn't know Mary Ruth had moved to Pasadena. As I dropped down Mulholland Drive to get back on the 405 north, I realized that I was clueless as to what I should do next. My game plan was shot because I assumed that Joanne would be there. How stupid was I? I thought for sure she was going to be there. She probably went to stay at some other hotel in Santa Barbara. That's probably what she did. I bet if I got on the phone and called a few hotels, I'd find her. I was so stupid and impulsive.

Earlier that day in the back of the limousine, with the Pacific Ocean out her window, Joanne called her sister Mary Ruth while making her third screwdriver. By the time Mary Ruth answered her phone, Joanne's tragic tears were dripping off her chin as she bellowed, "I left him!"

Mary Ruth was shocked. "You what?"

Joanne tossed down the whole glass in three gulps. And she kept pouring and mourning as she repeated, "I left him! There was this horrible earthquake this morning and the house fell off the foundation and now I don't have anything because we have no insurance and no kids and no husband, but I got everything," she said as tears fell down her cheeks.

She stuttered through her sobs. "I left him. I can't take it anymore. I'm done." She dropped the phone, covered her face, and wept into both hands.

Mary Ruth could hear her crying. "Where are you?" she asked.

In one gesture Joanne picked up the phone and mixed her next screwdriver. She answered, "I'm on my way to your house in Bel Air."

Mary Ruth sat up. "My house? I don't live there anymore. Well, not right now. I'm having it remodeled. Why don't you come and stay with me in Pasadena. I'm renting a big house with a few extra bedrooms and I'd love the company."

Joanne continued, "Well, Sister, I'm on my way. I'm in the back of a limo, passing Ventura, and I'm on my third, maybe fourth screwdriver."

Mary Ruth became alarmed. "You're only in Ventura and you're already on your fourth screwdriver? Girl, you've got to pace yourself. I'm sure that nice driver doesn't want you throwing up in his nice car."

As I drove back to Santa Barbara, I remembered the many times Joanne and I made this trip to and from Los Angeles. Whether it was to catch a plane out of LAX or see a concert or go shopping, I never resented the two-hour drive, until today.

As I drove alone, I made several observations about myself. Firstly, I could no longer use my home as my compass. That stationary landmark in my life, from which all things were measured, was no longer my citadel. It was no longer my pole star. There was no place right now that could comfort my agony, nor temper the chaos that raged through my life.

And secondly, I was having my own personal apocalypse.

My own personal revolution was destroying my life in front of my eyes. Because by all definition, description, and purpose, this was the end of my world as I knew it.

By the time I returned to the Hacienda Hotel, it was dark. I called the front desk to check for messages; there were none. I plopped down on the bed. I didn't know what to do. I had nothing to read and nothing to distract me but the television, so I turned it on but tuned it out.

I started thinking about my children. How I missed them. Words failed in describing how much I missed them.

Hours later, I stirred awake; I was still in my clothes and everything was still turned on. It was 3:21 a.m. I got up to turn everything off and then climbed under the covers. It was very quiet at that hour. I would be back to sleep in seconds. Or, so I thought.

Instead, I ran into the cold slab of reality that lingered just beyond my conscious brain. Oh, no. That reality hit me again, and I could not fall back to sleep. I suffered myself to the painful images from that day. From an unknown place deep within me came a bolt of despair, as I shouted at the top of my lungs, "What do You want from me?" I didn't realize I shouted until I had already done it. Eventually, I fell back to sleep.

At around ten in the morning, I slowly stirred. It was Sunday morning. The morning silence hung in the air with an unwelcomed loneliness. Should I go to church? No. Maybe? Of course I should go. But what about all the questions everyone will ask? I didn't have the energy to put up a front for all those people. People? They're my friends. Maybe going will do me good. Yes, that was it. So, I'll go. I knew that I couldn't help but feel better just being there. But, was I ready to see all the kids' friends? What will happen when they ask, "Where's Joanne?" What will I say? But it's probably exactly what I need. To be with my friends who love me. Maybe I can sit with Pastor Ryan afterwards, if he has the time.

By the time I decided to go, I had to rush out the door.

When I arrived, everyone was already in their seats, which was just the way I hoped it would be. An usher wanted to escort me towards the front, but I motioned my desire to sit in the back. I took the back pew.

The service started and I was hoping Pastor Ryan would give me a special message that would ease my pain. I listened, but I didn't hear anything that touched me. Too many memories of sitting in these pews with my kids blocked him out. Was there a chance that he might say something, anything that would lighten my pain and clear out some of my confusion? I tried paying attention, but he was preaching on a topic completely unrelated to anything I hoped to hear.

So I closed my eyes and thought of God. I told Him, "My pain runs deep." I looked at the bigger picture in life, and I had to go back to the days when I didn't have my kids; when I didn't have Joanne.

Looking at Pastor Ryan at the pulpit, I reflected on the conversation I had with Joanne about asking him to give back part of that half million dollar donation we made. Maybe, if I'd said yes to her, showed her I was a bigger supporter, maybe then she wouldn't have left me. But I told her money was no object. She knew we had money. I found more reasons not to ask for that money back than to ask for some of it to be returned. I found myself frozen in that thousand-yard stare. I was too beaten down to look up.

I had unwelcomed memories of the three caskets at the front of the church. Oh no. I felt that certain impulse. Oh no, I didn't want to cry. But it rushed up from my solar plexus to fill my eyes with tears. Why did I come? I should have stayed away longer. I took a deep breath. It'd only been three weeks since the kids sat here with me. We raised them in this church. Year after year, every Sunday these people watched my kids grow up from the time they were little. We sang together, prayed together, and worshipped together.

How could something so right go so wrong in such a short period of time? I didn't get it.

I prayed, "Because You told me to pray for those that hurt us, I pray, dear Lord, that You shower Joanne with Your love and drown her in Your joy, and deluge her with Your hope."

Off to the side, Ralph happened to glance around and notice me. When he saw that I didn't look right, he got up and walked over to sit by me. He squeezed my shoulder. This one single gesture of compassion sent me over the wall of self-control.

I bowed my head and poured my silent grief into my hands. Ralph helped me stand up, and he walked me out to the foyer. We kept walking out the front door to the outside. Away from everyone, the dam of my heartache broke wide open. Ralph hugged me and let me give in to my rush of crying. I didn't want this to happen here. I should have stayed alone in my room. The tears kept coming and I couldn't stop them.

Finally, I got my breathing under control and wiped my face. I cleared my throat and took a deep breath as I stepped away from Ralph. He was so great, he didn't speak a word. Through this whole scene, he didn't feel the need to trivialize it by saying a single word. He was truly my friend.

I took my keys out of my pocket. He asked, "Where are you going?"

"I'm going back to the hotel," I answered. I handed him Sara's cell phone that I had borrowed and assured him, "I'll call you later."

Back at the hotel room, I fell on the bed and stared at the ceiling while going over my shattered life. I was baffled how I went from there to here so fast. A few hours passed and all I did was sleep, cry, shower, and curl up on the floor with a blank stare.

In the late afternoon, I got up and drove to my house. Driving through Montecito, I took notice of the other houses, but I didn't see any damage that might have been caused by any earthquake. And then I got to my house and it was a disaster.

It looked dwarfed, having fallen three feet down to the slab. I drove up near the gas pump. I went to the fuel tank to see if it had lost any fuel. It had not, thank goodness.

I walked under the red "Do Not Cross" tape and went up to my garage. Getting a closer look at the cars, I saw their roofs were crushed down into the cabins. They were a total loss. Then I wondered what I could have left inside them. It didn't matter now; it was gone for good. There was shattered glass everywhere I looked.

I walked around the side of the house to the back yard and over to the veranda. Or whatever was left of it. One corner of the roofing had fallen. The support column fell straight down on top of our telescope, breaking it in half. There was more broken glass everywhere I turned. I looked up and saw that the chimney was split and ready to fall off the house from the second story. I was bewildered how and why my house was the only one damaged so severely? Was landfill so poorly packed that the house had no real gripping connection to the earth?

I looked out over the backyard and could almost hear the kids' voices playing in the distance. I turned to look as so many memories flooded my brain. What was I doing here? Why was I putting myself through this? Because I belonged here, this was my house.

I corrected myself, "You fool, not anymore. This *was* your house. It belongs to God now."

He just let me live in it and now He's taken it back. And that's all right, because He gave me many happy years in it and I thanked Him for the loan. I was just sorry I got so attached to it. Maybe not so much attached to the house, as to the home we created inside it. I prayed, "You want Your house, dear God? Take it. Oh, wait, You did that already." I stopped, shook my head, and realized, "It was Yours to begin with. You obviously did what You wanted to do."

I stared west at the setting sun, beyond the lawn, across the neighborhood, past the town, and over the ocean. Looking back at the eight years that we lived here, I must have stood there a thousand times witnessing the majestic view of the sunset. And it sprang on me that this was the last time I would have this moment in this place. Nothing was ever going to be the same, ever again.

This is where love found a home, and virtues were seeded in my children. And when the memory of Joanne surfaced I just wanted to leave.

Monday arrived in a haze of hurt and bitterness amplified by the sound of silence. All I did was mope in bed all morning and blankly stare at the television news. Ever since the kids' accident, I always thought that I could get through it all because I had Joanne by my side. She was my Rock of Gibraltar. The one person who I thought would keep me sane and on the right course was gone. Without her, how was I supposed to rebuild my life? Did I put too much faith in her, and less in God? Did my soul mate abandon our vows because...I honestly didn't know. How could she leave me? Wasn't everything enough? A saying came to me when River Phoenix passed away: "When everything was not enough." Every time I hear of a movie star or some other rich and privileged person self-destruct, I always think to myself: "When everything was not enough."

Did Joanne fall into that category now? Because I really did give her everything a husband could give, and then some.

Tuesday morning came quietly and calmly. I checked the cash flow in my wallet to see if I needed to find an ATM. I counted $132 so I didn't feel the need to go.

But I needed to buy some new clothes. I showered and shaved for the first time since Sunday. I got out and walked to a nearby restaurant where I ate a Mexican breakfast before walking up State Street to pick up some clothes.

It was already noon when I stepped into a store and bought myself a black gym bag, which I could start putting my things into. Back on State Street, I came across my bank's ATM machine and figured I might as well draw out some money. So, as usual, I took out the maximum, $300. I walked to Nordstrom to buy some clothes. By the time I tried on a few pants, and picked out some shirts and underclothes, it was about 4 p.m. When I got to the counter to pay for it all, the young male attendant rang up my tab of $288.

I handed him my Nordstrom card and it came back declined. I assumed the magnet might be worn out or some other technical reason. So I gave him my Visa, which made me confident, knowing it had a ton of credit on it.

But it too was declined. I told the young man, "I can't believe this happened twice in a row." I reached for my Louisville Slugger and handed him my American Express Black. I knew everything was going to be okay.

He turned to me and said, "It too is declined."

Okay, now something was not right. I took a deep breath. I decided that rather than embarrass myself in front of the people in the line and the attendant, I would pay for the clothes with the cash I had on hand. He put the clothes in a bag and I left.

I walked two blocks down State Street to my bank. I walked up to a teller to ask about my accounts. After punching the keyboard with my numbers, I was told, "This account was frozen."

"Frozen?" I asked in disbelief.

I turned and walked up to Brooke, the bank manager and someone I've known for years. I asked her, "What's going on with my accounts?" She punched my account numbers into her keyboard on her desk and told me that they were frozen as of 4:03 p.m. by a court in Beverly Hills. I was dumbfounded by the news and asked, "May I use your phone, Brooke?"

She said, "Of course, just dial 9 first."

When I got Ralph on the phone, he yelled, "Where have you been? I've been calling your hotel for two hours. I even drove by there and knocked on the door, but you didn't answer."

I said to him, "I'm calling you from Brooke's desk here at the bank on State Street. Do you know what's going on with my accounts?"

Ralph asked, "Are you sitting down?"

I took a seat across from Brooke and said, "I'm sitting down now."

He continued, "I got a call from a lawyer in Beverly Hills. Ever hear of a David Calvani & Associates?"

"No," I answered.

He went on, "He claims to represent Joanne in her divorce settlement from you."

Across the quiet open space of the bank, I bellowed at the top of my lungs, "She's divorcing me?" I realized the entire bank heard me.

Ralph said, "She is claiming, get this, in an affidavit that she believes you were trying to commit suicide in the boat accident. And that's why they froze all your credit card accounts and all your banking accounts, including your retirement accounts."

"For how long?" I asked.

"Until the divorce is finalized, I don't know, it could take a long while," he answered.

"What did she *not* get?" I asked.

"She got everything, Michael, everything," he said to me.

I couldn't believe my ears. "Hold on," I told him. I turned to Brooke and asked her to bring up my kids' savings accounts. She punched the keys to discover those accounts had zero balances. Begrudgingly I asked, "How much was in those accounts?"

She crunched the three closing balances and said, "Combined, twenty- four thousand three hundred dollars."

I put the phone back up to my ear and told Ralph, "She didn't forget to empty the kids' savings accounts to the tune of twenty-four thousand dollars." I felt the air get sucked right out of my lungs, again.

All I wanted to do was hide. Every time I went somewhere, bad things happened. Facing the floor, and with Ralph in my right ear, I heard him say, "I'm so sorry, Michael. Why don't I come and pick you up? I'll be at the hotel in fifteen minutes." And we both hung up. I handed the phone robotically to Brooke and stood up. The room seemed to disappear. Brooke asked, "Are you okay?"

I was keenly aware my blood pressure was zooming higher and higher.

All I could muster while suppressing my rage was "Brooke, thank you." I walked out of the bank and headed back to the hotel.

As I walked to the hotel, in a black fog with my new found funk, so many questions came racing forward. Who knew she was capable of what she'd done? How could I have ever thought she would stoop so low as to do this to me, and now of all times? Why didn't I think to get the kids' money out yesterday? It was never a question, until she pulled the *nuclear option* on me. And now it was too late. That's why they call it the *nuclear option*; there's no going back. And that's what she did. She slammed the door on the possibility of ever going back. But why did she have to lie about me? That's the part I couldn't believe. Did she think that I wouldn't have given her anything if and when we ever did get divorced?

I chastised myself because yesterday I locked myself in my hotel room when I could have been securing certain assets. Maybe moved some money off shore. But who knew she wanted a divorce? I thought she just needed time, not the rest of her life!

By the time I reached the hotel, Ralph was waiting for me. He met me at the door, which I unlocked to let us in. He started explaining that losing all my assets was based on Joanne's affidavit that "You attempted suicide, so the court froze all our assets, until the divorce is settled."

"Yeah, I heard that part." I fell back on the bed. I continued, "How could she do this to me? I can't believe Joanne could do this to me, and yet, she already has."

I stood up, grabbed the bedspread, yanked the whole bedding right off the mattress, and flung it across the room. It slid across a table and hit a lamp. The lamp smashed against the wall and everything went to the floor. That felt so good, I picked up the mattress and started lifting it off the frame.

Ralph grabbed my elbows and yelled, "You can't destroy the hotel room!" I didn't care what he said, but I caught my breath because I knew he was right. I couldn't destroy everything. God was doing that for me. Letting go of my arm Ralph said, "Come with me back to the house. You should stay with us. You know we have a spare room."

I continued in my utter confusion, "I just cannot believe that Joanne, the love of my existence, my best friend for most of my life, could do this to me. Where did it all go wrong? Where did I go wrong?"

I walked to the bathroom, looked in the mirror, and asked myself, "Where did you go wrong? At what point did you go and screw up this life so horribly and miserably that you have angered God to the point that He's taken everything?" I screamed at myself in the mirror, "What did you do?"

Ralph took my elbow and led me to a chair. He said, "Okay, I'm going to the front desk to pay the bill. You just sit here, or get your things together. We're leaving here in ten minutes."

I could not move or lift a muscle from the weight of so much chaos. I came up empty on searching for any cohesive thought process that would explain Joanne's erratic behavior. I confessed that she was right about one thing. I'd definitely fallen into a pattern, downward.

Ralph walked back in and through a blur of endless questions in my head I watched him put all my stuff in his car. I sat, disengaged from the world around me. The only thing I needed to succeed at was breathing.

Not only was my past a trail of broken lives, shattered dreams, and utter destruction, my future seemed completely in the dark.

Ralph helped me up from the chair. He walked me to the passenger door of his car. I got in. But then I looked over and saw my rental car sitting there. And that reality check brought me back to this world. I blurted out, "Holy cow, how am I going to pay for that?" When Ralph got in, I said to him, "I should return the rental car."

He asked if I was okay to drive.

I said, "Yes, you go first. I'll just follow you there."

At the rental agency, I started to pay the $120.90 rental charge, but Ralph pushed my cash aside and put the charge on his credit card. I thanked him sincerely.

When we got to Ralph's house, Bette came to greet us at the door. She gave me a warm and loving hug. I just stood there for what seemed the longest time. Bette admitted that she heard about Joanne and said some words of comfort. Ralph asked her, "Is dinner ready?"

Bette stepped back and answered, "Yes, I hope you brought an appetite, Michael. I also got your room ready and I want you to know that you can stay as long as you like. Just make yourself at home." Sara and Aaron walked up to say hello.

Sara gave me a hug and told me, "I miss Rachel. Sometimes something funny will happen at school and I'll want to call her 'cause I know she'd laugh, but then I remember I can't. And that really makes me sad. That happens so many times."

With my arm around her, I looked down at her and said, "I know, Sara, I miss her too. You were a good friend to Rachel."

Bette suggested she take me to my room.

We walked through the house all the way back to the guest room, which had its own bathroom. I pulled the clothes out of the Nordstrom bags and found a couple empty drawers. I placed the photo on the nightstand facing my bed. I thought to myself, maybe I could have Joanne airbrushed out of it.

After dinner, Ralph and I walked down the hall to his office. He listened to my string of woes and said, "I thought you two were going to be together forever. I never imagined that you were having problems."

I confessed, "I never saw trouble in my marriage either. Not until the kids' accident. The possibility that I would live out my entire life without Joanne was never in my universe. Not until the moment I heard it from you."

We talked until midnight, when we both gave in to exhaustion and called it a night. But before we left the office, he turned to me and assured me that I could stay as long as I needed to.

"Thanks, it won't take me long to get back on my feet and get out of your hair," I promised.

Alone in my room, I climbed into bed and wondered what I did to merit this cruelty. Apparently, cruelty comes in many shapes and spheres. It comes wearing the faces of people who love us. Or claim to love us. All I could count on was that this fall into the abyss did not seem to be stopping.

CHAPTER SIX

THE WORST WAS YET TO COME

The next morning I was awakened by the rustle and pitter-patter of children getting ready for school. I wanted to sleep some more, but nature called and I had to step to the bathroom. I looked in the mirror and saw that I had a red pimple growing on the right side of my neck. I wasn't surprised because I was under so much pressure, but at my age? I took a shower and stepped out of my room. The smell of coffee and the sounds of a family came from the kitchen. Bette, Ralph, and the kids greeted me with smiles and the offer of breakfast. I could see that everyone I talked with stole a moment to look at my pimple. Oh well. What could I expect?

Everyone left for their daily lives. Dazed and confused, I sat in my room, channel-surfing through the morning shows on TV. Regis and what's-her-name were funny enough, I could see why they're on TV. But truthfully, my favorite was Joyce, Regis's wife.

I decided to spend the day outdoors, so I locked up the house and started walking towards town.

After walking a few miles to State Street, I burned through several hours meandering through a popular bookstore. I went through every subject, every row, like I was doing inventory of the store. I just wanted to get my mind off this overwhelming load.

But I heard Joanne's voice in the back of my head asking Pastor Ryan for some of that money back. I asked myself, "Is it possible? Did I have it in me to ask him for some of that money back?" Was I now considering something that wasn't even a question a week ago?

Feeling the need for a change of space, I left the bookstore and walked back to Ralph's house. I went to my room. It was now late afternoon and I just wanted to take a nap. I fell asleep for what seemed like a couple hours when Bette came home with Sara and Aaron.

Eventually, I got up and read the Bible. I always loved reading Psalms. David infused his soulful poetry with inspiration that elevated his grief. But I felt like a defeated victim of circumstances that were beyond my control. What was evident was that someone else was at the wheel. Was it God? Was it Satan? Was it my sins that brought this evil into my life? Under the weight of these questions, I fell back asleep again.

Awhile later, I heard a knock on my door. Bette was letting me know dinner would be ready soon. In the background I was able to hear the sounds of a family. But it was not my family. I looked at the clock; it was 7:10 p.m. Holy cow, I slept away almost the last four hours. The room was dark, telling me the sun had gone down. I got up and straightened up the room like a good guest should.

When I got to the dining room and took my seat, everyone said hello. Ralph gave grace and was thoughtful enough to mention me in his prayer. We chatted while passing food around to one another. As everyone started talking about their day, I noticed that each one of them looked at my pimple. Gee, I'd forgotten all about it until I noticed Ralph, Bette, and the kids looking at it. Oh, well.

After dinner, I helped Ralph clean up the kitchen, and then I excused myself to my room. That's how good a friend Ralph was. I didn't have to explain myself. I closed the door behind me and turned on the TV. I went to get my pajamas, which I had left in the bathroom.

When I turned on the bathroom light, I caught myself in the mirror and noticed the pimple. It had become much larger and had turned from red to a bluish-green. I took a closer look. It was no pimple, that's for sure. Oh, no, this is why they were staring. I touched it to get a sensitivity level. Ouch! It was sensitive, all right.

Feeling the six miles I walked that day, I climbed into bed and fell into a hard, deep sleep. Who knew I could sleep so much?

The next morning I awoke to the sounds of the family getting ready for their day. I went to the bathroom and I noticed the pimple. Oh, man, not only was it bigger than it was last night, I could see another one coming to the surface on the opposite side of my neck. I looked like a freak. I cracked the bedroom door and called out for Ralph.

"Hey, Ralph, could I see you for a second?" When he got to my room, I showed him the second thing.

He heard the concern in my voice and told me to make an appointment with my doctor and he'd be back to drive me there. I agreed with his plan and he left for the office.

After the family left to go about their lives later that morning, I got on the phone and explained to my doctor what was happening. He told me to go straight to Dr. Bryant, a specialist in dermatology.

When I got Dr. Bryant on the phone, I explained my need to see him that day, and he agreed to see me that afternoon.

When Ralph picked me up for my doctor's appointment, I was aware that we didn't say a whole lot on the way there. I was probably overwhelming him with all of my recent drama. Or was it melodrama?

Ralph sat in the waiting room while I was led into an exam room. Removing my shirt and pants, I replaced them with a paper robe. Dr. Bryant walked in and introduced himself and proceeded to take my vitals. He said they all seemed normal.

Through a magnifying glass he examined the two pimples closely. He said, "Hidradenitis suppurativa, but they should not be on your neck. Or, it could be a carbuncle boil, but by just looking I'm not sure what kind of boil this is. I want to take a sample and close-up pictures of these."

I asked him, "Boil? Boils? Are they contagious?"

"I don't know yet," he admitted. He got a long cotton swab and swiped it on the boil at the eruption point. He continued, "But we're definitely going to run some tests." He secured the swab for the lab. "How many do you have?"

"Just these two," I said.

"I count three, including the one on your back," he said.

"Dang it, I thought I started to feel some irritation back there," I said.

"Why don't you stand up?" he said. He examined my legs. Ultimately, I had three boils.

"How long will they last?" I asked.

He lacked confidence in his answer. "Depending on the type...like I said, I'm not familiar with this strain just by looking at it, but some can last from a few days to six months."

"Six months! When do we get the lab results back?"

"In ten days. I have to send the samples to Chicago, they have the best equipment there."

At the front desk, Ralph paid for the visit and tests with his credit card. Where would I be without my good friend Ralph? The tab came to over $400.

After Ralph dropped me off at the house, I went to my room. In the bathroom cabinet, I found some Band-Aids. I put one over the first boil, as the second wasn't too bad yet. With a Band-Aid on each side of my neck I would look like Frankenstein. One was bad enough, but what choice did I have?

Bette announced dinner, and being a polite guest, I went wearing my Band-Aid. But I noticed the family atmosphere was a bit subdued.

I stuck to my room for most of the night.

Around eleven o'clock that evening, I got up to get a glass of water. I walked to the kitchen and relieved my thirst. I didn't want to stay too long, so I returned to my room. But as I passed a hall leading to the master bedroom, I could hear Ralph and Bette in a heated argument.

Bette questioned Ralph, "But in time there could be more than three and we'd never know."

"That's assuming," Ralph said defensively.

Uncharacteristic of me, I took a few steps closer to their door and heard Bette say, "Ralph, the other day Sara asked me if God is angry at Michael. I said 'no,' but that was before these boils. Now, I just don't know!"

Ralph stood his ground in my defense. "Bette, why would you even think of something like that. Nobody, but nobody loves God more than Michael does. He's just going through a really rough time right now. It could happen to anyone, and it happens to all of us."

"Yes, but not all at the same time," she countered.

Her words felt like punches. She wasn't buying his answers as she saw the abnormality of my broken life.

She continued, "I don't think it's a good idea for the kids to be exposed to whatever he has."

"What are you saying?" Ralph asked.

"Maybe he shouldn't be here right now. I'm saying that if it were just the two of us, it would be different, but with the kids here, who knows?"

"Who knows what?" Ralph quipped.

"Their immune systems may not be as strong as ours."

Ralph said, "You can't expect me to ask him to leave." Through the doors I could only imagine Ralph waving his arms when he told her, "We have a lot of this because of him!"

But when it came to her children, Bette was notoriously overly protective and nothing was going to change her. She dropped her mandate at Ralph's feet with the words, "But you owe it to your children and to me to protect us. Until we know what it is, we can't take that chance."

Her words pierced all walls of reason and rationale, because she was right. I couldn't expose Ralph, Bette, and especially the kids to whatever this was.

I climbed into bed and kept replaying her words over and over again in my brain. But one thing was certain. I was not going to put Ralph in a position to ask me to leave. He had too much love for me, and it would tear him up. I had enough dignity to do what was right, no matter the sacrifice. I didn't know what I would do. My only job was to fall asleep. And in my asleep I could escape from this misery, if only for a few hours.

But I was never far from this never-ending slide into an all-consuming torturous hell as I felt another boil protruding on my left side.

The next morning I found Ralph in the hallway. I asked him for a minute in my room. Privately, I told him, "I understand that because no one knows what these things are on my body, I should stay somewhere else. I haven't thought it through, but what is real is that maybe I shouldn't be here right now."

I could see the relief and sadness in Ralph's face. He sighed and said, "We'll think of something. Why don't you go back to the hotel, and I'll pay for a couple weeks stay."

"You'd do that for me?" I asked.

"Of course, it's not a question," he replied. "It's only for a couple weeks until we get the lab tests back and then we'll have you back here in no time."

"Thank you, Ralph."

Later that morning, he came back to the house to pick me up. Bette had graciously packed some food for me in a box, which she put in the car. I had my belongings ready, although in the back of my mind, I felt like I was forgetting something. I would later discover that I forgot the family photo. At the car, Bette, in a tender, motherly way, wrapped a scarf around my neck.

"Thank you," I said.

She shook my hand and said, "Take care of yourself."

Ralph drove me back to the Hacienda Hotel. We got out of his BMW and walked to the front desk. Ralph took charge and paid for two weeks on the room. When he handed me the key, I saw the hotel clerk look at me funny. I didn't realize the scarf had fallen off its intended mark and the blue-black boil was peering over the edge. But I saw the kid staring at it and I knew people were going to be afraid of me. I had to do a better job at hiding the boils. Ralph turned and asked if I wanted the same room. I shrugged and told him, "Sure, that's fine." I stepped out the door to get some air.

Inside, Ralph signed the charge form, and at $120.95 per night he took his receipt for $1,865 to cover the room for fourteen days.

I walked to Room 315 as Ralph pulled the car closer to get all my stuff out. After we emptied his car, I left him at the door. It was the middle of the afternoon and I was sure he had a million things to deal with at the office. I turned to him and said, "I really appreciate your friendship."

I went to shake his hand when he gave me a hug and said, "Don't be a stranger." As he walked to his car he promised, "I'll be by to check on you." I reiterated my appreciation for putting out the money for two weeks for the room. And then he was gone.

All I wanted to do was disappear. I closed the door behind me. There it was again, the silence. When I had a family, all that human static noise gave me a feeling of being home. How I missed the love that filtered through that background ruckus.

I dropped my gym bag on the floor and flopped on the bed. I fell asleep. I slept all afternoon and into the night. And then I slept some more. Because *anywhere* was better than here.

The next morning, Saturday, arrived with one more boil on my shoulder. I just wanted to run away. I wanted to run and run and run. And when I was done running for days, maybe weeks, maybe I would come out the other end as someone else.

But for now, I'd just stay in bed. It was safer there. But I couldn't stop living. I had to get up and put some life into this day. And where would I find the energy to do that?

I made the mistake of looking in the mirror. My own reflection stopped me as I looked at my face and into my own eyes. "You have to make this work," I said to myself. There isn't anyone to fall back on, I thought to myself. The words echoed through my mind. If I could get rid of these boils, I think I might have a shot at a comeback. I had to wait eight more days before I could call Dr. Bryant to find out the test results.

How much money did I have left? I looked in my wallet and found $130 and the receipt for $288 from Nordstrom for the clothes I bought. I would return the clothes for the cash.

But I still needed to buy a turtleneck, and soon.

Sometime the next day I wrapped the scarf around my neck and left for Nordstrom to returned the new clothes I purchased. Thankfully, no one gave me any attitude. This brought my cash reserve to $430. I looked at their piles of turtlenecks and found them too pricey for a man in my situation.

I thought I could do better at a second-hand store. I'd passed one many times called Oscar's Reincarnated Clothes.

When I got to Oscar's I found a black turtleneck shirt that fit just right. I looked for another, but couldn't find one. So I bought the shirt for five dollars and went to the restroom to put it on.

Later, I stopped at the corner to pick up a newspaper.

Back in my hotel room, I spent the rest of the day looking for a job and making phone calls. Eagerly I set up two interviews, one for a driver and the other as a nighttime guard at a local factory. But what was I supposed to do? Claim I have no resume? Because if they looked at my professional history, they'd throw me out the door. Do I have to create a fake history? What am I, nuts?

That night, I felt another irritation. I woke up. I turned on the light to discover an oncoming boil on the top and in the middle of my right hand. "NO! Not on my hand!" I blurted out in frustration. How was I supposed to hide a boil that's sitting on top of my hand? Oh, no, this was not good. I turned off the lamp and fell back on my pillow.

It seemed my life had become a perpetual cycle of asking the same two questions: "Why is this happening to me?" and "When does this stop?" My anger, confusion, and loneliness ganged up on me suddenly as I grabbed the pillow and screamed into it, "Why are You doing this to me? I know *You know* what You're doing to me, but I don't understand!"

And the worse moments were those very frightening first few seconds when I first awoke. Every time I woke up, the wrecking ball of torment dropped right on top of me just when I became cognizant that I was back in this world. If only I could just sleep my life away.

I became depressed. I had never been depressed before. Is this what it was like, to not want to move?

Then I remembered this same painful impression on my heart from the morning after my father died. I woke up that morning with immeasurable sadness. And with such a huge question: "How do I go on without my father?"

And here it was again: "How do I go on without my family?"

On Sunday morning, I decided not to go to church. I couldn't freak out people when I looked like this. But I couldn't stay in bed all day. I got up, showered, and stepped outside to get a newspaper. In it, I found a couple places hiring drivers, and I thought, "I could do that." But what address would I put on the application? I guess I could put Ralph's, I was sure he wouldn't mind. No, his neighborhood was too rich. I could just pick some random address from some regular neighborhood. Could I do that?

I returned to Oscar's in hopes of finding gloves. I had to hide this thing on my hand. Deep in a box full of winter gloves, I found a pair of black driving gloves. They were just what I was looking for.

Another Sunday afternoon dragged by. Sunday afternoons used to be my favorite time of the week. Some of my best memories took place on Sunday afternoons. But today it all felt so lonely.

Another day wasted in my hotel room. I looked out the window and could see that the sun was going to be setting soon. I could see a sliver of the blue ocean from a couple blocks away. Maybe a walk along the beach would do me good. I needed to get out for a while.

I walked down to the water's edge just south of the pier. I liked being at East Beach when the sun was real low out on the horizon line in the ocean. That's when you can look right at it.

I took this moment to pray for my three children. Eventually, Joanne came to mind. She was a monumental disappointment. Yet, she was the very woman I loved and adored for decades of my life. So I asked God, "Just how am I supposed to pray for the woman who helped dismantle my life?" How was I to forgive her for leaving me like this? Because I could never find it in me to let it go, I figured I'd just let God do it.

I told God, "Between You and me, You have enough forgiveness for both of us."

I thought this was all Joanne's fault. Wait, this was not about the blame game. That's not what this was about. It was bigger than that. There was no blaming anyone. Nor did I believe that this was about one singular thing, or about one particular lesson. There's a holograph of dynamics at work here, yet nothing sufficiently apparent to articulate an intelligent line of thinking.

Sitting on the sand as the sun dropped beneath the horizon line, another day in hell turned into another night of despair and desperation. As the beautiful northern sky grew darker and finally slumbered into night, I came to the very harsh realization that I didn't know anything. Every perception of this world had been completely twisted. I could no longer relate to this world the way I used to, and I was at a loss of how I was going to fit in.

I lay back down on the sand for hours on the dark beach, looking at the stars for answers.

"Consider the heavens, filled with God," I said to myself. As I lay there, I pieced together the little intricate details of the night the kids were taken. Mentally, I returned to New Year's Eve and I could trace the prevention of this nightmare to one singular moment when I should have thought, and acted. But I didn't.

I recall stepping into the doorway at the mansion, just as it was starting to rain. Rain. As I wiped the water in my hand with my handkerchief, I should have realized in that moment my duty was to call John and tell him not to drive, and that Sara should call our local taxicab to pick her up. It would have been so easy.

The tragedy didn't have to happen! But it did. My wisdom shut down because I was so caught up in the superficial glamour of that New Year's Eve party. My lapse of judgment destroyed my family. Is that what it was? Was it my fault? Could I go on living having unintentionally killed our three children? When all I had to do was call John and tell him not to go because it was raining? But I was swept up in the gloss and buying into the delusion of the evening. It was one more thing to compute in my brain, but I wasn't listening and missed the chance.

I returned to the hotel room later that night, as I didn't want to be out on the beach too late. I had heard of a recent incident of college students getting mugged at night on East Beach.

I had no appetite, and this in itself was slightly upsetting. Wasn't that a symptom of nearing death? No appetite? No, don't let these thoughts get away from me. I had to learn to control my thoughts, and not let them run rambunctiously through my mind to drag me down further into depression, and worse, insanity. Someone could go crazy losing everything like I had lost. But that's no cause to lose my faith, my mental clarity, and fundamental cheerful disposition. Because frankly, that may be all I had left. And who knows? Before my life is over, I may lose those, too.

Why didn't I see this coming? Why didn't I see any of this coming? How would or could I, or anyone else for that matter, have seen this coming?

Inside the small hotel room, days faded into nights, and nights turned into days. Night number four turned into day five, and so forth. I didn't venture out but once a day, in the late afternoon and at night, to eat. Just by eating cheap fast food to fill my stomach, I had diminished my money down to three hundred dollars. Another four days passed in this one room I called home. How did I get here?

The night before I was to call Dr. Bryant, another boil erupted on my forearm. I hated those nights, as I became a total insomniac. Over the past week the boils spread throughout my body. I counted a total of nine boils.

Finally, the day arrived when I was to call Dr. Bryant for the test results. I found the nearest pay phone to make the call first thing in the morning.

He took my call right away and asked, "Michael, how are you?"

I answered, "There are nine now." I cleared my throat and swallowed nervously. I went straight to the question and asked, "What did you find out?"

"Not anything definitive, meaning it's not an identified strand. And because of that, I don't know how to treat it," he confessed.

I asked, "You don't know what it is?"

He stammered for words and said, "I can't even prescribe an antibiotic ointment because it has the potential of becoming an accelerator. I do not want to mis-treat it, or it could carry it quicker over your body."

He was stumped. I was checkmated.

He kept speaking, but all I heard in my head was "I'm damned if I do and damned if I don't. Was that it? Was this checkmate by God? Was this what He wanted?" I interrupted him at whatever point he was trying to make and asked, "What can I do?"

He said, "I would just be guessing if I told you what to do."

"Can you at least tell me if they're contagious?"

He admitted, "I can't make that determination, I don't yet know enough about it."

There was a lapse of silence in our conversation as I felt my helpless condition getting worse. Exasperated, I asked, "So you're telling me that there's not much anyone can do because you don't know what it is?"

"Michael, that is basically correct. If I can do more tests with the cultures I already have, I can send them for further research, and maybe in time, we can find more answers."

I said, "More answers? You haven't found *one* yet. And you're the specialist." Suddenly, the phone booth seemed to warp around me as I noticed the hot sun hitting me through the glass. More tests meant more money, I thought to myself. I said, "Doctor, I don't have the means with which to finance more tests."

With disappointment in his voice, he said, "Oh, well, when you're able, when you have the means to get those tests done, please give me a call and we can get you in here."

I just hung up the phone and walked away. Was He killing me slowly? Was I going to die? I had to get back to Room 315 and that was all I really had to remember. Walking down the sidewalk, I prayed out loud to God, "Don't let go, don't let go, don't let go. Don't let go of me, please."

I repeated the words, ignoring the passers-by. "Don't let go," I begged. I could not have cared less who heard me. In that moment, I felt like I was the only one on earth. And in that moment I fell into the ranks of those people who talk to themselves as they walk down the street, not caring who hears them. We all know who they are, and now I knew I had become one of them.

Several days passed and I seemed to be almost wasting my life away doing nothing but hiding in my room.

And then one night I got a boil on my back that kept me tortured all night. And it seemed like they kept coming. With every night came a new boil somewhere on my body. I was mystified why it only happened at night.

And then one morning I awoke to the jab of reality: my last day in this hotel room. Two weeks had passed since Ralph dropped me off. I sighed, realizing that I didn't know where I was going to be laying my head that night. I had been thinking about where I might go after my two weeks were up and the only place I could think of was the Santa Barbara Men's Shelter. I didn't know anywhere else to go. I sat on my bed watching the clock. It was 11:40 a.m. and I still had to get my few things into the gym bag before twelve. But I had no energy to face reality as I fell back onto the bed. I had to allow myself some pity. Deep from within, I felt a well of emotions swelling up because I could no longer hide in my cave, Room 315.

My silent tears fell as I lay frozen, in a muted panic. I had to find somewhere else to hide, where no one would see me. "Come on, stand up," I said to myself. A large lump swelled in my throat, and as I swallowed, more tears came down my face. I didn't know what was out there for someone like me. But I had to be stronger than this, that's for sure.

I told myself not to dwell on anything big right then. Just find the courage to walk through that door. It was 11:55 a.m. and I knew I had to get up. So I sat up and took another deep breath. I stood up and started putting my things into my black gym bag. I crammed a blanket into one end of it. Yes, I knew I was stealing it. What the heck, because I knew God was not watching. I took one last look around the bathroom and dared myself to look in the mirror. Would I find courage there?

I looked in the mirror and asked myself, "Where is your courage?" I got up closer to the mirror and looked myself straight in the eyes from about two inches away. I said out loud to myself, "This is what you have become." I could only remember the man I used to be, the father I used to be, the husband I used to be, and all I wanted to know was "Where did he go? Where is that man I once was?"

At last count that morning, I tallied fourteen boils. The only ones I couldn't hide were the first two on my neck and the one on top of my right hand. So I was guessing that I'd be wearing my turtleneck and gloves for the rest of my life. However long I may have left.

I grabbed my gym bag, faced the door, and sighed. Again, my next step was into the unknown. It was 12:05 and I went for it. I opened the door and stood there for a second, taking in the bright light of noonday and a deep breath of crisp ocean air. I stepped out, pulled the door behind me, and walked away.

My first stop was the post office. I had to forward all my mail to Ralph's office.

My second stop was my church. As I walked across the empty parking lot on my way to Pastor Ryan's office, I remembered the many happy conversations we had with friends in that parking lot. I recalled loading the buses when the kids went to summer and winter camps.

I stepped into the outer office where his secretary, Wendy Schmidt, greeted me warmly.

Pastor Ryan invited me into his office. I apologized for dropping by unannounced. "Michael, you're always welcome anytime. It's always interesting when you come by," he said. He sat down behind his desk. He asked, "How are you, Michael? I've been praying for you and Joanne during this challenging time."

"Thank you, Pastor Ryan, but just to let you know, Joanne filed for divorce about two weeks ago, and my house fell off the foundation in an earthquake, and I have boils on my body that I know you would rather not see. Should I go on? Didn't you ask me, 'How are you?'"

Pastor Ryan sat there with a look of shock, sympathy, and sadness. "Yes, tell me, keep going," He said.

"I have these boils all over my body, and my expert doctor among doctors doesn't know anything about them. He doesn't know how long they'll last. He doesn't know if they're contagious. He doesn't have any answers. Nothing."

Pastor replied, "I'm very sorry, Michael. I know God has a purpose that we may not understand. It's like when an athlete reaches a new record, he or she strives to do even better. You must find the fortitude to expand your faith."

I was a bit stupefied, so I asked, "Faith? What does that mean to a man who has lost everything? Joanne was claiming that I tried to kill myself on my yacht. You remember the *Oh Happy Day*?"

He nodded, remembering the times we took him out on the ocean.

I continued, "She's bearing false witness that I tried to kill myself out on the boat, and because of that lie, she was able to convince a judge in Beverly Hills to freeze every penny I have. And I can't even sell anything just to make some cash. So I was wondering and hoping and praying that there's a chance I could get back some of that large donation I made a couple weeks ago."

Pastor Ryan looked down and away, breaking our eye contact. "It's been more like a month. And as I recall, you did say that you heard God speaking to you in your prayers, telling you to make that donation. Am I right?"

"Did I really say that? Yes, I did. And, yes, He did say that. I probably said it before He took away my children, my wife, my job, my house, and *my life*! I probably said a lot of things before all this happened. But what He did not say was, quote, 'Give them a half million dollars.' So maybe if we went back in time, I would have just donated, say, $400,000. Then I would still have $100,000 left."

"But we can't go back in time. I can't return any of that. Besides, it's already gone to the church's national headquarters in Atlanta," Pastor Ryan said, rejecting my request.

"Atlanta! You mean the money I gave to *this* church in Santa Barbara was sent to Georgia?"

"Michael, in turn we'll be getting that money funneled back here for the construction."

"But I just thought it would have stayed closer," I told him.

"Have faith," he offered.

"Have faith?"

"Michael, God does not try a man beyond what he can handle."

I looked him in the eye and confessed, "Pastor, this is more than I can handle." I added, "Do I look like a man who is coping? Have faith? What does that mean to a man who's lost everything?"

"It means you have to believe harder," he said.

But I was baffled by the shallowness of his words. I replied, "Have faith? After all I've been through, this is your counsel? Pastor, where's your compassion?"

"You don't have to insult me, Michael," he said, embarrassed. He stood up, indicating our meeting was over. "Is there anything else?" he asked. I squirmed in my chair before I got up to leave.

I stopped at the door and turned to him, thinking I might find something to say. But at the last second, wisdom reigned and I kept my mouth shut. I remembered this was a house of worship. And I would not be denigrating Pastor Ryan, or God, in His home.

But in a flash, that wisdom was torched by my burning anger. I walked over to his desk, looked him in the eye, and said, "Go ahead, build your youth center with my money, but if you put Joanne's name on it, I'll burn it down." And in that frozen moment, and through my searing eyes, he could see my resolve.

I turned and walked out the door.

I walked across the parking lot and knew that I would never ever come back.

I worked off my anger by walking. I headed to the ocean and started walking south along the water's edge. I just walked and walked for miles south along the ocean. I didn't care if I ended up in Ventura, thirty miles away, or Mexico.

If God wanted to kill me, He would have done it by now, right? How would I know what God would have done by now? But what's to say He won't do it tomorrow? Remember, I am a fool and I don't know anything about God's decision-making process. Stop thinking this way. I'm not dying, but if I do die, I'll see my children again, and sooner. Wasn't that enough to want me to stop clinging to this life?

No, this was much more than that. It was bigger than, say, if I had stolen money from the company, which I never did. This was bigger than if I had had an affair, which I didn't. I was monogamous with Joanne from the first day we kissed. When you find the perfect woman, no one else will do. I loved her every day of my life when we were together.

What happens to all that love? Where does it go? Does it just evaporate never to be thought of again? Does it hang in the air and die from lack of memory? Is that what keeps love alive? Memories?

Does love die by the lack of attention?

I had watched fear completely overtake Joanne. She was just overwhelmed. She couldn't find the fortitude to get through this. It was too much for her. Imagine how much better I would be coping if she hadn't taken all our money. The whole thing overwhelmed her and she fell apart. Oh no, there, I did it; I found myself feeling sorry for her. I hit that sympathetic button in my heart for her for just a second. Shutting off nineteen years of love like a spigot wasn't easy. Wait a second, I was not finished resenting Joanne. I reserved the right to harbor my anger for her a lot longer than a month, two months, or maybe two years. Or even two decades. I had to consciously stop thinking of her.

Down around Carpinteria, I finally looked up and saw that I had walked about twelve miles. I hardly noticed. But I guessed I should be getting back up to town, so I turned around and headed north.

With about ten miles left to get back to town, the sun set over the ocean. Across His big sky, God was changing color filters from yellow to orange to green and blue to purple and finally to black. The ocean took on a whole other personality at night. The stars always seemed to shine brighter over the ocean. I looked up to find Orion straight overhead. Of course, that's where it always was in February.

I walked a few miles while staring out over the dark waters. The lights on the oil rigs just off the coast made good markers to tell me how far I'd walked. I kept walking for another couple hours and I was getting kind of tired. I was tired of everything, but basically I was tired of walking. And I was tired of carrying this gym bag.

I went to lie down on a sand dune, at the bottom of a set of stairs leading up to some kind of building, about twenty yards away. I couldn't make it out in the dark.

I got the blanket out of my gym bag. I opened the blanket and wrapped it around me. I turned my gym bag into a pillow and stared at the stars. Only a month ago I had a life full of happiness, love, and security. But that was all gone and here I was on the sand under a blanket I stole. I muttered, "Thank you, dear God, for this blanket." And then, under a galactic night sky, I was lulled to sleep by the sounds of crashing waves.

I dreamt I was walking happily on the beach with the kids and Joanne. I was having such a peaceful dream until...

...I heard the voice of an old woman, "Hey, young man, get up and go get a job." I opened my eyes and discovered it was the next morning. The old woman continued, "There are plenty of jobs out there." Then she started poking me with her beach umbrella.

I yelled back at her, "OUGH, get away from me!"

But she kept bellowing, "Get a job!"

I yelled back, "Are you hiring? Because I would love a job!"

She swiped at my feet with her nasty umbrella and then hollered out, "Go get yourself a life! Go on!"

I had to stand up to get this old woman out of my face. As I stood, she backed away and I mocked her pompousness, "Yes, and I'll pray for you too!"

As the old lady walked away, I could hear her say under her breath, "God, that made me feel better."

Why did an 80-year-old woman with her lethal umbrella make me her target? Do I have a bull's eye painted on me? I figured it's about seven in the morning, give or take two hours. I didn't really care.

"Oh, God, that was rude," I said to myself. I lay back down and curled up under my blanket. I was not ready to get up. And then I sort of recognized the setting. Because I got here in the dark of night, I didn't really know where I dropped to make camp.

I looked out over the sand. Hey, I've played on this beach before. So, I turned around and I saw that it was the Biltmore Hotel. I was near the bottom of the stairs that I'd run up and down quite a few times. The stairs are on a gradual slope up the dunes to the patio restaurant. Oh, no, these people here know me. Impulsively, I stood and looked up at the restaurant. Thankfully, there was no one there looking back at me, only a busboy setting the tables. How many times have I had lunch on that patio?

I crouched back down and counted the $61 that I had left. How long would this have to last me? I shouldn't have spent so much at the hotel. Whatever, I would get an egg burrito somewhere. Aah, forget it. I didn't have to have breakfast.

Hours later and back in Santa Barbara, I spent a couple hours in Ortega Park, but I had to look into getting shelter for the night.

Twenty minutes later I turned the corner onto Yanonoli and arrived at my destination. I knew that no one from my other life would ever come down here. I also had to remember that this was only temporary. It's not the rest of my life. I had to believe that, but then what did I know? I might even die here. I stepped into the lobby of the Santa Barbara Rescue Mission.

I looked around to find an attendant. I noticed him behind a desk inside a glass office. I walked up and knocked on his door. He waved me in.

"Can I help you?" he asked.

"Yes, I need a place to stay. Just for a short time. How does this work?"

The attendant looked at me like he was scanning me, compiling a profile on me. "You've never done this before, have you?" he asked.

"No, I've never been in this position before," I replied sheepishly.

He organized some forms and handed them to me, along with a pen. He told me, "Go make yourself comfortable in the lobby and fill out these forms, and then come back." I sat down at a table to complete the questionnaire.

It had the usual questions. The address line stumped me. I figured if you're here, you most likely don't have an address. And yet, I did have an address, but if I put 970 Santa Ynez Road, Montecito, he was going to laugh me out of here for insanity. So I left it blank.

But I was stumped when it came to the part about my health. I didn't know. I was confused. Deep down I did not believe these boils were contagious. I was almost certain of it. I hadn't seen the slightest evidence that they're contagious. So, I was going have to lie. I didn't like to, but if I thought they were contagious, then I wouldn't be able to stay here. So I marked this "no." I returned to the office.

"I'm Ted, resident manager," he said.

"I'm Michael Whiley," I said returning the introduction and the forms. Ted motioned me to take a seat. He looked up from having taken an overview of my forms.

He crossed his arms and lectured me, "There are a lot of rules in this place, and that's the only way it can function. You can stay as long as you abide by the rules. You line up outside, and never before 4:30 p.m. Generally, you never get the same bed two nights in a row. So don't be territorial. Your shower schedule will be between 7 and 7:30 a.m. Don't show if you're late. But since this is your first day, I'll check you in now, and you can shower now if you'd like, just keep your valuables nearby."

Ted showed me to the dorm room and around the facilities. He showed me to my bunk bed, and left me by the showers. He said, "Go ahead and shower, but afterwards you'll have to leave until we open tonight at 5:30."

"Sure," I replied.

"I'll be in my office," he said, leaving me. In the shower room, I closed the door leading to the hall. Each shower stall had a small space to change clothes behind a door. I dropped my bag to the floor and turned the shower on to let it get warm and then I undressed. Reaching to close the door to my stall, I caught myself in a full-length mirror about ten feet away. For the first time I could see the full onslaught of my boils. I had a couple on each leg, lower and upper back, a couple on my right shoulder, my arms, neck, and hand. I prayed, "I just don't know what I did to deserve all this. What did I do? Tell me!! I want to know! What are You doing to me? I'm the one who loved You when it came time to feed the orphans and widows. I was the one who drove to Mexico to make sure children were fed and had beds to sleep on. I made sure that every child in church went to summer camp, to do what? To praise Your name. That was me. Is there someone I haven't forgiven? Tell me and I'll apologize. I've never cursed you."

I confessed that I was living my worst-case scenario.

The private shower stall gave me some relief from the outer world. The water falling on my face blended with the tears. I had become so emotional lately. Who could blame me? But when does it stop? When does the crying stop? When I was done, I dried myself off and headed for the street with my gym bag, my only possession, filled with crumbs from a past life. But I was clean and grateful.

Five-thirty came around and I walked into the shelter showing my number. I headed to my bunk, took off my shoes, and climbed up. I lay there with all my clothes on. Some of the other men hung out by their bunks and chatted with one another. I just lay there staring at the ceiling, not much for conversation. I was very tired so I fell asleep right away.

I was having a comforting and peaceful dream about flying. I loved my dreams when I flew. In those dreams, my whole body worked as one unit and lifted off the ground at will.

In my sweet and serene dream, I was flying by a lake, roughly twenty feet above water level, when an attendant rang the bell at 6:45 a.m., rudely awaking me. It was the onslaught of absolute rudeness.

Oh, no, this reality again.

I didn't think I wanted to shower that morning. After all, I did shower the previous afternoon. I would be back that night and I'd shower the following morning.

I spent the early morning hanging out by the pier and then I headed to the library, where I realized that the only good card in my wallet was my library card. And I hoped I wouldn't screw that up. I read the *Wall Street Journal* and nearly every current newspaper. I meandered through the science section and came across *The Universe and Dr. Einstein* by Lincoln Barnett. Dr. Einstein was such a genius. How could one brain hold so much complexity? After a couple hours into his Unified Field Theory, I was ready to get up and stretch. I understood his principles rather well, because Barnett masterfully turned complex ideas into simple words. I checked the book out.

Again, I browsed Oscar's Reincarnated Clothes and found a pair of sweat pants. I also picked up a batch of new socks, which left me with about $19.

I walked over to Alameda Park where I found a large tree that offered shade and so I settled under it. I looked up at the branches high above the ground. It was a magnificent show of nature. I wondered how long I was going to be at the mission. I considered whether or not I should call Ralph or any of the guys, but I talked myself out of that. Who wants to be around someone with boils? I doubt I would. I was sure Ralph told them everything.

I got to the mission at 4:45 p.m. and took my place at the end of the line. The others around me were talkative, but I hid behind my newspaper. It's not that I thought I was superior; it's just that I didn't want to come out of my shell. I just wanted to hide in my own thoughts and be a mystery. Because that's what life had turned into for me, a complete mystery.

During the evening I continued reading Einstein's book where I left off in his Unified Field Theory. It's the beginning of understanding the string theory, also known as the "rubber band" complex, meaning that everything has a connection to everything else in the universe by these nano-rubber bands. Maybe that's where I should go look for God; in the sub-atomic particle? Perhaps inside me somewhere a particle of God stirs the electrons that keep my heart beating and my lungs breathing. That's my point: how could God not know this was happening to me?

The next morning I showered in one of the private stalls. The first thing I did was lock the door. I took off all my clothes, and as I reached up to hang them on a hook, another resident opened the door and saw me totally naked. Although it was for only a split second, he could plainly see that I was covered with boils. He closed the door apologetically. But my secret was out. I went to turn the lock harder to make sure it was secure. I did not want that to happen again. I was so careful about it, but it still didn't latch. I continued with my shower, and when I was done I started to collect my stuff.

A half hour later I was ready to leave and scan the job listing in the paper. I even considered getting some breakfast. Walking through the lobby, I saw Ted wave at me through the glass. At first I thought he was just waving, like good morning, so I waved back. But I saw that he was waving for me to come to his office.

"Good morning," I said.

"Good morning, Michael. Please have a seat." He frowned and said, "A little while ago, another resident guest came to me and let me know that you might have health issues. Is this true?"

My heart started racing, and I could feel a lump building in my throat. I couldn't hold it back and nervously swallowed. "Yes, it is," I confessed.

A little agitated, Ted said, "I'm sorry, Michael, but on this form you marked 'no' in a box you should have marked 'yes.' So, please be very honest with me. Are you HIV positive?"

I looked him straight in the eye and said, "No, I am not."

"Then please tell me what you have," he said.

I looked at him and weighed response options in my head. By process of elimination, telling the truth was the only option. "The doctor said he didn't know, honestly."

Ted asked, "Now, be very honest with me, did the doctor say if they're contagious?"

I replied, "He said he didn't know, but based on the people I've been around, there's absolutely no evidence that it's contagious."

Ted sat back down and slumped over his desk. "Michael, I'm sorry, but because my duty here is to the whole community, I'm afraid I'm going to have to ask you to leave. Until your doctor can tell us it's not contagious, you'll have to find other accommodations."

Hoping I could change his mind, I reaffirmed, "But I haven't seen another person get this from me, really." And in my desperation, I blurted out, "God..." And then I stopped myself. I asked myself in my head, "Am I going to pin this on God?" Yes, absolutely. I told Ted, "God has it in for me." I kept going. "God has turned my life upside down and He's why I'm here in the first place."

With a spin of his head, Ted asked, "What?"

"God has it in for me. Just me, it's not anyone else," I said in my defense.

But then I took a step back and looked at myself from outside of my body; I saw myself in a black turtleneck and wearing black driving gloves at 8 a.m., when we all knew I had no car. I was looking like

James Bond hiding out at the rescue mission. And I was hearing myself blame God.

Ted had to think I was crazy. What else could he think? He frowned and said, "I'm sorry, Michael, when you get your health issues under control, you can come back."

I got up and graciously thanked him for the couple nights of shelter. I turned and walked out. The irony of dropping off so many clothes and stuff here over the years and now being told to leave boggled my mind.

I was not going to be angry with Ted. He was not the cause of my woes. He was just looking out for the other guys, and I couldn't blame him. He was just doing his job. But I didn't know where I was going, again. He didn't even buy the God part. I really did think for a second that it was going to work, but it didn't. It was another hard landing on the cold slab of rejection.

Everything I touched was hell-bent for broke, and the needle of my life's compass had spun uncontrollably south. The building blocks of what were right and justified were now lying on the ground in pieces. I was going to have to go it alone. But who knew for how long? It could be days or weeks, I didn't know.

Isn't there scripture that says "To lay down your treasures before God"? I laid down my treasures. Oh boy, did I ever lay down my treasures for God.

But inside my heart, I knew I didn't.

God took my treasures away from me. I didn't voluntarily give them to Him. It's not like God came to me and said, "Psst, Michael, I want you to give up your three children to Me." What would I have said? No? Yes? Take me instead? But God would have replied, "But that's not who I want." And hence the choice was taken away from me. So, no, I did not lay down my treasures before Him. He decided to take them back.

CHAPTER SEVEN

THE WORST WAS YET TO COME
PART II

I walked over to the railroad tracks and took them north. I decided that I would walk the tracks until I could walk no farther. So, I just walked and walked. After a few miles the tracks passed by the airport. Another hour later I passed Isla Vista, but I didn't care. My feet led the way and I just went along.

A few miles past Isla Vista, the tracks ran right down on the beach. Fifteen miles from my starting point, I came across El Capitan State Beach, and then I collapsed.

This was just what I needed. I got away from everyone and had a beautiful beach to myself. Maybe there was a chance I could sleep here tonight. I sat at a picnic bench a few feet away from the sand and opened up the newspaper and my library book on Dr. Einstein.

I checked out the shrubbery along the edge of the park and saw there were a couple spots that might be able to hide a campsite. Over the next couple hours, I saw the sheriff patrol cars drive by a few times, checking on things. I didn't want to get arrested. These guys would arrest you first, and then take pity on you later. I really didn't want to get arrested.

What a beautiful beach. I should have come more often when I had a life to bring with me.

I asked God, "Is this a test? Is that what this was about? Is that it? Just tell me. Just let me know and I'll be totally fine with it. You just say it, just say it, and I'll be totally fine, because I know You are listening. So, if this is a test, then I have to be accepting of my plight. I have to be okay with dying."

I also believed that the true me was separate from my string of calamities. Calamites come and go, but the real me must surmount this outer world of disasters. Can I go through this and not change the fundamental traits that make up who I am?

I just wanted to know why He was doing this to me! Or, have I done it to myself? Which was it?

I enjoyed my escape into the book as I hung out for most of the afternoon. But I had to deal with where I was going to sleep, if not there. With the cops coming around so often, I reluctantly started walking the same tracks back towards town.

A couple hours later, I turned in at an opening in the shrubbery as the sun was starting to set. Behind some bushes, I found a clearing that would shelter me for the night. I made my world on the ground there in the quiet loneliness of night.

The next morning, I continued down the tracks back to town. Just inside city limits, I found a perfect hiding spot, tucked in between Los Carneros Park, the freeway, and the railroad tracks. It was a good spot, noisy at times, but private. If you close your eyes, the sounds of the passing cars could almost sound like crashing waves. And I was going to need more than what I had. I was going to have to go hunting for things. But for right now, my blanket would have to suffice.

I spent the next several days gathering large cardboard boxes from behind department stores. I used those for my flooring. I got in the habit of going shopping in back alleys at night, and sleeping most of the day. I didn't want people seeing me rummaging through their dumpsters during the day.

Sometimes I found other useful things. One evening in the back of a hardware store I found a tarp. Over a day or so, I gathered enough rope to string across four trees to make some shade over the camp. At night, it protected me from the dew.

One day I discovered I was down to my last four dollars. Holy cow, just sitting there I realized I still had my wedding ring. I got up and walked over to the pawn shop called Opportunity Shop and hawked my wedding ring. He offered me $45.50 for it.

I countered his offer and said, "Really? It's a nice ring. How about $55?"

And he replied, "Not a penny over $45.50."

"I'll take it." He handed me two twenties and a five. I took off that ring that had no meaning to it. It was gone and I didn't care. Wow, a quick forty-five bucks. This could last me another week.

On my way back to camp, I came across a homeless woman. She was holding a cup in one hand and a baby in the other. She sat on the sidewalk, begging. I kept walking. And then I asked myself, "Wait a minute. Who am I, if I don't give that woman something?" I turned around, walked back to her, and gave her the five-dollar bill.

She lit up and said, "Thank you." I turned and walked away. Ten steps farther, God, being God, in a flash of a thought challenged my compassion and I realized that this woman was begging for two people, herself and the baby.

I turned around and walked back to her. I took the five dollars out of her cup and replaced it with a twenty. Who was I to say no to a six-month-old baby living on the street? "God bless you," I said.

She smiled while looking up at me and thanked me repeatedly.

I continued walking. Funny, I considered the irony of me telling someone, "God bless you."

If practicing random acts of kindness, despite all of my misery, would help me remember who I was, then I must practice it more often. I could do the little things that would put a smile on someone's face. Or, I could do good things without expecting anything in return, not even so much as a "thank you." Wasn't that the core value of giving? To give without expecting anything in return?

After all, I was now a citizen of the invisible nation that I was starting to see living in America.

A couple days later, as I walked down an alley one afternoon behind a Chinese restaurant, I saw an Asian man step out to smoke. With nothing to lose, I walked up to him and asked, "Do you work here?"

He nodded yes.

I asked, "Do you know if they're hiring?"

He took a long inhale and with almost a smirk he said, "Yes, we need a dishwasher boy, but you're no boy."

"But anyone can clean dishes, right?"

I could see by his look, he'd rather not agree with me. "We pay minimum wage, and most important, all you do is wash dishes. Can you start now?"

"Oh, yes, I can start right away."

He led me into the kitchen and to the sink where there was a mountain of dirty dishes piled high from the previous two days. He said, "Old dishwasher quit. He was a boy. Wait here." He walked away, leaving me alone.

I figured there had to be a pair of dishwashing gloves around there somewhere. I found the standard yellow gloves under the sink. I put them on.

He came back and said, "You're hired."

I got started on chipping away at the mountain of crusty dishes. In no time I was sweating like a dog. But hey, I was making money and with no questions asked. This was good. Seven hours later that night, at around nine o'clock, he came back around and said to me, "You come back tomorrow morning at eleven o'clock." And then he handed me $50.75.

I smiled, took his money, and left. Hey, I could get used to this, I thought to myself on the way home.

The next day I arrived a few minutes before my shift, and as I was changing gloves from my black driving pair to my yellow dishwashing pair, an older Asian man came in the back and surprised me. He saw the lesion on the top of my hand and looked at me with disdain. I put the dishwashing glove on clumsily and smiled at him. He turned and walked away.

I chastised myself that it was just my luck that he would have appeared that very second, and I should have been more careful. I got down to washing the dirty dishes that had arrived after I left the night before. I assumed the lunch crowd would start anytime soon.

The day went smoothly as I kept to the kitchen. And the piles of dishes kept me busy all day.

When nine o'clock that night came around, my smoker friend walked up to me and said, "My boss says you have to not come back."

"What? Why?"

"He says you have bad hands," he answered.

"But I'm wearing gloves," I protested, showing him that I was wearing the yellow gloves.

The man shook his head and said, "I'm sorry, he's the owner." He handed me $65.25 and said, "Good luck."

Without taking off the yellow gloves, I grabbed my stuff and walked out the door.

Outside by the big trash bin, I removed the rubber gloves and tossed them in. Just when I thought things might be looking up, I was reminded of that "pattern" Joanne warned me about.

Ten days of doing nothing drained my funds down to five dollars. That's all, five dollars and some change. I would have to start asking people for money. How do I do that? Where do people do that sort of thing? Oh, my God, listen to me, I was breaking apart. No, I passed that point months ago.

I went to the train station to hit up the tourists coming into town. I didn't know how to do this. "Just smile, Michael," I said to myself. "Just smile and people will give you money," I repeated to myself. Did I need a cup? Some guys used cups. If I used a cup, would people think I was a professional beggar? But I wasn't. Or, should I just use my hand? I would use my hand. My gloved hand, that is, so as not to show that boil and scare them away. I got plenty other stuff working to scare them away.

Seeing a young couple get off the train and noticing that they started walking towards me, I targeted them as my first ever attempt to beg. As they passed by I took a deep breath and asked, "Excuse me, could you spare some change?" But they totally ignored me and walked right by. They heard me, they saw me, but they didn't look at me. A little bit of me died right there and right then. But no matter, I would have to do it again.

I saw a young man in his twenties walking nearby and I asked, "Excuse me, can you spare some change?" He dug into his pocket and pulled out a few quarters and handed them to me. "Thank you," I told him. Hey, it worked, I thought to myself. The kid continued walking and I was seventy-five cents richer. Wow, seventy-five cents. My whole perspective was completely dwarfed by memories of withdrawing three hundred dollars at a time out of ATM machines. What was I thinking?

I continued begging, and every rejection was like a little needle that dug into me. But there were some who gave. In an hour I decided to use a cup. Money can be dirty if you think about it. I was up to more than five dollars, so I guessed I was a professional now.

I was tired of begging the very day I started. But such was my punishment for whatever it was I did. However, I did rack up fifteen dollars, and with that I could buy hygiene stuff and a couple of meals. And that was just one day. I was feeling better already.

If the Bible defined hell as "separation from God," how could I ever be separated from God? If God is the very air I breathe into my lungs, how could I be ever be separated from Him? He, who hears everything. Even my very whispers could be heard on the moon if He were standing in a crater there. He is the very colors I see and the ocean I bathe in. How could He be so close and watch my tortured soul and emotional anguish, and do nothing about it? I wanted to know.

I knew that God knew who I was already. When I die, death will only be a passing doorway. I know that when I die, I will see God Himself, in all His infinite forgiveness, waiting for me on the other side. And I don't see how He could turn me away.

It may not be much, but I would claim that I was a soul who tried to carry His attributes into this human experience. I tried to ease the pain in others. I supported the poor and the vulnerable, and I learned long ago that the supreme purpose of man is to love God first, and to serve one another as "He serves us." Not in a subservient, demeaning way, but equally addressing everyone as an extension of ourselves.

That is the core of everything I understand to be what Christ meant when he said, "Do unto others as you would have them do unto you."

When will we live that code? When will we let go of the old eye-for-an-eye mentality that imprisons us to cycles of hate, war, and violence? We must try to live in this code of life. Could we live in that mindset every day of our lives? It's how we should approach the people we work with, the people we live with, and the people who come up to us and beg us for the crumbs of our fat life.

I returned to my camp in the afternoon and finished reading the last chapters on Dr. Einstein. Are we walking evidence of his Unified Field Theory in that we are connected to one another?

I never understood why religion, now and throughout history, never approached science as God in creation. He is the nano and the sub-atomic. He is the infinite space and all that fills it, and *that* is science. Nothing exists without Him and that is science. He is the very gravitational pull that moves the atoms. Holding all things together, He is spirit and nature doing a cosmic dance together.

My repetitive life turned into more days of begging at various places, which also included the bus station, Ben & Jerry's Ice Cream, a couple Italian restaurants, and sometimes a popular bookstore. I kept up with the *Wall Street Journal* as part of my routine, and whatever other journals that would keep my mind sharp.

In Santa Barbara, March was always reliably wet and cold. I wished I could burn a campfire for heat, but that would attract unwanted official interference.

Were my memories all I had? I noticed I spent a lot of time remembering my past life. Because looking at me, you'd never think I'd been anywhere. Is that what people thought when they saw me? Or did their eyes glide over me as if I were invisible? Did they quietly pity the rotting man who slid into hell on earth? Were they thinking to themselves, "Thank God, that's not me"? Or did they ponder, "See, that's what happens when you do so many bad things and fall out of favor with God."

The fact is, they were all thinking all of those things. I know because I used to think all those things. How many times did I ignore the needy when all they wanted was a little help? Where are they now? I'd find every one of them and beg their forgiveness and give them what I could if it would satisfy God and get me out of my humiliation.

Was that it? Wait, I was bargaining with God.

Okay, so what's the lesson? That I should give to the needy no matter how little I have? No matter if I have almost nothing? So, when I do have something, think of another less fortunate soul because they are an extension of me? Was that my lesson?

Was I being ostracized from a real life to learn what it's like to be impoverished? Because this was not living! Or, was I missing the point? Was there a point?

Was the lesson to embrace life, ignore the big mysteries and continue make believing that I was happy? Was I cursed to awaken every morning to no purpose? I even missed getting up and having to get ready to go to work.

But who knew how much longer I had to live?

Rejection resurfaced every morning. From my waking moment, I was on a path of rejection. My life was painted with it. Everyone who saw me mentally built a defense and pretended I was invisible or waved me off with a hand gesture or a shrug of their shoulders. It didn't even have to be spoken. That's how easily people discarded me. Yet, I stood there with all the feelings, intelligence, and dignity that would match anyone else's. But I had become invisible. Even standing right in front of people, I had no presence. And I had to laugh to myself because "I used to be somebody."

There was a time, when I came across the desperate and homeless I mentally took an eraser and pretended they weren't standing there as I walked by them. Yet, sometimes I'd go out of my way to help them out. I know I did many times. So, I can't be too hard on myself that I would rewrite my own history in my head, just to satisfy a jaunt down pity lane. No, I was not going to do that. I had to watch my mind and carefully monitor my thoughts. Because how could I forget "I used to be somebody, and I still am. And I used to tithe, and I still do."

Was I looking at a life ahead of me filled with unending questions? Is that where this leads? Was I to wander aimlessly through this pit the rest of my life? Must I roam and beg the rest of my living days? Will I ever rid myself of these boils? What if I don't? What if I have to go through every day of my life thinking I've wronged God? How will I ever know if I have, or not? If I have, then why must it be a mystery to me? Was I asking too much? And what made me think that God even knows I'm alive? How could He not know that this calamity has destroyed my life? Couldn't He see everything that I was looking at? Couldn't He feel the pain I lived with everyday? Wasn't He the very electricity in my heart muscle that made it beat?

Was my lesson to learn that the material world is not mine to own?

Curiously, I wondered if I'd ever be in a relationship with another woman again in my life. Was that it? If God is all about love, then why was He putting me through this? What did I do to deserve all this misery? Was I supposed to learn that only God could give me real happiness? I didn't know I was living a false happiness before, because it sure felt real.

Who knew God and I had issues?

Who knew giving the church half a million dollars would upset Him? But did any of this make sense? No. None of this made sense and that's the great privilege of being the Almighty. He can do, and does do whatever He wants. We are born and we die at His whim. And everything in between called life is known to Him. But the one advantage God has over our own sense of what is right, is that He can see the infinite possibilities and we can't. He has the advantage of time-travel and knows what lies ahead. We don't. But this reasoning doesn't make anything better, or easier in the here and now.

Weeks melted into one another, and another month went by as the days and nights meandered into April. Although nothing changed in my routine or fortune, it was the beginning of spring, which brought warmer temperatures and more fog. A lot more fog. And a lot more questions.

If God was the very ground I slept on, and the very branches that gave me shade, then why couldn't He see how miserable and heartbroken I was? Just short of killing myself, I couldn't imagine what worse thing could happen to me. And we know what happened the last time I asked that question. Or was it Joanne?

Somewhere in the middle of the night I felt a blister on the bottom of my right foot. I wasn't sure, but I thought it might be another boil. I couldn't be certain in the dark in the middle of the night, but just the thought of a boil on my foot worried me enough that it kept me awake for a few hours.

When I finally woke up late the next morning, I started thinking about what I had to get done that day. When I stood and took two steps, I was hit with a shot of pain in my right heel. I sat right down and examined my foot. Sure enough, and of all the worse places, there was a boil on my right heel. I stood to test the degree of pain. I could only take a couple steps and it hurt badly. I had to walk on the ball of my right foot, making sure I didn't put any weight on my right heel. I swore to never ever ask that horrid question again.

Having to keep my heel up off the ground made me walk funny. Since I had to keep my right heel completely off the ground, I was hunched slightly to the left to help alleviate the weight off the ball of my right foot. Walking straight up was nearly impossible.

A few non-eventful days went by with the same routine. It was evident to me when I looked at my reflection that I'd lost probably twenty, maybe thirty pounds since this all started. Peddling for change hadn't been all that successful lately. Some days were all right and other days were pitiful.

One beautiful April afternoon as I was sprawled out on my cardboard, I heard rustling in the bushes. I sat up, anxious to know who was coming in my direction. Three Mexican migrant workers came out of the bushes talking Spanish. I discovered they were making their way up to the Central Valley to pick strawberries. After a few meager attempts with my gringo Spanish, we seemed to all get along. A couple of them spoke enough English that we figured how to communicate. I asked, "How long are you staying here?"

My new roommates told me, "Oh, no, we're not staying."

Another of them said, "We like Santa Barbara, but we don't like the police." They all laughed.

One of them noticed the boil on my hand and said, "That is a bad pimple, man."

I had taken off my gloves on my way back from peddling.

"Oh, it's nothing," I replied.

We hung out for a while, jabbering in Spanglish when one of my new Mexican friends said to me, "Hey, gringo, you hungry?"

"Yeah, I'm hungry," I replied.

"We're going to bring some food back for you when we come back, all right?" he offered.

"Sure, gracias, when you come back," I told him. Shortly after talking amongst themselves, they left.

A few hours later in the dark of night, I first noticed them by their drunken laughter. And then I heard rustling in the bushes approaching camp. Giggling like little schoolgirls, these macho Mexicans had too many shots of their friend, Sr. Patron. They crash-landed in the campsite in a good mood and with bags of stuff. My new best friends brought me a huge plate of Mexican food, loaded with everything. I turned on the dim lantern, so we could see. It smelled so good I just wanted to dive in. And with fork in hand, I was ready to. But in a flash of lightning, I was stopped by a profound sense of appreciation. I closed my eyes and said, "Thank you, Lord, for this meal, I appreciate it." Yes, the Lord and I were still on speaking terms, no doubt about it. Of course, I thought it had been kind of one-sided lately.

They offered me a shot of tequila. Tequila? I didn't drink alcohol. But I guess with food, it would be all right. No, it would accentuate the depression. "No gracias," I replied. Ha! Tequila and me - never happen.

The guys sat on the ground and logs as they settled in for some more drinking and banter. We exchanged stories. I had the best ones. They couldn't believe their ears when I told them I used to have a yacht, a bunch of cars, and my own gas pump. They looked at me and howled the night away. They could smell me a mile away, and thought I was so full of crap you needed a plane to stay above the level of stink I was making. But no matter, they loved the stories. We laughed. I ranted about the most expensive and luxurious times of my life, and they screamed laughing. The absurdity of my life drowned out any glimmer of truth, and I could see that these guys took it for shear entertainment. I knew they thought I was making it up, so after a while, I shut up. I kept the boils part to myself. I didn't want to scare them off.

And the tequila kept making the rounds. I was amazed that I understood a lot of what they were saying. I didn't speak Spanish other than what I picked up living in Southern California.

When the laughter mellowed out, one of them pulled out a tightly folded space blanket. Space blanket? They all slept huddled together on a space blanket. Why didn't I think of it?

It was fun having people around, even if they spoke another language. As I lay down, I realized that these guys didn't judge me. Being humble migrant workers at the bottom of the food chain, they just lived spontaneously and practiced non-attachment. Gee, come to think of it, that sounded like my life. And with that, I turned off my brain.

The next morning I woke up in a pretty good mood. Of course, good was relative. But that morning I woke up to a beautiful blue sky. And the smells of the wet foliage were pleasant enough. I saw that the guys were gone already. They must have gotten up really early. I didn't even hear them leave. Oh, well.

I wondered how much money I had left. I thought I had about ten dollars. So I went to count it. I kept it in the gym bag, but I couldn't find it. I looked everywhere, but it was not there. It took about ten seconds to cover everywhere it might have been. Oh, no. Was it possible? Did they steal my gym bag? Why would they do that? I lifted a cardboard flat covering some buckets to find a dark blue gym bag. It was similar to mine, but I didn't even notice it the day before. I opened it to discover used and dirty clothes from one of the migrant workers. Holy cow, he took mine by accident. Oh, no. It was probably still dark when he picked it up.

What was in my bag? Let's see, there was my pair of pants, a turtleneck shirt, my underwear, socks, hygiene stuff, and things like Band-Aids and glow nets for the lantern. Wow, I was going to have to work harder and longer to replace all that stuff.

And immediately I went begging for some change. I raised four dollars in a couple hours at various places. I was not comfortable staying in one place longer than ten or fifteen minutes.

One night while rummaging through the alley behind State Street, I found a framed mirror. Who knew mirrors were so heavy? I lugged it back to camp.

The next morning, I propped the mirror against a tree. I sat down and looked at myself in it, which took effort and bravery. Was this a man? No, it was some repulsive excuse for a man. I couldn't understand how I had come to this point. I knew that I had watched my life fall, stumble, and crash into this abyss. I couldn't explain why it happened. I could only explain how it happened.

I looked to see if the boils were any bigger. No, the ones on my neck stayed the same size. I counted the same number of boils. I looked at my face. I looked haggard and tired. The lines in my face had grown deeper. My eyes looked like they were permanently bloodshot, and my hair was totally out of control. Having gone five months without a haircut resulted in a tangled web. I hadn't taken notice of my appearance in weeks and weeks. I had no idea who this person was that I was looking at. I asked the man in the mirror, "Where did you come from, and how did you get here?" Looking at myself, this troubled human, was not anything or anybody I recognized.

And yet, I am somebody. Simply, because God is the very electric pulse that gives life to the nerves that looked out through my eyes, giving them the intelligence of vision. And looking at this man in the mirror, I realized God is the intelligence that said to this brain, "This is you. And you are somebody."

I didn't have to go back to look at my material life to say, "Hey, I used to be somebody." I didn't need that. Freedom, is that what I was looking for? Did I give You, God, the impression that I wanted to be free from the burdens of that other life? I hope not, because that was not the way it was at all.

Days of merely surviving passed one into another. "Where was God? Where did God go? Where was He?" I asked myself. For days I went looking and searching for God, and I found Him right where I left Him last: *everywhere*.

I woke up late one morning and saw myself in the mirror and instantly decided I no longer wanted that mirror. It served its purpose and I just wanted to get rid of it. I laid it face down under a bush where I wouldn't step on it. It was time to go out and generate some revenue.

By one o'clock I raised about seventeen dollars. It was a good day, even though I really hated doing this because I thought some people were genuinely scared of me. I was warm under my turtleneck, but I had no choice. Any day I had to go begging was a bad day.

I stopped for a cheap burrito at Selma's Joint. After eating my only meal of the day, I had about twelve dollars left. That ought to be good enough to feed me the following day, and maybe even the next day. Maybe I should go back to camp. I was tired. And what I really wanted was just to stop doing this for a while. So, feeling ahead of the game, I headed back to camp.

As I turned the corner at Castillo and Cota Street, there was a gas station. I saw a woman walking towards me on the sidewalk in front of the gas station. My thought was, "I made enough today, I'm off duty, just keep walking." I weighed in my head if I should ask her, or not, for her spare change. The answer in my head said, "No, just keep walking." But against all my guidance, I stepped towards her and asked her for her change. In the four seconds it took her to reach in her purse, in the corner of my eye I saw Ralph pumping gas into his BMW. Bette sat in the front seat. I looked at her at the same second she turned to look at me because Sara, who was sitting in the backseat, was pointing right at me.

I turned and limped away in the direction I just came from. I tried to walk normally, but the pain in my heel was just too sharp. I knew they saw me. I just had to get away.

When I finally got out of their line of sight, I made a couple turns and went down an alley. I knew they didn't want me coming near them. I didn't want Bette's pity. She was not to blame.

"Slow down," I told myself. So, I got out of the alley and sat on a bus bench to catch my breath. Wow, that was close.

When Sara saw Mr. Whiley and alerted her mother, she belted, "Look, Mom, it's Mr. Whiley." She pointed at the strange looking, hunched over, skinny, homeless man with four inches of beard and wearing a turtleneck on a warm April day. When Bette looked over, she didn't want to see the resemblance, but she did. And she was fairly certain it was Michael. But being overly protective, she didn't want Sara to think that. So Bette contradicted Sara saying it wasn't him. Bette again boasted of her keen eyesight and delivered a final judgment that it was in fact not Mr. Whiley. Sara gave up her position and reckoned her mother was likely right, again.

Why didn't I listen to myself? I knew I should have just kept walking, but "NO" didn't register with me. I didn't think Ralph saw me. But I knew Bette and Sara did and would be telling him that they saw me looking like this: limping and looking really pitiful. Why didn't I just keep walking like I planned? What made me stop for that woman's change? I didn't want to. But I heard fear in the back of my head: Oh, but you still have to replace all that stuff that was in your gym bag. And in that one brief flash of doubt, fear ruined my day.

Acting on intuition is wisdom. Wisdom works even when we don't know it's working. And I failed wisdom. I headed back to camp, as I had done enough damage for one day.

One night, in May, I woke up in the middle of the night and went shopping. I took whatever suited my purpose and selected only the best quality second-hand products any dumpster could offer.

I had tired of desperation owning my name.

And for whatever reason, I kept this nocturnal schedule for weeks. I slept all day until four o'clock, then I hit up the exiting restaurant crowds at various locales and bars. I never stayed too long. But by doing that routine over a few weeks, I raised enough money for my meals and a daily *Wall Street Journal*.

Sometime around Memorial Day, around two in the morning, I was rummaging through a dumpster behind Saks Fifth Avenue and found a current edition of the *Robb Report*. Aah, my subscription finally caught up with me. It's a rich man's penny saver. Looking to buy a six-figure car? A ten million dollar yacht, or a jet perhaps? How about an island for her on your anniversary? If it's expensive, it's in there. To my shame, I salivated at the images. I couldn't wait to study it page by page the next day in the sunlight.

The next morning it started raining. The blue tarp covering the camp held the water at bay, but the storm was loud and fierce. I could only hope the tarp would hold. After a few minutes of the angry rain, it dwindled down to a sprinkle and eventually stopped entirely. I found the *Robb Report* and opened it to the first page. I lost myself inside the driver's seat of a 2003 Bentley Arnage T. New, it listed at $230,000. But with all the add-ons, the asking price was $270,000.

Pages later, I settled down in my lounge chair on an island in Fiji for only $4,000,000. What a deal. However, it's not big enough for an air strip so I'd have to pass.

Hours later I got up to stretch. It was a beautiful afternoon, but I went back to sleep for a nap. I woke up a couple hours later and started thinking about food. I hadn't eaten since yesterday.

At State Street and Haley, I panhandled for change from passers-by for about ten minutes. Since there was a good chance someone might drive by who knew me, I couldn't stay long.

As I walked away from State Street, I stopped to look at my reflection in a store window. All I saw was a broken man. I had to find redemption. For whatever I did, whatever misunderstanding I had with God and my universe, it needed to be clarified. If it didn't happen while I was alive, perhaps in death I would find the answers to my questions. Was that it? Was my death the only thing left? My nothing existence was the only other card that the Dealer of Life had not turned over, yet.

I walked into a discount store and bought some essentials. I picked up some canned beans, tuna, and water. When I got back to camp I dropped everything when I heard a rustling in the bushes.

And then it stopped. Was it an animal? A person? A cop? I figured I might as well say something. With the deepest voice I could muster I asked, "Who's there?"

I heard more rustling.

"It's just me," replied the stranger.

"Who's me?" I asked.

Out of the bushes came a transient-looking man. "It's just me, I'm just passing through," he said.

"Who are you? Are you alone?" I asked.

"Yes, I'm alone and my name is Gabe. And I don't take up too much room. I don't talk a lot, unless you're up for talking."

My first impression was that he was decent enough. But at this point, what do I know about judging character? I figured I would let him hang out here for a bit. Not long or overnight, but for a bit.

"Sure, all right, you can hang out for a while," I told him. He sat on a log. I noticed he was sporting sturdy boots and warm, layered clothes. Oddly, his clothes looked new and clean, like he just stepped out of an L.L. Bean catalogue.

Gabriel has changed out of his Versace and into his hiking armor.

CHAPTER EIGHT

ENTERTAINING A STRANGER

Gabe looked over at me and asked, "Do you have any food? I've got some bread I picked up from a bakery little while ago." And from the inside of his jacket he pulled out a modest loaf of French bread.

"Yeah, I have a can of beans." Then I chastised myself mentally for being too inviting. I explained to him, "We can't warm anything up because I can't start a campfire. See, when cops come through here, they're just looking for a reason to kick me out of town by claiming I'm a fire hazard. But I'm not, so they pretty much leave me alone. So, Gabe, I'm Michael." I opened the can of beans and with a clean plastic spoon I dished a portion into a Styrofoam bowl. He broke off some bread and handed me a clump.

"So, tell me, Michael, how long have you been here?" he asked.

"Let me think," I answered. In my head, I clocked my life backwards in time and said, "About five months. Do you live in Santa Barbara?"

"No. I'm on my way east here in a bit," he replied.

"Oh, got that travel bug, huh?"

He chuckled, "Seems like I never stop. I can't actually remember the last time I stopped for longer than a few hours. What's your story?"

I see there's no getting around avoiding the subject, so I tried to keep it vague. "Well, my story is kind of complicated. Life threw me some curve balls," I told him, hoping he would leave it at that.

But he kept prodding, "Like what?"

"I lost everything. My children were killed, my house destroyed, and my wife left me. I thought she was my soul mate. What soul mate would leave me like this?" I asked.

Gabe answered, "I'm sorry to hear that. But Michael, do you want the real truth? There are no soul mates. God is your only soul mate. Humans are not soul mates to one another. Who do you call out for when you need help? Do you call out for your soul mate to come and save you? Or God?" he asked.

He reiterated, "There are no soul mates other than God."

Sarcastically, I retorted, "Now you tell me."

Gabe sensed my bitterness and with a sympathetic tone replied, "I'm sorry to see you suffering so much. Many men of God have suffered trials down through the ages. They were living through the mystery that is God. Do you believe in God, Michael? Yes, I believe you do. In fact, I'll even wager that you're a man of God."

"What makes you think that?" I asked.

"I can see Him in your eyes," he replied.

With a bitter tone that is beneath me I said, "Well, I think God took a vacation from the subject that is my life."

"They all felt abandoned by God," Gabe professed.

"Who's they?"

He took a deep breath and said, "*They* are the courageous and faithful lovers of God. *They* were sometimes famous, but most were not. *They* were spiritual warriors who felt God had abandoned them. But God was never far."

"Well, I'm assuming that you're not going to be here very long, so let me show you," I said. I dropped my trousers and showed him the boils up and down my legs. I pulled off my turtleneck and turned around to model the punishment God sent my way. I asked, "Why would God do this to me? When all I ever did was love Him?"

"Remember Michael, it is in the fire that gold is purified," he said.

I considered his words as I put my shirt back on. And I thought, well then what does that make me? I said, with a laugh, "So what does that make me? Then call me twenty-four carat." It wasn't much of a chuckle, but just enough. And like a fire that spreads quickly, my laughter grew. Wow, I was laughing. Looking at the absurd, extreme polarities of my life, my laughing got out of control. My sides started to hurt. For a minute I escaped it all, unattached to this identity and pain. And through my hearty laughter, tears filled my eyes. Gabe had brought laughter back into my life, if just for a few minutes.

For the next couple hours, we talked about courage and strength. We talked about the fortitude and resilience of man, individually and collectively. He spoke of forgiveness and how one becomes empowered by it. He suggested that I not go too hard on God, because if I'm still alive, then God must have a plan for me.

I asked, befuddled, "Plan? If this pit I've fallen into is part of His plan, then why doesn't He let me in on it?"

Gabe asked, "Michael, do you remember Joseph from the Old Testament?"

I nodded.

"How do you think Joseph must have felt being sold by his own brothers to those passing slave traders? But look what God did with his misfortune. Turned him into the king's right-hand man, and he saved tens of thousands of lives over seven years of drought."

I looked at Gabe and asked sincerely, "How am I supposed to have faith? Where am I supposed to find it? How do I lift my faith to where I'm not blaming myself for all this tragedy and misery? How?"

He crouched down to my level and said, "Let me suggest that you live every day practicing the presence of God. By attuning your attention to the I AM presence within your heart, you can communicate directly with the Infinite. God's perfect plan will come to pass every time regardless..."

Cutting him off I bellowed, "Where do you see a perfect plan?"

"Believe that everything that happens to you is part of a plan. It maybe unknown to you, but there is a plan," he said seriously.

"I just don't see it."

"Michael, you are living that plan. How can you not see it?"

I contested, "If there is a plan, it must be obscured by the walls of misery and agony He sent my way."

"Don't judge your life, and especially don't judge your relationship with God, just by one chapter," he said, trying to soothe my anger and confusion.

After another hour, Gabe stood up and declared, "It's time for me to go. Thank you for your hospitality." He stretched his right hand to shake mine, but then gave me a hug. As he hugged me, I thought to myself that no one had hugged me for months.

Gabe hadn't judged me once this entire time. He broke from the hug and said, "Remember, time has no effect on God, so you have to be very patient, and..."

I know what he was about to say, and in unison we both said, "...have faith." I watched him turn and walk back into the bushes from where he came.

I lay back down on my cardboard bed, and I could tell by the light that the sun would be setting soon. Wow, the afternoon just flew by. I pondered the high points of our conversation. Gabe was interesting and gave me a lot to think about. I did laugh a lot today.

The sun disappeared quickly and it got chilly really fast. I got up and dropped the flaps that kept the night wind out of my shelter.

I could see the stars in the east. "If You are so close, why do You seem so far away?" I asked God rhetorically. He didn't seem to care. That's not to say He doesn't care, or at least He just doesn't *seem* to care. But what do I know? I looked at a very bright star and thought, from the very light of that distant star, You could be watching me.

And then a very strange thing happened. I could hear the wind, but it was very still. The distant wind whispers became more evident as they got louder, and yet everything remained still. I was amazed at the phenomenon: the sound of wind, but everything was still. And just then I was hit by a blast of warm Santa Ana winds. The temperature shot back up as I grabbed my stuff from flying everywhere. The tall palm trees swayed as their fronds were tossed violently back and forth.

I ran around securing my stuff from flying away when a large palm frond crashed like a missile to the ground with a loud bang about an arm's length from me. Startled, I shouted, "Oh my God!" At the realization that I could be dead, I burst out laughing. The thought of getting harpooned by a palm frond cracked me up. I busted a gut laughing at how close I just came to having a ten-foot palm frond drop on my head at a hundred miles an hour. What a way to go. After all this, I get killed by a flying palm frond? The thought just kept me laughing. Suddenly, all the lights in the neighborhood went out.

And for the first time in my life, the wind came alive to me. The neighborhood vibrated with a subtle panic as magic seemed to waft through the electric atmosphere. Even the stars shone brighter.

I weighted everything down so it didn't fly away. These warm winds must have been clocking about thirty to thirty-five miles an hour and I'd guess the temperature was in the eighties. The loud winds howled through the camp, the shrubbery, and the trees.

I lay back on my cardboard bed (weighed down by some big stuff) and covered my head and face with my blankets. I hunkered down with my back to the intense winds.

Sometimes nature takes on a character, and these winds brought with them a tenor that I would characterize as blissful. I wanted to stay in this good vibe I got from Gabe. There was something different about him, but I couldn't put my finger on it. I learned a lot that day. I wasn't going to worry about anything that night. I was just going to fall asleep and shut this world out for a few hours. And maybe dream of what God might be planning for my life. And besides, it was just another night of going to sleep semi-hungry. I had learned how to turn off that feeling.

———————

About five weeks later, sometime in early June, I was walking in the back alley behind Monty's Office Supplies on Anacappa Blvd. It was late at night and I found a pile of discarded *National Geographic* magazines. I could not believe someone was throwing these away. These timeless stories and photographs could transport you anywhere around the globe. At least the magazines should have been given to a library.

I turned away from the dumpster and right into a police cruiser stealthily making his approach down the alley with no headlights on. When he reached me, he turned on all his headlights and flashers. He got out right away. "Drop that stuff right now," he barked while pointing at me.

I dropped all the magazines. Holy cow, my heart started racing a million beats a minute. That always happened when I was near cops.

He said, "You are in violation of city code 8762. What is your name?"

"Michael Whiley," I answered. He shined his bright flashlight at me, blinding my sight of him. He got closer and started sniffing around me.

"Is that alcohol I smell?" he asked.

"No, I don't drink."

A "humph" of doubt came out of him. With his hands on his waist ala General Patton he asked, "Where are you from?"

Figuring I had to tell him the truth, I said, "Montecito."

The cop belted out, "Haa, and I'm from Beverly Hills! Do you have any ID?" I reached for my wallet and handed him my driver's license. He shined his flashlight on it and then on my face. I looked nothing like I did when that picture was taken. "Did you steal this wallet? Because this sure is not you and you sure don't smell like you live in Montecito."

"That's me," I told him.

"Like I said, did you steal this wallet?"

"No, that's my wallet and that's me in the picture, honestly," I pleaded with him.

"Yeah, and I suppose all these credit cards are yours, too?" he asked.

"Yes, but they've all been cancelled."

"I bet they have. Of course, no doubt you tried to use them," he replied.

He took my shoulder and spun me around, taking my right arm behind my back and handcuffing me. "You're making a mistake, that's really me," I said. When he turned me around to face him, I looked at him closely. I thought I knew this guy from somewhere. Then it dawned on me that it was the same policeman who drove us to the morgue that horrible night six months ago. Nothing I said was going to change the situation right then, so I was going to go with the flow. Besides, I was handcuffed, and there was nothing I could do anyway.

He put me in the back seat. This could be the same back seat we sat in, in that other life. I just shook my head; there were so many things going through my mind, I didn't want to deal with them. I thought, I'm done with life. Or, is it done with me? How did I go from there to here in half a year?

He pulled into the back lot of the Santa Barbara Police Station. He got me out of the car and we walked to the entrance.

After we entered he took me over to the holding pen and handcuffed me to the bench. I sat feeling like a leashed animal and smelled like one too. I leaned back, as who knew how long this was going to take? I didn't care. I had all the time in the world. No wonder he didn't recognize me. All I had to do was remind him of that night and he'd know it's me. He was a participant in the three-act horror that New Year's Eve.

He came over and uncuffed me from the bench. I thought he might take them off, but he didn't. "Follow me," he said. I followed him to his desk. "Sit," he told me. I took a seat next to his desk. He sat in his chair and picked up my wallet. "I don't want this to last all night, so please be truthful about this. Where did you steal this wallet?"

"My name is Michael Whiley, my home address is 970 Santa Ynez Road, Montecito, California 93108."

"Cut the crap! You just memorized these details," he bellowed at me.

I knew I was going to have to come clean. So I told him, "I'm surprised you don't remember being at my address."

"What are you talking about?" he asked.

I cleared my throat and swallowed. My face and voice tightened up as I looked him in the eye and answered, "You don't remember coming to my house last New Year's eve? You drove to that address on that night." He looked stumped as I continued, "When you came to tell me that my three kids were dead. You drove me and my wife...my *ex*-wife...to the morgue."

By the changing look on his face, I could see that Officer Marcus did remember. He shifted in his chair. I took a deep breath and looked away. Just having this moment reach back in time to that event stopped me from saying another word. I was looking at someone who was actually there that night.

He looked at me, looked at the photo on my driver's license, and said, "I remember this man."

"I do, too."

"Some nights you never forget," he confessed. "This is you," he relented. "What happened?" he asked while taking the handcuffs off.

"That night was the beginning of the end of me. This all started the second I saw you standing in my front door. From that moment on, my life has been on the express elevator drop into hell," I professed as if I were incriminating him for being the messenger of death.

My story took about twenty minutes to tell. Just speaking the words that described my life exacerbated the pain. He continued shaking his head in disbelief of the story of my woes.

He tore up the paperwork he started. "Come on, let's get you out of here," he said. On our way to the exit he stopped and offered me a free shower. I gladly took him up on his offer, but I made him promise to watch the door while I showered. He did.

In the privacy of the county jail shower, I washed my body for the first time in weeks. When I was done I dried myself off with county towels Officer Marcus gave me. Unfortunately, I only had my same smelly clothes to put back on.

When I came out of the shower, he said, "I'll walk you to the door, and here's your wallet back. If I were you, I'd cut up those credit cards. You can't use them anyway."

I replied, "Yes, I should do that."

When we got outside on the street, he reached for his wallet, took out forty dollars, and handed it to me. "I'm sorry I can't drive you anywhere, and this is all I got."

"Wow, thank you very much. I do appreciate it," I told him.

"Good luck," he said to me before heading back inside.

As I headed back towards camp, I went back down that alley and picked up those same *National Geographic* magazines. When I got there I found the stack just where I dropped it. As I stood in the spot where I was two hours ago, I realized that by getting picked up by Officer Marcus, I ultimately ended up ahead with a hot shower and forty dollars. Is that the answer and the meaning of life? To watch life turn negatives into positives?

About three weeks later, on a sweltering June Sunday, curiosity got the better of me and I went to stalk my old church-going friends. I limped all the way to my old church. It was noon, hot and muggy. I was still wearing my black turtleneck shirt. Yes, the one with the long sleeves. But I'd still rather suffer the heat than expose my boils and watch people run from me.

I turned the corner and saw the church and parking lot from half a block away. Cars were starting to leave, as the service had just let out. I limped closer and hid behind a bush where no one could see me. Over the next few minutes I watched members mulling around and talking as they walked to their cars in the parking lot. I saw Larry and his kids walk to their car. I watched Terry and Adam chat with Ralph and Bette. Eventually they all left.

Despite the heat, I decided to walk up to Montecito to see what condition my house was in. Was it still there? I headed back to Montecito along the hot paved road. As I limped past the Vons Market in Montecito I looked totally out of place. If any cop were to drive by, I'm sure he'd stop and harass me.

On Olive Street, I limped past the "white castle," the ornate French chateau that fascinated the kids. They would always turn to look at it. I stopped on the opposite side of the street and got a good long look. It's really a beautiful structure and you can tell the architects really went the extra mile. I wondered if the people living in such opulence were happy. I hoped so. I hoped they savored every particle of their life, not having to worry about basic human survival necessities. As I imagined the people who lived inside, I visualized God's Divine Light blazing in their hearts. So, I prayed for their happiness and that God would shower them with His love. I turned and kept walking.

I finally got to Santa Ynez Road and I could see my property in the distance. It had a chain link fence around it. When I got closer, I saw nothing but a slab of cement that was the foundation. The surveyor, Sam, must have cordoned off the gas pump. That was smart.

I tried to convince myself when I said, "I'm glad I came today." Why did I feel like I had to justify limping four miles to come and see this? Why did I feel like I had to justify everything to myself? Because everything and everyone I touched fell into this pit with me. That's why Ralph and Bette didn't want me around. And that's why Joanne didn't want me around.

Has this changed the inverted microscope through which I look at myself? Or, permanently unfocused the panoramic lens through which I look at the world?

I held onto the chain link fence and rode the tsunami of my anger.

I imagined what was our home, and I saw death. Death in every way: death of life, death of dreams, and most painfully, death of love. And yet, as I looked back at who I was, I could say that I wouldn't change anything. I looked deep and searched hard, and I couldn't find anything I'd done in this life to warrant such hostile acts against my existence. And that's a bold statement because I no longer subscribed to the idea that this was my fault, or that I was to blame. Impulsively I shouted, "I'm not to blame! You can't blame me for this!"

I didn't do this to myself. I believed that given who I was, because of my love and respect for life and an affirmed yearning for God, I was not responsible for this implosion. Greater forces were at work. Things like this just do not happen by freak chance. God had to know that He was doing this to me. And now that I believed that profoundly, I was ready to go through this battle for as long as I could.

I didn't care for much, because much did not care for me, and that gave me the advantage.

Having nothing, and with nothing to slow me down, I felt like I was getting a head start. But whatever kind of race I was in was unknown to me.

Recalling Gabe's talk about faith, I stood with a new resolve to get through every day of life. As I gazed upon the wreckage that was my home I prayed, "Dear God, it was Your house to begin with, You are the very materials that were used in the construction, so how could You not own it? If all You want to give me is the air I breathe, my heartbeat, the sunlight I love, and maybe a daily meal, then that's fine with me. That's okay by me, on the condition that You never stop loving me. Oh, Lord, not even You can break my faith."

I once read a book on the art of negotiations. I understood that a strategy known is a strategy annulled. Once the opposite side knows your plans, they are dead on arrival. So, as I looked at the ruins of my life, I saw that this is "their" game and I was just a pawn. And yet, it's because of Him that I was still alive.

I would gladly have given up this life right now in exchange for fifteen minutes more of that other life that was filled with beauty and love. I would make that trade in a split second.

It's God who dazzles me in His sunrises and sunsets every day. It's God who nudges a stranger to reach in their pockets to give me change. It's God who moves the clouds across the sky. It's God who said that when we call on Him, He'll be listening. Well, if that's so, I hope I'm keeping Him awake at night.

It was late afternoon when I started down the hill. I made a right on Butterfly Lane and neared Larry's house. It was a nice house near the bottom of Montecito. I had an overwhelming feeling of reaching out to someone, maybe him. Maybe I should just let my friends know I was alive.

When I got there, I hid behind a tree to check things out first. The big windows in the living room allowed me to see inside. I watched Larry's daughter, Rebecca, walk in front of the window to do something, and then she looked up and saw me. She stared at me. Our eyes locked on to one another. "Oh, no," I thought to myself.

Then she ran out of the living room. Maybe I should have knocked on the door and said hello. Was I crazy? No, Larry would probably like to see me and tell me how things were going at BriMar. Then I saw him walk through the living room and up to the front door. She must have told him I was there. He came out the door and walked up to the edge of his driveway.

Larry saw me. And just as I was about to step out from behind the tree and say hi, he yelled, "What are you looking at? You just get yourself down the hill and over to your own part of town." He kept going on, "Don't come snooping around this neighborhood."

I was shocked by the icy response. I was stunned; frozen, actually.

"Did you hear me?" he shouted. He really didn't recognize me.

I thought, should I say something?

"Don't make me call the cops!" he said threateningly.

And that's all he had to say. I turned and left. No effort at any explanation, I just had to get away. I never saw that side of Larry before. I was taken aback by his whole reaction and the fact that he didn't recognize me. He didn't have a clue. What did that mean?

I didn't want to become sad just because Larry didn't recognize me. I didn't want to be sad for his reaction in that it showed an ugly side of Larry. That in and of itself could have made me sad. So what? "It doesn't matter," I said out loud to myself. I had to always stay in control of my emotions, and that started in my head. "Don't think too much about it," I told myself.

I just had to change the channel in my mind.

I strolled down Channel Road to the beach and spent an hour watching the sunset, and then night fell.

Hunger was calling me to work. At a couple restaurants in Montecito Plaza, I raised some change for food. There's an unwritten rule about no loitering in Montecito--unless you belong, of course.

I thought about generating some cash at Vons. Maybe not! What was I thinking? Begging at my old local grocery store? I was not thinking right. Someone would for sure recognize me. But I had to stop pretending that I looked anything like I did before. The sad truth was that I was not recognizable with this long beard, scraggily hair, gaunt face, and rags.

What did I have to lose? I kept my distance and stood by the plants. Nearby a bakery-deli was still serving customers. A few people dotted the tables, drinking their nightcaps. I stood a bit apart, and every once in a while someone would come walking by and I would politely ask if they had any spare change. Most people contributed, some didn't.

After twenty minutes, I had enough for a sandwich and drink at the adjacent bakery. When I could see that no one else was at the counter, I placed my order and waited outside. After retrieving my meal, I settled at a table outside. I could see people going in and coming out of Von's. I considered how many thousands of times I walked through those very doors, but in another universe. And who knew that one day I would be standing there begging?

A heavy fog rolled in.

As I ate my sandwich, I considered how I was continuously learning that life gives us absolutely no guarantees. Not one. Not even in a happy marriage.

I realized there are no guarantees if it has to involve another human.

How much longer was I to suffer like this? Wait a second! Wasn't it hours ago that I committed myself into this arena where I'm the pawn? That's right. That was me. And listen to me now. Maybe I was tired and should just find a place to lay my head.

I limped around the shops looking for a little shelter from the fog. I knew I wouldn't find it in a doorway as there were too many cops coming around. I thought that the bushes across the street might be safer.

As I crossed the street, I saw an open spot in the bushes near the sidewalk. I crawled into it and hid in a fetal position. The bushes protected me from the wind. I was tired from my long walk. I just wanted to fall asleep and wake up at first light in the morning to be on my way.

Closing my eyes did not shut out shocking images of my flattened house, Larry's angry face, and him pointing at me. I reached for sleep to overtake me. And perhaps in my dreams, God could work to heal my wounds. Perhaps in my dreams, I could find an answer somewhere. In any case, sleep would steal me away from there.

I dreamt I was playing volleyball on East Beach with a whole bunch of people at an evening barbecue. We were all having fun when…

…It felt like someone kicked me. I woke up to someone falling over me on the sidewalk. During the night my legs had rolled out of the bushes and onto the sidewalk. I looked up and locked eyes with a jogger half standing, half stumbled over. And then the stranger said, "Michael?"

I immediately recognized Adam. Oh, no, I thought to myself.

"Michael!" he shouted in elation.

I realized I had to say something. "Adam?"

He helped me up. "Michael, it's really you. I can't believe this. Wow, it's you. I have to call the guys," he said while giving me a hug. "We've been talking about you, and wondering whatever happened."

"I'm okay," I said, lying to his face.

Before I knew it, he reached for his cell phone and called Larry. He told Larry that he found me down by the shops. And then he hung up.

I didn't know what to think. Was this a good thing? Maybe not? Maybe yes?

Ten minutes later Larry showed up. He was excited to see me, but I could tell he was having a hard time with my smell and appearance. But the three of us got into his nice perfumed car anyway.

He drove us to, of all places, East Beach, where we met up with Ralph and Terry. I had no input on planning this unexpected reunion.

We gravitated to a picnic table. Ralph gave me a warm hug. Terry came with a bag of his clothes for me. It was good to see all of them. I realized I was going to be with my friends, and my whole disposition changed to hope and excitement.

I said through my grin to Larry, "You remember some guy watching your house yesterday?"

Larry's light bulb went off and he said, "Oh, my God, was that you? Why didn't you say something?"

I answered, "I was about to, but I didn't want to embarrass you in front of your family."

Ralph asked me, "Did you ever get the test results back from Dr. Bryant?"

I caught myself looking away and then confessed, "He said they didn't know anything about anything and had no treatment. He was clueless. But hey, I'm still alive."

Larry piped in, "Praise God."

Ralph told me, "I've been working on your divorce, and the date is set for November."

"November! It's only June. You mean I have to wait another five months?" I bellowed.

"There's no way to speed it up," he said apologetically.

Looking at Larry and then Adam, I asked, "How are things at the company?"

Larry offered a fast, "They're fine."

Adam looked at him quizzically and asked, "Are you kidding me? Cut the crap." Adam looked at me and said, "It's been miserable. We haven't closed a deal this year yet. Morale is lower than it's ever been in the eight years I've been there. That's how things are at the company."

I admitted to them, "Somewhere in the back of my mind, I sensed something didn't go right with that Pentagon bid. I have no evidence, but it's just a gut feeling."

I noticed Terry looked around at the guys, and lowering his voice he asked me, "Let's be real here, Michael, we love you, we're your friends, but what did you do?"

"What did I do about what?"

Adam reaffirmed our friendship before he quizzed me, "You've always been there for us, but what did you do to make God so upset?"

"Nothing," I replied instantly.

Larry folded his hands parental-like as he said, "Well, you must have done something."

"What are you talking about?" I asked, dumbfounded.

Terry explained it all when he said, "It's like the wrath of God is all over you."

"Ah, I get it, you think God is punishing me and now you want to know what I did to deserve this. Like I haven't asked this question before?"

Adam replied, "It's the only explanation for all the bad things that have happened to you."

I asked, "You mean there's an explanation?"

Terry reminded me of the sequence of my life's crisis: "First the kids, then the boat..."

Larry helped him out when he chipped in, "...then the house."

And even my most valued friend in life, Ralph, threw his stones with, "...and even Joanne turned against you."

Adam finished the list with "...and is it true you have boils?"

Hearing the calamities of my life spoken with such false accusatory tones, I was ready to reveal the soul searching I had uncovered. I told them, "I know, I know what you're saying, but I've searched out my actions of my past, my attitudes, my thoughts, and I can't find anything that would warrant this wrath...don't you think I've raised that question? I ask it every day of my life."

But Terry's curiosity wasn't satisfied when he reminded me, "God doesn't punish us for nothing."

"I know that," I told him. "I also know that I can't find any reason I would have ever given God to bring my life to this." I can't believe my good feeling was shot out of the sky with daggers of accusations. I continued, "I can't believe you guys are coming down on me like this. I may not be alive to see Labor Day, and you're giving it to me with both barrels. You act like you didn't know who I was at the time."

Ralph said, "We're just trying to help."

Looking right at him I asked, "By shooting the wounded? Where's your compassion?"

Larry defended their ignorance by claiming, "God is a just God. You had to have done something."

I shook my head in disbelief and reminded him, "Of course He is a just God, but He's God. He can do anything He wants, even if it goes beyond natural law or logic. He doesn't have to answer to anyone for approval."

There was a second of silence until Adam found his voice. "God doesn't like flashy stuff."

I would agree with this, so I asked him, "Yes, and what is your point?"

Larry answered my question, giving me the impression that they must have had this conversation before because it almost felt like it was rehashed. He asked me, "Remember that Sunday barbecue when Pastor Ryan brought out that blown-up check, praising you for your generosity? That was a bit much, wasn't it?"

I suspected one day that whole thing was going to come home to roost and now here it was. "That was not my idea! Pastor Ryan and Joanne planned that behind my back. In reality, I gave that check to Pastor Ryan in the privacy of his office. Joanne meant well, but personally, I was embarrassed, so how could you throw that at me?"

Terry asked, "How was your relationship with Joanne? Was there anyone on the side?"

I couldn't believe Terry would think such a thing. Indignant, I answered, "Are you accusing Joanne of having an affair?"

Terry shook his head and said, "Not Joanne, you!"

I shook my head in disbelief, thinking where in the world would I have ever found the time to have an affair, even if that was in me. Which it wasn't. Between the office, kids, wife, boat, friends, and then on top of all that, throw in an affair? Who's got time?

Adam reminded me, "You were a VP, you had the big house, cars, yacht, you had all the big toys, you strayed."

Larry quipped, "You strayed."

Terry finished, "It happens to the best of us."

Adam confessed, "It would happen to me and I don't even have all that stuff."

"Guys, I sincerely loved Joanne with every fiber of my being. I never ever would have cheated on her," I said.

In a hushed tone, Terry asked me, "Did you take money from the company? That maybe only you and God know about?"

"I can't believe I'm having this conversation."

"We're your friends, you don't have to be so defensive about it," Ralph said to me.

"Defensive?" I retorted. "Do you guys suffer from collective amnesia?" I realized this group mindset wasn't going to change no matter what I said. I could see this road coming to a dead end. I had to get away.

"I'm out of here," I said getting up.

Ralph said, "Don't go, Michael!"

But I just had to get away from this hostility. I told them, "I don't need to defend myself to people who know better. You were *there*."

Terry caught up to me to offer me the bag of clothes, but I didn't take them. I just kept walking with my limp towards the water and heading south down towards the beach, and away from them.

I was confused. Why would they think I was messing around or stealing from the company...or pissing off God one way or another? Weren't they in my life at the time to know better? I was just mad. What I hoped was going to be a good day turned to poison from where I least expected it.

I turned up Channel Street from the beach and headed back towards my property. I needed to see it again. It would anchor me back to my center. Maybe just being there may soothe my anger. Perhaps some memory from there would strengthen my resolve. I didn't know.

As I limped up Old Mill Road, for some reason I decided not to turn up my street, Santa Ynez. Rather, I just kept walking. I turned right on Cold Springs Road and onto La Paz Road. I slipped by the local private college, Westmont, and continued up the hill. I thought about my ex-friends and realized, "Yesterday they weren't in my life and today they're not in my life, makes no difference to me." And with that I tried to separate myself from any attachment to the idea of friends. And with them gone, so went the last thread of hope I had to ever reclaim my old life. How much further must I fall?

CHAPTER NINE

HIM

When I finally looked up from my anger, I discovered I had walked a couple miles up into Montecito. I was close to the Tea Gardens. Maybe I'd go up there and hide with my anger.

I saw the chain link fence, and when I was sure no cars were coming, I climbed over it. I scurried up the hill from tree to tree in hopes no one driving by would see me. I made my way to the paved road and started up hill. The road curved sharply and upward. It's a steep walk, and after about fifteen minutes the hill levels off and you arrive at the Tea Gardens. Three arches are smothered in flowers and smells, sitting alone overlooking the world. Blossoming purple irises hang from the trestle, creating a canopy of beauty worthy of heaven.

I took in the breathtaking view and wished God would just take my life. That He would grant me the mercy to let me die. And perhaps rejoin my children in heaven.

Did I have the nerve to throw myself off this ledge? The 300-foot drop would be a quick death. But why was I thinking like this? Because I had no purpose and nothing to live for might be a good reason. All I lived for was to endure another day of pain and suffering. So what would be the point? But If I showed up at Heaven's door too early, what would they say? "You're not supposed to be here, yet. Wait outside." Outside where? And then wait for what? No, I didn't want to get there early. I'd wait for that door to come to me.

The slab of cement was covered with purple iris petals, red bougainvillea petals, and green leaves. It looked very fairytale-like. I sat down with my back against a column and faced the ocean. I knew now that there really was no one I could turn to for a second chance.

All I had left was a silent God.

I got on my knees, feeling the need to plead my case to Him, yet again. "Even my best friends have turned on me. Oh, God, I come to You because I deserve some answers. Can a man fall out of favor with

You for no reason? Is Your love so fickle? One day it's on, the next it's off? Do you find pleasure in my suffering? If I have done something wrong, something evil, TELL ME! But I've kept myself clean in every part of my life. You've taken everything from me without any reason. I'm innocent. Besides, how does this make You look? I mean, look at me, God, I'm Your worst PR move, *ever*!"

A warm breeze swirled around me. It got stronger and wilder. The wind turned fierce, turning into a little dustbowl. It picked up the flower petals and leaves about six feet in front of me. The whirlwind got bigger and stronger. I stood up and took a step back away from it as it was now about ten feet wide and spinning in a tight circle. I was amazed by the sight when I heard a voice speak to me. I wondered if I was hearing this voice from inside or outside my head? It was coming from outside of me and in a second I knew whose voice it belonged to. Without so much as a thought, I dropped to my knees as He answered my questions.

The voice asked, "Do you think My image depends on you? Where were you when I exploded the sun into existence to bathe the earth with light? Where were you when I showered the earth with comets to create oceans? Where were you when I collided the moon with the earth to keep the earth on its axis? And where were you when I lifted the land above the ocean surface? Where were you when I sprayed the night sky with the Pleiades and Orion? Who has put wisdom in the mind, and understanding in the hearts of men?"

I was so awestruck, I didn't remember breathing.

He continued, "You question the source of all that has ever been, or will be? Are you attempting to correct Me and question My judgment? This I will tell you. Through these trials you have proven your love and faithfulness. You are no longer a child, but a son to Me, and I will bring forth more gifts than before because you showed yourself to love the Giver of the gifts, more than the gifts themselves."

The whirlwind stopped in an instant. The petals and foliage that were caught up in the air fell to the ground in a cone-shaped mound. It was over.

He spoke to me. God just spoke to me. I sat up and put my hands on my lap. I noticed that I didn't feel the boils on my body. I took off my glove, and I saw the boil that was there a minute ago had disappeared. I stood to check my other boils to find that they were all gone. I'd been healed. In that minute God came into my life and forever changed the very particles of my being. I got back on my knees, laid my forehead on the ground and gave the most sincere thank you of my entire life.

The whole experience of hearing God speak to me was more than I could take in and not get emotional. I felt tears filling my eyes as I noticed a coldness coming from within my body. It wasn't an outside chill, but an inside cold that could not be heated by the hot June sun. I sat shivering in the 90-plus-degree heat. It was nothing like I'd ever experienced. I was genuinely cold in this milestone event in my life. I held myself to counter the very real cold I was feeling from within. I thanked Him for revealing Himself like that to me. I promised never to second-guess Him again. I knew beyond all doubt that this was all one big test. He wanted to know if I really loved Him, and I really did. I could still feel His presence.

After about an hour, the cold sensation went away. Finally, I stopped shivering.

The hours went by as the sun crossed the sky, and although He wasn't speaking or making whirlwinds, He was in the sunlight and He was in the ocean air traveling thousands of miles across the Pacific before He breezed by my face. And I knew that He will never ever lose me, or forget me. And I wondered what He meant when He said, "more gifts than before."

I sat recalling the images that exploded into my mind as He spoke. Should I try and write down the words He spoke to me? Will I want to share this with others? Or should I keep the whole experience to myself and treat it as a private matter? What if I told people and then they didn't believe me? But why would I care? I knew it happened and that's all that matters. Period. The end. So maybe I will keep this to myself until the right time comes to share it with anyone. If that day should ever come.

The sun was setting and there was no better vantage point to see the grandeur than where I was. I found myself smiling. I was smiling because all the pain and woe that I'd endured for the past seven months was worth those two minutes with Him.

As night fell, I stepped outside from under the canopy of flowers to gaze at the stars. As I looked up at them I thought to myself that God was watching me from the stars of Orion. He will always know where I am by the light of the seven stars of the Pleiades, the very star systems He mentioned. He is the very light that traveled across the cosmos, ending here on earth, in the Tea Gardens.

Hours later, and ready to fall asleep, I walked over to where He appeared earlier. I flattened the mound of flower petals and turned it into a bed. I lay right down in that holy spot, covered myself with my dirty blanket, and fell asleep.

God was at that very moment flying his Gulf Steam G650 at 70,000 feet above Montecito. High above the twinkling lights of the Pacific coast, He smiled gloatingly and yelled, "Lucifer!" In an instant, Lucifer was dropped on the floor of God's plane in a bent-over, kneeling position right in front of Him.

Satisfied, God said, "I have my answers, Lucifer. I know, and now you *must know* that you are wrong, again." Although Lucifer tried to speak, God, being the very life-force that Lucifer would use to speak, denied Lucifer his voice.

"What's going on?" is what Lucifer would ask God if he could. But God continued the force field on Lucifer and wouldn't even let him lift up his head to look at The Almighty, however hard Lucifer may have tried.

Wanting to make certain Lucifer knew his miscalculations, God declared, "I have concluded that after losing everything that I had blessed him with, Michael never turned away from the Giver of his gifts. He never said My name in vain. He never spat in My face, like you said he would do. And now you must pay for the balance you owe. I proclaim that neither you nor any one of your evil legions will ever go near him for the entire remainder of his long life or the lives of his children for ten generations."

The devil fell through the floor of God's aircraft. God sat there smiling. He took a deep sigh and realized, "It's time to get to work." He walked down the aisle towards the door. He knew He had to clean up the chaos and disasters in Michael's life that Lucifer had concocted.

In the early predawn light at the Tea Gardens, God appeared walking up the driveway on His way to the arches. He was dressed in a white dinner jacket and black formal pants. Lying on the slab before Him, God saw Michael sleeping soundly. He looked up at the canopy of flowers and savored the smells. He tiptoed around the sleeping man and went over to the railing.

He looked out over the grandeur of His morning and He smiled. He took notice of something down at the bottom of the hill. With His all-seeing vision, He changed His perspective and saw Michael's four friends playing golf at the Montecito Country Club.

The fresh grass was particularly fragrant to Ralph, Larry, Terry, and Adam on this perfect morning as they teed off on the third hole. Ralph teed off first and put his ball dead center in a sand trap just left of the green. As they each took their turn, every one of them put his ball in the same sand trap. They chalked it up to the wind coming off the mountain.

While riding in their golf carts along the fairway, Ralph said to the other three, "I told Bette about our encounter with Michael. She said she didn't understand why someone as smart as Michael couldn't pick himself up."

"It's more complicated than that, Ralph, you know that," Terry said in Michael's defense.

Ralph replied, "I know that, Terry. But in the end, don't we all have to take responsibility for ourselves?"

"Yes, but Michael is one of a kind," Terry retorted.

Larry used a golf club to emphasis his point. "It just goes to show you, it could have happened to any one of us."

Adam admitted, "Thank God it didn't happen to me. There's no way I could have handled it. I probably would have killed myself, really."

At the sand trap the guys looked down and discovered the four white balls all clustered together. Quizzically, they looked at one another and shrugged. Adam asked, "How does that happen?"

The wind suddenly picked up around the guys and they reached for their hats. The wind moved into the sand trap, picked up the sand and spun it into a whirlwind. The four golf balls went flying in all directions. The wind sucked up all the sand and formed itself into a tightly shaped whirlwind about ten feet wide. The four guys marveled at it.

Then God's voice was heard coming from the whirlwind of sand. He said, "I AM angry at the way you have treated my son, Michael. You have judged him unfairly and heaped condemnation on him. Like fools, you criticized him through your own eyes. You are full of betrayal, doubt, greed, and fear. Your wisdom is of man and not of Me. Do you not know that My thoughts are higher than your thoughts, and My ways are not your ways? Now, go find him and don't go empty-handed but with offerings worthy of Me. For until he prays for you, I will not hear your prayers."

And then the sand instantly fell to the ground in a cone-shaped mound. The four guys stood frozen. They just got a double dose of earth shattering realizations. The first was realized by Adam when he said, "We heard God talk to us. Can you believe it? That was God's voice talking to us."

Larry understood the second earth-shattering notion when he said, "And He's really, really mad at us."

Ralph was also shocked, saying, "There was a distinct tone in His voice that says we have upset Him."

They all started shivering at the same time. The four friends experienced the same cold that Michael had experienced the day before.

Terry asked, *"How do we go through life knowing we've angered The Almighty? How do we live with His anger waiting around every corner?"*

They just stared at the cone of sand with the exposed brown dirt surrounding it. Besides the bizarre coldness everyone felt, the sand trap was evidence that something other-worldly had just happened. Adam took out his cell phone and tried to take a photo of the sand trap, but he was shaking too hard to steady his hand for a clear picture. Frustrated, he said, "It was like, like Moses or something. Isn't that what it was like?"

With his head hanging in shame, Ralph realized, "God just spoke to us. He talked to us like He was right here. And He was. We were in the presence of God. He's really upset with us." Ralph sat down on the grass, hugging himself from the cold he felt inside. Terry, Larry, and Adam huddle around him.

Shivering, Larry said, "It doesn't matter what we did in the past, we have to ask God to forgive us and do what He said."

Adam agreed, "That's what we have to do."

As all four men openly shivered, they unabashedly confessed their short-comings out loud to God. They sat huddled by the sand trap, now in need of a grounds crew.

From the railing at the Tea Gardens, God saw and heard their wailing. He smiled, then realized something odd. He reached in His pants pocket and pulled out a big handful of white sand from the sand trap. He dropped the sand on the ground, folded His arms, and in His best Jack Benny impression, said, "I hate when that happens." And then He left.

The sun had been up for at least an hour when it was as if God Himself nudged me awake to a new day. I opened my eyes and remembered where I was. I floated in the blissful experience from yesterday. I looked again and confirmed that the boils were really gone. I sat up and folded my hands together and offered Him, "My most sincere gratitude for healing me, for appearing before me like that, and for answering my questions. Thank You for Your compassion. I know Your wisdom goes beyond my own comprehension."

My new understanding brought with it a clearer light for a new day and a new chapter in this life. I was no longer a child, but a "son" and I was going to have to learn what all that means, because I really didn't know. I hope I don't let Him down. But what the next step was, I wasn't sure. Maybe I wasn't supposed to know.

Within minutes after darting out of the country club, the four friends met at Ralph's house. At once, they all started telling their story to Bette.

Shortly thereafter, Larry's and Terry's wives showed up. Bette poured coffee for the group of people who had suddenly gathered at her house at 8:10 in the morning.

The guys talked above one another in telling what they saw and heard. Suddenly Terry's voice came blaring above the others: "You heard Him, He said He'll never answer another prayer from us until Michael prays for us."

"What does that mean?" asked Bette.

Ralph looked at Bette and explained to her, "All that we have could go away if we don't find Michael."

Terry bellowed, "How could we have let him down?"

Again, they all started talking at once, chastising themselves.

Adam stood up like a coach. "Stop it! We ALL failed him. So, we just got to suck it up and find him. That's all we have to do to make things right with God. We have to find him!"

Terry said, "Wow, God actually talked to us today, guys. And the tone of His voice scared the hell out of me."

Ralph smirked and replied, "Wasn't that His point?"

From outside the circle Bette said, "I failed everyone. I kicked him out of the house because I was afraid." You could see Bette's posture shift as she dropped her head in shame and started tearing.

Larry said, "That must be the 'fear' part God talked about. I didn't understand that until this moment."

Bette replied, "We're going to have to organize a search." Her guilt motivated her assertiveness. They all nodded and murmured agreement to whatever plans Bette came up with. She got out her street map of Santa Barbara and figured that maybe they should start with the shelter and the parks. She offered to cover the beaches and coastal areas.

Larry asked, "So when do we start? I mean, I've got to get to the office, and maybe I can take the afternoon off to help look."

"Let's reconvene this afternoon with a plan," Ralph suggested.

Adam reminded them, "He's not looking to be found."

Ralph replied, "Well, I'm taking time out from my life as I know it to find him. I'm going to start looking for him immediately."

Terry gestured his hands in defense as he claimed, "I've got responsibilities that I just can't drop. I mean, my life still goes on, right?" He looked to the others for support, but found none.

Ralph shook his head and offered, "Sure, Terry, keep your nice little life going until you watch it fall apart. We all have to be equally committed to this, or we might not get out alive."

Larry turned to Terry and said, "Let me remind you of John, Rachel, and Edwin." His sobering words had its intended effect on the room.

Terry remembered himself and said, "Yes, of course. You're absolutely right, this is about sacrifice. Very well, I'll take two weeks off starting today, this afternoon. I have to let them know. And I'll cancel all my appointments."

Adam ribbed Terry, "Yeah, and you can cancel your life as you know it until we find him."

"I get it, Adam," Terry retorted.

Ralph looked to Larry and Adam. He asked them, "Are you in?"

"Day and night," Adam said.

Hours later, inside Adam's car in the parking lot at BriMar, he and Larry discussed their approach to taking a large chunk of time off. They were both going to cash in two weeks of accrued vacation.

Adam and Larry each sent messages to the head of H.R. via email to this effect. So, in their respective offices, they wrapped up last-

minute business and canceled all their appointments for the next two weeks.

Taking initiative and even surprising herself, Bette went to the auto club office where she gathered materials and tips from a travel counselor. He marked her map with the various parks along the hillside running the length of Santa Barbara. He also pointed out the waterfalls behind the hills of Montecito.

When everyone showed up at noon at Ralph's house, Bette passed out the maps. She also gave everyone a list of landmarks and significant locations, such as the train and bus stations, key pedestrian corners, major boulevards, and shopping centers. They divided the city into zones.

Trying to be upbeat, before they split up Adam said, "If he can be found, we're going to find him."

The seven adults got into seven cars and headed out in seven different directions.

———

I'd been held captive by beauty in God's Tea Gardens for the whole day. Soaking up the love vibration God left in this space, I was filled with a sense of bliss I'd never felt before. For most of the afternoon, I just hung out by the railing, taking in the glorious view. For the first time in a long time, I believed everything was going to be okay. I didn't know where it was all going, or what the outcome would be, but it was going to turn out all right.

"And if it doesn't?" I questioned myself. What if I should go begging every day for the rest of my life? Then that would be okay because all I would ever have to do is remember when He came to visit me. That's all I would ever have to do when I'm feeling down.

In time, the tapestry of the setting sun relented to the starry night sky. If only I could live here forever. But I can't. However, I thought I would steal one more night of accommodations. The entire day passed and I forgot to think about food. I hadn't eaten anything all day. But if I didn't think about it, it didn't bother me. I lay down in the same spot to sleep and wondered if He was looking at me by the sunlight reflecting off the moon.

The manhunt lasted the entire afternoon. The search posse drove in circles around the city. Up and down the same streets and boulevards too many times to count. And too quickly it was time to pick up the kids from schools and day care. Thus, the search had to be postponed until after dinner.

But feeling his spirit agitated, Terry didn't stop looking for Michael on account of dinner. He sat on a bench on State Street. While holding a plate in his left hand, he ate with his right. He wondered what Michael was eating tonight; that is, if he was eating at all tonight. He chose this spot because he could see the bus station on Carrillo St. and still watch the active pedestrian traffic on State Street. When he saw someone of interest, he used his binoculars to get a closer look. He continuously looked up and down the boulevard, all the while replaying in his head his morning's encounter with The Almighty.

But then Terry thought that this was the last place Michael would ever come since it's so busy and crowded. He wouldn't be hanging out here. So, Terry went to the men's rescue mission on Yanapauli Street. He observed the coming and going of men up and down the street. After a couple hours, he called it a night.

The next morning I woke up with the sunrise and smiled at another day of living. And most importantly, I woke up to another day of living without the boils. No, it wasn't a dream. God actually came down to heal me personally. I innately started the day with a prayer and a smile. I knew this was the day I'd be going down from the mountain, as they say. I hoped I wouldn't act too weird.

I stood at the railing and looked out. How could anyone ever get too much of this? I knew my campsite was about six miles away, so I egged myself to get going. I walked away from the arches and down the paved driveway.

In times of trouble, all I will ever have to do is to replay the voice of God, look up here and remember.

From my pants pockets, I pulled out three dollars and forty cents, all I had to my name. I walked down the curvy road to the fence. I hid behind a tree to see if anyone was coming. I scaled the fence and climbed down to the street side. I continued walking down La Paz Road.

Across town this same morning, Adam started searching for Michael in his zone. He drove around and around. When he got to Maple Street, he pulled into Maritza's Mexican Food and saw a homeless man sleeping near the entrance. He got out of his car. But upon closer inspection, Adam saw that it was not Michael. He left the man sleeping.

Simultaneously, Terry returned to the Men's Rescue Mission and parked across the street. He fed the meter and sat in the passenger seat, watching the men slowly exit in the early morning. A couple hours later he gave up and went to another site.

I could walk normally again. Without that boil on my foot, I rediscovered it's a wonderful thing being able to walk upright. Three blocks of mansion after mansion down La Paz Road, I reached Westmont College. And for some reason, I was suddenly on campus. Within just a few steps I was wowed by an extraordinary large French ornate mansion. Built in another era of architectural dynasties, it was now the administration building. I walked through an arch to the right side of this structural beauty and found myself in a courtyard with a magnificent water fountain. I ran my hands in the falling water and shook them off. And then I considered splashing my face. Did I dare? Who would deny a man in need of some water? I reached out with my hands and splashed my face. The chilly water sent shockwaves through me.

As I gazed into the pool of the water, I happened to notice a piece of paper lying on the bottom. I looked closer, and the printing looked like a dollar bill. I estimated the depth of the water to be about twelve inches. I rolled up my sleeve and I realized that I didn't have to wear this turtleneck any longer, thank you Lord. So, I reached down to the bottom and retrieved the dollar. I untwisted the bill and saw that it was a twenty dollar bill. I looked up and said, "Thank you." Then I realized the humor of finding that money right there and then. It had to have been Him. I started laughing. And it's funny how I walked right to it. He put it there, or *caused* it to be put there. My laughter built. And the more I thought about it, the harder I laughed. How funny was God, to put that there for me? I laughed so hard, tears welled up in my eyes. And the laughing tears brought soulful tears, as I knew that He's really, truly, always with me.

I put the wet bill in my pocket. "Wow, there's a twenty dollar bill in my pocket," I thought to myself. I started my new life, whatever it may be, wherever it may lead, with twenty-three dollars. Sensing I should not hang out there too long, I got up and left.

I walked back down the trail running along La Paz Street to the corner. I turned right on Hot Springs Road, and took the back roads to town.

An hour into my walk back, I reached the commercial part of town. I stepped into a second-hand clothing store and bought a couple tee shirts and a pair of shorts. At the end of my spending spree I had nine dollars left. Who knew I could suddenly be so rich? And you should have seen the look on the attendant when I handed her my wet twenty dollar bill. She frowned and asked, "You didn't pee on it, did you?"

"No, it's holy water," I replied, sincerely and with a grin.

After changing into some summer clothes, I walked out the door with my dirty clothes in a bag. On my way home, I stopped at the first restaurant I came across. I was so hungry, it didn't matter what kind of restaurant it was. Alas, it was a Mexican joint, Maritza's Mexican Food. I gorged on a hefty three-dollar breakfast burrito.

At around noon, I reached my camp. It looked just as I left it a few days ago. But the last time I was there, I was far more miserable, so I can truly say that things were looking up. It wasn't the Tea Gardens, but it was home.

Bette spent most of her morning on the phone with a variety of local papers, placing ads in the "Missing" section. Ralph was in his office making duplicate copies of Michael's picture. He put his cellular number on the Missing Person flyer.

Over lunch at Rusty's Pizza, the hunting party convened to exchange notes. Ralph handed them stacks of flyers to paste everywhere in their zones. After filling their stomachs, they were on the road again.

Bette continued her afternoon search of walking up and down the same beaches. And then she'd have to sit down for awhile. She used her binoculars often.

Ralph drove by Ortega Park, and with his own binoculars searched across the acres of grass for Michael. Throughout his zone, he stopped to put Michael's missing picture in laundromats and grocery stores, and on trees and lampposts. He thought if Michael saw his picture and recognized Ralph's cell phone number, maybe he would call. "We should be so lucky," he thought to himself.

After dinner, they resumed the search. After dark, the guys left their wives at home to stay with the kids. The hunters searched the back alleys and walking paths as part of their routine.

Days were consumed by the same routine.

One evening, Larry walked up and down streets paralleling State Street. A block away, he saw a man who resembled Michael. Based on the last time Larry saw Michael, this man could possibly be him. Larry hurried to catch up. The man turned the corner. Larry hustled faster to the corner. The man turned on to State Street as Larry scurried up closer. When Larry got to within touching distance of the man, he asked the stranger, "Excuse me, do you know the time?"

The man turned around and said, "I don't know and I don't care."

"Thank you, anyway," Larry said, hiding his disappointment.

I spent the next few days in my camp. I just wanted to be alone and replay the memory of that whirlwind over and over again. I never wanted to forget the nuances of that moment of my life. Maybe I should write down everything I remember Him saying. So I wrangled paper and pen and started writing.

Over a couple of hours, sentences turned into paragraphs. And the paragraphs turned into pages. I contemplated the gigantic concepts He spoke about. Over the next several days, here and there, I was able to reconstruct verbatim everything He said.

Day after day, the manhunt for Michael went on around town and throughout the neighborhoods. It continued relentlessly, and was now taking a toll on the hunters. The search went deep into the second week. And some in the posse felt like they were ready for a change of zones. But they all agreed that it was best to keep the same zones for familiarity.

Terry and Adam turned their search into exercise by buying bicycles. For days, they rode up and down the bike lanes, forever looking for Michael.

At the end of the second week, Ralph was feeling pressure from his partners at the firm to return to his obligations. But he was not budging. He knew the price of failure at this task. He understood the personal, family, and professional ruin that lay ahead if they failed to find Michael.

Bette and the three other wives were getting tired and resentful of this newly added pressure to their already hectic and busy lives.

On the Friday afternoon of the second week, the group met at Larry's house. They had to consider that the "off time" from their jobs was all spent, and they still had not found Michael.

Ralph reiterated that everyone's sacrifice must be shared equally amongst all of them, not just some of them. Larry, Adam, and Terry were concerned for their positions if they had to take more time off. But when Ralph reminded them that they should remember the words from God as if it happened that morning, they knew they were going to have to make other arrangements.

Terry went to see his boss at the real estate office. Terry was a lousy liar and didn't explain himself well when he tried to describe what he had to do without sounding like his religion had taken him over the cliff.

But that didn't stop him from confusing his boss, who told Terry that he could keep his job, but he just wouldn't get a salary until he came back. And he gave Terry a full month before he would begin to find his replacement. It was a take it or leave it kind of deal and Terry's only option was to agree, as he hoped his family could survive on their savings.

Over at BriMar, Adam and Larry both got the same empty ultimatum from Charles. Charles reminded them that the company needed them at this critical time, and expressed discomfort that the *two of them were doing this at the same time. He suspected they were out looking for other jobs, or starting another company. Officially, HR labeled it as a non-paid sabbatical.*

So, with as much intensity as the first day of the manhunt, the four men and Bette went out to find the elusive Michael Whiley.

One unsuccessful day turned into another. And then another. And without showing an ounce of results, the third week went by.

The fourth week showed no results either. However, it brought an interesting statistic when five of the seven got traffic tickets, including Terry and Adam while they were on their bicycles.

Everyone's patience and endurance were being tested. They had become short-tempered, sleepless, and sick. Privately, they each worried that they may never find Michael.

One early Saturday morning in late July, Ralph served the kids breakfast while Bette was still waking up. When she arrived in the kitchen looking for coffee, Sara asked her if she would take them to the beach. Bette complained that she had been at the beach every day that week. But figuring time with the kids would be good for all of them, she gave in.

After waking up one morning, I thought I'd like to take a long walk. It was a beautiful morning and would likely be another perfect day in paradise. I thought I'd walk up the railroad tracks and maybe mosey up to El Capitan Park. Once there, I'd likely find some place to sleep overnight. So, I packed my bags and took enough provisions to last me through the next day. I started walking the rails and followed it around the curves of the coastline.

I eventually reached El Capitan beach in the early afternoon and boy I was ready for a good, refreshing swim in the ocean. I was sweating like a hound dog. There were other bathers dotting the beach.

After claiming a small parcel of sand for my stuff, I took everything off but my Bermuda shorts and went running into the brisk water. The initial jolt felt icy cold and invigorating. As I waded deeper into the water, I recall the night I nearly died out there.

But no one was going to die today, I thought as I plunged head first under the water.

Bette pitched their beach umbrella and chairs as Sara and Aaron raced for the water. Bette yelled, "Sara, keep an eye on your brother." Bette sat down to read her magazines. She looked around and saw a few people strewn across the large beach, at the same time keeping an eye on her kids. She put down her magazine and sat up. Casually, she folded her hands together to pray. Alone, she prayed, "Dear God, please hear my heart and prayer, oh Lord. I know You say You're not hearing our prayers, but I pray that You bless Michael. Bless him with Your protection, that's all." And with that, she sat back and stared out at the ocean and her kids. She reached for her binoculars to get a closer look at them.

The water was exhilarating and powerful. I gave the waves my back and faced the beach. I swam farther out to where I felt a comfortable distance.

From out there, I got a panoramic view of the shrubbery surrounding the park, allowing me to gauge the best spot to make camp that night. I also remembered the park rangers making their rounds. I'd have to get farther down the beach, and then after dark I'd retrace my footsteps back there.

I swam for about fifteen minutes and realized I was a bit far north from my spot. A couple kids were swimming, and the tide pulled them closer to me. I could tell it was a girl and a boy. Hearing them talking to one another, I thought I recognized their voices. I turned to see Sara and Aaron.

Sara looked over at me and immediately recognized me despite the beard. "Mr. Whiley, is that you?" she asked.

"Sara? Hi, is that Aaron, too?" I fired back.

"My mom and dad have been looking for you," she said excitedly.

"Really?"

Sara continued, "Yes, day and night. In fact, Mr. Whiley, they've all been looking for you."

"All the time," Aaron chimed in.

"Hi, Aaron, how are you?" I asked.

"I'm fine," he said, moving his arms to stay afloat.

"Aren't you guys a little too far out?" I asked.

Sara said, "My mom is on the beach. You should come with us. Oh my gosh, they've spent the last month looking for you."

"Really?"

"We need to tell my mom we found you," Sara said.

"Where is she?" I asked.

Sara spun around to face the beach and pointed at Bette sitting under an umbrella, looking at us through her binoculars. Finding the coincidence of discovering the kids out here in the water, I easily saw God's hand in the moment. I recalled His words, "and the children shall lead." So I agreed with Sara, and we made our way back to shore.

Through her binoculars, Bette checked out the strange man swimming by her kids. She noticed the kids and the man coming out of the water. He kind of had Michael's physique, she thought to herself. She refocused the lens to get a better look at his face. Startled, the bearded face looked a little bit like him, too.

As we all swam back to shore, I enjoyed catching up with the kids. I quickly pondered the chance meeting out here in the water. I could barely make out Bette sitting in her chair.

Bette got out of her chair and made her way closer to them. She tried walking and looking through the binoculars at the same time, but that was useless. She stopped, put the lens to her eyes, and could clearly see that it was Michael. She ran towards them while shouting his name. She kept running and yelling his name. Unashamed, she freely made a spectacle of herself.

When she was ten feet from me, Bette dropped her binoculars in the sand, stretched out her arms wide and gave me a hug. "Oh, Michael, it's you, it's you, it's really you," she shouted. And without letting go of me for a second, she cried and apologized, "I'm so sorry for how I treated you. I'm so ashamed of myself, and I just want to thank God that He gave me this chance to say this to you in person. I'm so sorry! I was just afraid. Will you forgive me?"

The profound impact of her sincerity triggered me to return her hug. I held her as she gripped my torso. About two inches away from my face she screamed, "We found you!"

CHAPTER TEN

THE WIND AT MY BACK

"Bette, thank you but you don't need to apologize, you were just looking out for the children," I said, trying to ease her guilt.

I could see that she was looking at my legs, and through her sniffling she said, "Michael, you look good, and those things went away."

"Yes, those things are all gone, never to return," I replied confidently.

"How wonderful," she exclaimed.

When we all got to their spot, she went straight for her cell phone. "Ralph?" she screamed into the phone. "I found him! I have Michael! Yes, he's right here!"

At his usual surveillance spot in Ortega Park, Ralph sat on the grass with his cell phone to his ear, watching everyone walk by. He ran to his car on hearing the news.

Bette handed the phone to me.

Ralph asked, "Michael, is that you?"

"Yes, it's me," I answered.

Ralph asked, "How are you? I'm so sorry I behaved like that back at East Beach. I disrespected you, but I want you to get Bette to drive you back to our house right away. Would you please let me talk to Bette?"

I handed the phone back to Bette. "Where are you?" he asked.

"I'm at El Capitan, meet us back at the house! Call the others! Call everyone!" She hung up the phone, turned to me and asked, "Michael, will you please come back to the house with us?"

At first, I was not sure if I wanted to do this. "I wasn't planning on going back into town so soon," I told her.

She cleared her throat and said, "Michael, something happened to Ralph and the guys while they were golfing about a month ago. And I know that they would very much like to tell you."

She drove us back into town and to their house. By the time we got there, I could see a few cars in the driveway. After getting out, I followed Bette towards the front door. But before we even got close to it, the door opened and out came a flood of people smiling and jubilantly greeting me. It was my very own gang of four friends and their families smothering me with hugs and laughter.

Everyone would eventually verbalize their realization that the boils were gone. They all talked at once and patted, squeezed, or hugged some part of me. Between the few families, I estimated there must have been about a dozen people there, all laughing and talking at once.

We filled Ralph's large living room. He took charge and settled everyone down. He turned to me and said, "We had an experience about a month ago." Ten minutes into the story of what happened at the golf course, I started to understand that God was really determined to make things right. And He was starting with my very own friends. It was His love emanating through these people in front of me. He didn't have to show Himself to them, but He did. And He did it for many reasons.

Terry handed me a page with typewritten words on it. The same day they witnessed the spinning sand, they wrote down what they remember they had heard. Between all of them, they were confident they got every word down on paper. As I read it, I recognized the personality of God in the words, just as when He appeared before me. I questioned whether or not I should share with them my short time with His Omnipresence. Why not?

I started to tell my story. I started from when I walked away from them and how I made my way up Olive Mill Road to the Tea Gardens. From my backpack, I pulled out my hand-written account of what He had said to me. I read the words to their amazement, and by the time I was done there wasn't a dry eye in the house.

I was amazed to find out that they all had put their lives on hold to find me. Terry walked up to me and said, "Michael, I'm sorry for discarding you so easily. Please forgive me."

I stood to hug him and said, "It's okay, Terry. It's all over."

He continued, "Looking back, all I could remember about myself was just being money driven and I didn't stop to see how I could have helped you."

Larry came over to me. He looked down at floor and shook his head, and with a grim look on his face said, "I really don't deserve your friendship, and if I had it to do all over again, I would do it completely differently. So, if you could get past my ignorance and betrayal, I'd like to be your friend again."

I looked at Larry and remembered the day I hired him. I knew he was a genuine man who walked the talk of what he felt in his heart. So letting this go was easier than I thought. I told him, "Larry, don't be so hard on yourself. I'm not."

Adam stood and took a second to find the words, and when he did he said. "Uh, I just want you to know, Michael, that I wasn't sure why things were happening to you, the way they were. In front of all of our friends, it doesn't matter what my doubt perpetrated in my mind, just know that I regret every minute of it. And I'm really sorry." Adam sat down. Terry's wife gave him a hug.

I squirmed in my chair, not feeling like I was owed anything. Yes, I remembered getting angry at them on East Beach a month ago, to such a degree I thought I'd never see them again. But if they hadn't been the way they were, I might not have retreated to the Tea Gardens, and I would have completely missed my time with God.

But I thought to myself, when God wants to appear to me, the time and place will be dictated by His whim, not because of something someone else did. Just as I was about to open my mouth to say something, Ralph cut in.

Ralph said to me, "You know, Michael, I would never want to intentionally hurt you in any way, but looking back, I completely failed you. I let fear fill my house." I noticed he wasn't looking at me but down at the carpet. He continued, "I should have led my family with faith and not with fear. I would like to say I am deeply sorry for the way I treated you and behaved."

I stood up and walked over to him. "I understand your fear. After all, I'm the one who lost my children." I gave him a hug. "Ralph, you'll always be my friend," I assured him.

"And your room is still vacant. It's got your name on it."

I was stumped. I never thought when I started out that morning that it was going to bring me to this pivotal point in time.

The afternoon passed as we exchanged stories and caught up from our time apart. After hearing of their sacrifices and challenges in searching for me for a month, we all found it most ironic that it was the children who found me. This simple connection God orchestrated out in the ocean seemed like yet another slap in the face to the adults. I imagined God was reminding us of the importance of being like His children.

After much banter, I was amazed by the rush of time; it was almost sunset.

Eventually, the four of us wound our way to the quiet privacy of the backyard, when Larry asked me, "Michael, would you pray for us? Like God said to, you know. I don't think we're out of the woods until you pray for us."

I felt like a door had just suddenly opened and whatever we put before God, He was going to make happen. Wow, I felt Him watching us. I felt Him hearing us. And as I was empowered by His presence, I knew beyond all doubt that not only was He here with us, but that He was going to make things right.

As I looked at my brothers in God, since we all had made the acquaintance, I know that it was only His love reaching into us that could have created this moment right now. When only weeks ago it was unthinkable. But that's God for you. Playing with opposite polarities like they're a spinning magnets.

I closed my eyes and held my friends in a group hug. In my most sincere voice, I prayed aloud and gave grace for His friendship expressed through my closest brothers. I also thanked Him for His protection and for His wisdom.

Later that night, after dinner, we congregated in Ralph's office. When everyone settled, Ralph informed me that they were ready to help me out financially.

I was touched by their generosity, so I asked, "What are you talking about?"

Ralph said, "We're going to pool our resources and support you financially until you get back on your feet. This is what we should have done in the first place."

Terry offered, "We're getting you an apartment or house or…"

Adam interrupted him, "…And a car. We've already talked about it. We're going to lease a car for you."

"Whatever it takes to get you back on your feet, and however long it takes," Terry said.

"Thanks, Terry," I replied.

Adam chimed in with, "Even if maybe one day one of us has to move in with you."

We talked into the night until it was time for everyone to go home.

When I got to my old room, and for the first time since that afternoon, I was actually alone. I dropped the packages from Nordstrom that Adam had picked up for me in the late afternoon. He had disappeared for a while, and I came to find out he had gone to Nordstrom and picked out some basic clothes for me. I dropped my dirty and worn backpack right next to the clean white Nordstrom bag. The clash of these two objects symbolized two opposite worlds. I called this moment "When Worlds Collide."

I saw, still on the night table, the perfect photo that was taken onboard the *Oh Happy Day*. It sat right where I left it. Funny, it hadn't moved an inch. How could I have forgotten it? A part of me was almost glad I did forget it. I sat on the bed and took off my shoes. And then I went to the bathroom.

I switched on the light and there I was, again. Catching my reflection dead center in the mirror, I took a good look at myself. I remembered that the last time I stood looking at myself in this very mirror my life was in a tailspin. And that was only eight months ago. I was not that same man anymore. It's not the months or the years, as they say, it's the miles. Wow, to go from there to here in eight months felt like I just went a million miles.

Slowly, I came to understand that what happened to me at the Tea Gardens was a pivotal point from where everything else would be measured, calibrated, and calculated for the rest of my life.

I got into bed. I sat upright and held my hands firmly together in earnest prayer. Feeling the gratitude swelling up from deep within, I said to God, "Dear God, I know You are in all of this. You orchestrate my coming and going. I just want to say thank You. Words fail to describe the ocean of my gratitude." I opened my eyes and saw the photo on the night table.

I reached for it and brought it to my chest to hug it. "And dear God, You are the protector of all children, and I ask You to protect mine, wherever they may be in Your Heaven." I caressed the images of my children.

I put the photo back on the night table and continued praying, "And dear God, I pray for Joanne, that you guide her to wisdom and embrace her with Your love so that..." There was a knock on the door. I got up to answer it.

It was Ralph. "Sorry to get you out of bed, but here's a tray of water and snacks. You know, just in case you get hungry or thirsty."

"Thank you, good night," I replied. Ralph put the tray on the night table and left. After closing the door, I stood there feeling the weight of the long walk I had done that day, and I plopped myself on the bed.

I stared at the ceiling and chuckled to think that when I woke up that morning, it was the last time I was ever going to sleep on the ground. Fighting my excitement, I slumbered into sleep.

The next morning I slept in late. I stirred, but didn't recognize anything. It took me a few seconds to remember I was in Ralph's house. I turned and came face to face with my family photo. I felt grateful to still be alive. I stretched and sat up with a smile.

I started the shower to warm it up and went for my new clothes in the Nordstrom bag. The shower felt great. Washing my body, I recalled the last time I showered here, in this spot. I had three boils, and no matter how bad it felt, the worst was yet to come. But I knew that was all behind me.

In the kitchen I found a note attached to a set of car keys from Ralph telling me they went to church. It also said to meet them at Larry's house for a barbecue lunch.

I made my way to a barbershop. This was my first haircut in more than six months and the barber started by cutting four inches off my beard all at once. Poof, it was gone. It took about an hour to trim and shave me clean.

When I showed up at Larry's house, they all teased me about looking like my old self again. But I knew they were being polite because I had to be at least thirty to forty pounds lighter.

On Monday morning I got out of my room and made my way to the kitchen where I found Bette just coming back from the store. She greeted me warmly and offered to make me breakfast. I realized it was already ten in the morning.

Just after breakfast the phone rang. Bette exchanged a few words, indicating Ralph was calling. She handed me the phone. Ralph asked, "Hello, how did you sleep?"

I replied, "Like a king."

Ralph jumped in with, "I heard from Joanne's lawyer this morning." Startled back to reality, I caught myself sitting upright at attention. He went on, "They're proposing a settlement offer of fifty percent of all stocks, bank accounts, bonds, gems, insurance, cash, property, and real estate. Basically, your total assets are currently valued at $5.2 million. In November, the expected settlement court date, you'll be entitled to $2.6 million dollars in various forms and cash."

I told Ralph, "I'm stunned! And to think that I ate because good people gave me their spare change."

"I'll pick you up at noon, be ready," he said before he hung up.

Later, as I sat by the door waiting for Ralph, I asked myself, "Is she not entitled to fifty percent of everything?" Was I so vengeful that I would contest her equal share of our family assets? What family? By the time she took everything and went into hiding there was no family.

But if I could walk away from this nightmare with $2.6 million to start out with and never have to see her again, I would be okay with that. Come to think, I'd be very okay with that. The polarized conditions of my life this past year were so absurd.

At noon, Ralph picked me up in the driveway. On our way into town he asked, "Would you be interested in a personal advance against the $2.6 million?"

Initially, I was puzzled by the question. "I don't understand. Like an advance? Like a loan?"

He fumbled for an answer, "No, well yeah, but without the interest. I figure come November you could pay me back."

"Gee, thanks Ralph, that's really nice of you. How much were you thinking?" I asked him, not knowing where the invisible line was drawn in the sand.

But all he came up with was, "How much do you think you need? Now, remember, we're still paying for your apartment, car, utilities, and..."

"And cable?" I asked throwing it out on the table. Laughing inside my head, I thought to myself, "I have to have cable."

"And cable. Remember, it's just a loan, a zero interest loan," he affirmed.

I mulled it over in my mind. We're in the middle of July, so I have four, maybe five months to go. Maybe six months before it's all settled. "Okay, I'd be happy to take you up on your offer for the loan. What do say...fifty thousand dollars?" I asked.

Ralph coughed and choked, being taken by surprise.

"Is that too much?" I asked.

He replied, "No, yes, no, I just didn't think you'd use it to start a new company, just something to get you through until November. But to answer your question, no, it's fine. How would you like that?"

"It'll have to be in cash, you know," I answered.

"Yes, I know. Let's get you some clothes before we go to lunch."

When we got to Nordstrom I said to Ralph, "I can't afford this just yet."

"Relax, this one's on the house. Now just get yourself a few pairs of pants and shirts and let's get out of here...oh, and you'll need some shoes."

While we were busy checking shirt sizes, pants sizes, etc., I said to Ralph, "I really appreciate this."

And then his words hit me when he said, "I'll even throw in the time I spent on dealing with Joanne's lawyers over the last five months."

His words might as well have been a bazooka. I was confused. I asked, "What? Wait a second! You were going to *bill* me for the time you spent dealing with Joanne's lawyers?"

With his lawyer skill of trying to change the subject he said, "Like I said, I'll throw that in, and we'll just forget about it. Do you like this blue shirt?"

He turned and kept shopping, but my curiosity was too much. I asked him, "How much was it?"

He looked at the tag and said, "Sixty-seven dollars."

I asked, "Not the shirt, your bill!"

"You don't want to know," he answered.

Now I had to know. "Yes, I really do," I told him.

He nodded his head in disbelief and said, "You don't want to know."

"But I really do," I insisted.

So he looked to the ceiling and said, "Forty thousand dollars. It was my standard rate, but like I said, it's forgotten..."

And that's when my disbelief cut him off again, "...Wow, just think, while I was out there begging for spare change just to eat and keep some food in my stomach, you were ringing up my tab to the tune of $350 an hour!" I had to consciously inhale as my view of absolute irony stood in front of me. I also found it funny, but I had to contain my laughter.

"As I said, never to be mentioned again. Except maybe once," he confessed. He looked me in the eye and said, "Would you please let Him know that I gave this to you as my gift?"

Then I remembered that Ralph had given me many gifts. I realized he wanted to make sure that God knew he did this for me. And the truth was, Ralph's time was valuable and that really was a gift. It was not about the money. He was taking care of my business while I was out there. I looked at him and warmly put my hand on his shoulder and said, "Ralph, I thank you for your generous gift and I will surely thank God on your behalf for allowing His eternal abundance to flow freely through you."

Relieved, Ralph let out a sigh and said, "Thank you."

"No, thank *you*," I said.

Within twenty minutes I had the basic essentials. I picked up a pair of tennis shoes and dress shoes. Ralph threw a third pair of shoes in the basket. I told him, "You know I can buy this stuff tomorrow after you get me the cash. You don't have to spend any more."

Ralph waved me off. "Just get it. Get it all. It doesn't matter. You can't break the bank in fifteen minutes. Not even at Nordstrom."

By the time we got to the restaurant, the three other guys had already arrived. The guys talked about getting back into the swing of work after being away for a month.

I figured it was as good a time as any to bring up my deep and dark suspicions and see if anyone would bite. I said to them, "As you all know, ever since I heard that the Pentagon bid failed to hit its mark, it struck me that something wasn't right. I can't tell you what it is, but, from what I gather, the numbers were too high. Was I right?" I turned to Larry and Adam.

They both nodded yes. "That's what we were told," Adam said.

I looked at Larry and asked him, "Do you still have your friends at the Pentagon?"

Larry affirmed his connections with a smile and a nod.

I continued my baiting with, "All we need is a copy of whatever they got." I reminded Larry on the sensitive nature of the objective. "You don't have to do this if you don't want to. If you don't want to, just say no. I'll understand."

Larry took a deep breath and said, "I thought you were going to ask me something hard." We all chuckled and I said, "We're not done yet." Then everyone stopped laughing.

"Adam, are you still pulling rank over there at the IT department?" I asked him. He nodded. I continued, "I'm thinking that whoever sent the bid inside the Fed Ex box probably came in at some odd hour. Do you think you could get a printout of who let themselves in the doors during, say, the holidays?" I could see the wheels already spinning in Adam's head.

"Sure, I should be able to do that," he answered.

"Thank you, Adam."

During lunch we spoke of my divorce settlement and timeline. I also told them of the generous financial offer Ralph gave me earlier. I explained that as of the following day, I'd be able to start paying my way through to November. They immediately countered my words with explanations about promises to God, and that it was a non-subject.

Ignoring me like I was invisible, they conspired right in front of me and agreed amongst themselves that their financial commitment ran through to November.

I relented my position and accepted their generous gift for renting my apartment and paying for the lease on the car.

Ralph snootily mocked me, "And he made me promise to pay for his cable today!"

Adam bellowed his triumph, "And we're paying for your cable!"

"I can pay my own cable, thank you very much," I said graciously.

But Terry had to add his own cleverness when he said, "Not if you never see the bill."

Again, another round of "Haa!" followed by a round of fist bumps, like teenagers with credit cards.

I couldn't win this one. "All right, all right, you can pay for my cable, and thank you."

When the check came, each of the guys went for his wallet. Without a second to think about it, Adam put forty dollars in my hand.

Larry looked at him and said, "I'll match your forty, and I'll raise you another twenty." And Larry put sixty dollars in my other hand.

"Okay, I'm in," Adam said, laying another twenty to his forty.

Terry shook his head and looked in his wallet, like it's his hand of cards. He asked, "What's on the table?"

I told him, "sixty and sixty."

"You mean I got to come in with sixty dollars just to start?" Everyone nodded. And then he belched.

Waving my arms to change the atmosphere, I said, "Yeah, lucky me."

Frowning, Terry laid down his bills right in the middle of my two hands stuffed with cash. "Here's your measly sixty, and I'll raise you another forty." An audible reaction came up from the table.

Adam countered with, "I'm out."

"So am I," admitted Larry.

Everyone looked to Ralph. He opened his wallet and looked inside. He emptied out his wallet. Fifty dollars.

"Shoot, that won't even get you into this game, homey," Adam said, taunting him.

Terry piped in, "You'll need at least one hundred to get in on this round, dude."

Ralph frowned, "Do you take ATM?"

I looked to Ralph and asked, "Can I trade in that ATM card for room and board?" We laughed.

With fists of cash, I knew what it was like to be Tony Soprano as people handed me their money with a smile on their face. But my boss was The Boss of all bosses. Because my Boss brought me everything I hoped for...and if and when I screwed up, my Boss didn't throw me away with the morning trash.

When the tab came, Terry picked it up and said, "It came to $85, any cash on you?" They all looked at me. I chuckled at this absurdity.

Ralph smirked at Terry, "Are you going to make Michael buy us lunch?"

"With our money, yeah," he answered.

Larry piped in, "That's not your money anymore, because it's his money now."

I jumped in and said, "Hey, I don't mind." I count out the bills to pay for it.

Larry pushed the money back and yelled at me, "No! Put your money away! You're not buying us lunch." He turned to Ralph and said, "Ralph, you got a credit card you need to baptize?"

Ralph gave him a look and said, "Somehow I knew this was going to make its way around to me." We all laughed, including Ralph, who bought us lunch.

Afterwards, Adam and I went to pick up my new leased vehicle. I thought to myself on the way that it wouldn't matter what kind of car I got. I was actually going to have wheels again. I could be mobile and productive. I might even get a job as a driver or messenger. Funny how the "desperate me" called out for attention. I had to continuously remember that it was over.

When we got to the car lot, we found that the only car available was a red Crown Victoria. It wasn't what Adam had ordered for me, but since it was only going to be for a few months, it was no big deal. It was just short of a living room on wheels. And I took it, gladly. Adam handled the details with the clerk. Within a few minutes the paperwork was all completed. I signed where I needed to and he handed me the keys. Wow, what once seemed so distant and far removed from my life came so quick and easy.

Outside, I turned to Adam and with a hand shake and a hug I thanked him. I looked at the car and was wowed by the idea of "freedom." I checked out the back seat to see if I could fit back there if I ever had to sleep in it. But why was I still thinking like that? I was going to have to get over my "desperate me" perspective.

I drove over to Terry's office where he met me in the parking lot of the real estate agency where he worked. We took his car to go house hunting. He wanted to get me into a house, but I figured that $3,000 a month for a house, split four ways between my friends, would come to $750 each. On top of the car, etc., they were shelling out over a thousand dollars each for maybe five months. So out of respect for their promise, or agreement, with God, I was going to let them do this. But I wanted to keep the costs down, and a house was out of the question.

I told Terry, "I'd prefer a two-bedroom apartment with a nice view, and that's all I need. And that's all I'll take. I'll need one bedroom for my office and the other to sleep in." I reiterated my appreciation.

And in a matter of about an hour of looking, we found the perfect two-bedroom apartment and it came with a loft. The sky-high two-story window looked onto a huge, beautiful maple tree. And for $1,700 a month it was easier to swallow.

Terry signed the papers and wrote the nice landlady a check. Although we still had five days before the beginning of August, she agreed to let me start moving my things in the next day.

Terry looked at me, and I could read his face. I know he was thinking, "What things?"

And in my head, I said to myself, "All the things I'm going to buy starting tomorrow to fill this place up."

When the landlady handed Terry the keys, he put them in his pocket. I wondered why he wouldn't hand them to me? I mean, I was the one who was going to live there. But in my new wisdom, I kept my mouth shut and continued my attitude of non-attachment.

When we got in his car, Terry pulled the keys out of his pocket and handed them to me. He said, "I just want to say how sorry I am for not doing this for you sooner. I'm sorry God had to step into the situation and remind me how many times you were there for me. So, just don't forget about me, Michael, like I did you."

Comforting him, I said, "How could I forget you? How could I forget today and this time we spent together looking for an apartment? Believe me, this was a milestone day in the life of Michael Whiley and you were a part of it."

He drove us back to his office. I thanked Terry again and gave him a hug for helping make the apartment happen. I looked at my new red Crown Victoria and said, "If there was ever a car made for an old Jewish lady living in Miami Beach, this is it."

I drove back to Ralph's house, and like a family enjoyed a night of Bette's good cooking and Aaron's antics. I told everyone I found an apartment and they asked for details. Bette inquired, "Does it have a washer dryer hookup?"

"Yes, Terry was smart enough to ask about those details. And he signed the papers. I move in the first of the month," I told them. But for a second, I pondered the enormity of having an apartment. That feeling didn't make sense to me because I've lived in much bigger houses. And with an unconscious swipe of my hand across my forehead, I snapped out of it. It was a whiff of fear, which must be a left over from the pit I was in.

That's why it was so important to me at all times to have control of my thoughts. And not let my mind indulge itself with blame, guilt, or self-pity.

Ralph asked, "Is that the leased car in the driveway?"

"Yes, and I'm very appreciative of that gift, thank you," I answered.

And before you know it, the third day of my new life was over and I was tired. I went to my room and prayed. I thanked Him for this day and for everything. I fell asleep basking in pure gratitude.

The next afternoon found me enjoying a conversation with Bette in the living room when I heard Ralph's car pull up the driveway.

When he walked into the house, he was pulling a modest sized carry-on suitcase on wheels. "Let's go to my office," he suggested. We excused ourselves as Bette left to pick up the kids from school.

We sat on the sofa. I unzipped the suitcase and tossed back the flap. There it was, fifty thousand dollars in mostly twenties and fifties.

Ralph said, "It's all I did today. I had to go to eight different banks because I didn't want to take out more than ten thousand dollars from any one bank. Banks have to report all transactions for more than ten thousand to the IRS. And since this is a no-interest loan between two friends, it's not their business."

I just stared at all this cash. Wow. Then it hit me: the colossal gap between the two worlds, that of having abundance and not having it. I was the living human laboratory that went between the two worlds so suddenly. And with just barely enough faith, I traversed those canyons to and fro, and back again.

And what this meant more than anything was that I will never have to beg again. That it was all over. I stood up and gave Ralph a big hug.

"I can't find the words," I told him. My eyes filled with tears and I said, "I'll never have to beg with outstretched hands in hopes that strangers might find a pinhole of compassion to search their pockets for change." That was all gone. And over the coming days and nights, I repeated this realization in my mind.

In a side pocket of the suitcase, I pulled out a box and found a new wallet. Ralph said, "I figure a new day ought to come with a new wallet."

I just wanted to go save the world. Save it from the hunger I became accustomed to. Save it from the poverty I endured. Save it from the illness I had suffered. Save it from itself.

I rolled the suitcase to my room and dropped it by the bed. I rejoined Ralph in the hall on our way to the family den. He suggested, "You should keep it in the upper cabinets of the closet. The kids don't need to know it's there."

After dinner, I planned to surprise the wits out of someone. Since I had my own car, I could actually go visit people. I decided to drop in on someone who might be able to do me a favor, if she doesn't have a heart attack when she sees me.

Back in my room, I went to the suitcase and hovered over my bank. I pulled out a few thousand dollars, stuffed hundreds in each pocket, and crammed my wallet with the rest. I thought, I don't need this much money. Don't be crazy, I'll never spend this much. I know, that's the point. So I took it anyway.

Upon arriving, I parked the car and walked up to the modest house. I took a deep breath and knocked.

When she opened the door, Claire shouted, "Oh, my God, Michael!" and slammed me with a hug.

I returned the greeting with a hug and an apology for dropping in on her unannounced. She invited me in. As I walked into her living room and looked around at all the normalness, I thought it was just a beautiful thing to behold.

"How have you been?" she asked.

I replied, "I'm doing great."

"Wow, I'm so happy to hear that. Would you like some tea or coffee?" she offered.

I suggested we go to a coffee shop. She agreed and collected her essentials.

I pointed out that I was driving the racy, red, old lady's car. But it has a keyless entry, so it's got to be okay on the cool scale. I welcomed her into my mobile living room unit.

It didn't take Claire long to confess her confusion. "I heard so many rumors. I didn't know what to believe."

Thoughts shot up through my head like a pinball machine. "Please don't tell me, I don't want to know what they were," I said jokingly.

She shook her head in disbelief, "I can't believe I'm sitting here with you."

At a quaint coffee shop, we ordered drinks and caught up on her life. She told me she had stopped by the house recently but it had been flattened.

We talked about her transferring to another department after I left. She brought up the low morale at the company. "It's everywhere, Michael," she said. She waved her hands in anxiety while confessing, "I don't know how much longer I'm going to be there myself. To tell you the truth, I've been looking around."

At the risk of being rude, I knew I had to ask her for a favor while she still had her job. "Claire, I need a favor from you, and if you don't want to do it, I'll completely understand. You won't have to explain yourself. What I'm looking for is a copy of the Pentagon bid out of my old computer. Would you happen to know what they did with it?"

"I can probably find out. But once I locate it, what then?" she asked.

"I need to find the last approved version of the Pentagon bid. If there's any chance you find it, could you print that out for me? I know it's asking a lot, considering it's about 230 pages. But if there's a speck of doubt that you'd rather not do this, just say so and nothing will change between us."

"I'll be happy to do it for you, Michael. It may take me a couple days to find your old computer, and then I'll have to find the time to wire it so I can print it out. Let me come up with a plan. Is there a number where I can call you?"

This simple question stumped me and it showed. I answered, "Uh, I'll have a new number tomorrow. I'll call you with it." Note to self, get a cell phone.

I told her I was in the process of moving into an apartment. When she asked me about the actual process of moving in, I explained that I was starting from scratch. I had nothing but a backpack, a handful of clothes, and a framed photograph of my family to claim as my own.

Her eyes grew wide with surprise. "Oh my gosh, where did it all go?" she asked.

"Well, that's a good question. I guess God just took it all back and I had to learn how rich I really am without having anything", I answered. I just didn't feel like I wanted to get in too deep right now, so I changed the subject. And then I thought maybe she could help me decorate the apartment and fill it with stuff. I asked her, "How's your decorating skills?"

But she could see through me and my attempt to change the subject. She admitted, "I try and have fun with it, but I'm not that bad, I'm all right I guess."

Over the next hour, I relished rediscovering someone I had once known. Claire shared her many ambitions. I felt hopeful and a bit rejuvenated in her company.

I dropped her off at her house and told her, "I'll call you with my new cell number." And once again, I extended my appreciation to her for going out on this limb for me.

"Only for you, Michael, I always said I'd do anything for you. I guess this is it," she said before getting out of the car.

I drove home thinking about how fast things were moving. I was surprised at my eagerness to fill an apartment with things. Things and I still had issues. There was a part of me that disdained things. Materialism distorts our soul's journey and steals our priorities. It lacks true satisfaction and will let us down in the end, every time. I spent the last six months telling myself I don't need things. And thankfully, in His grace to show Himself to me, I found what I needed.

Life is not about what we have, but who we are. And who we are can be tangibly measured by how we treat others.

I turned the car around, drove to State Street, and parked. I walked to my usual spots where only days ago I stood begging. I hung out just waiting for anyone to walk up and ask me for money. Many did. And I gave it to them generously. I headed up State Street and there was not a person in need who I didn't walk up to and offer some money. Whether a teenage runaway or an old bum, I didn't care. I handed it out like candy. I was just a walking ATM machine for the poor, no pass code required.

And in this moment I realized that this is what Christ would do if He had a pocket full of money. He'd walk the streets helping the poor and not be judgmental about it. He would not judge them by their appearance or by their smell. Rather, he would see His Father's light shining in their hearts. Because after all, how could He forgive His assassins if it were not for Him seeing God's light in each and every one of their hearts? So I looked at the destitute and that is Who I saw.

After another half hour of tithing, I went back to the car.

I drove around looking for the needy who had not found indoor shelter by this hour. I drove up and down alleys looking for people to give them fifty or a hundred dollars. I pulled up to them, cracked my window, and handed them a bunch of money. I said "God bless you" and drove away. After an hour of drive-by tithing, as I called it, I guessed I had given away a few thousand dollars. I was tired.

When I pulled into the driveway at Ralph's house, I got out of the car and looked up at the night sky and waved at the Pleiades. Inside, I made my way to my bedroom and put the leftover money back in the suitcase. Although it was not much, I didn't want Bette to find hundreds in cash when she emptied my pockets at the washing machine. That would be rude. Not to mention very funny.

The next morning, Bette bought me a new cell phone. Since I had no credit card, she offered to put the whole thing on one of hers. I promised to pay for the monthly bills.

Of course Ralph was the first person I called to give him my new number. And while I had him on the phone, I asked him for everyone else's phone numbers. One more step into a life I recognized, and yet I saw so many people enslaved by their cell phone. I enjoyed the freedom of not having had one for eight months. But the freedom turned to isolation.

So now it was time to rebuild my Rolex, uh, I meant my Rolodex.

I called Claire with my number and suggested that I hire her to help me put the apartment together. I needed someone to help me buy new furniture and arrange it in my apartment. She was willing, but refused the money. She insisted, "I'd rather do it just for the fun of it. No, I cannot accept your money."

"Aah, innocence," I thought to myself.

Saturday morning came and I was out the door early. When I picked Claire up at nine o'clock, she carried a clipboard like a portable office. She was Outlook in tennis shoes. We stopped for bagels and coffee, and ordered it to go. We returned to my empty apartment to show Claire.

She exuded excitement over the big open space above the living room created by the loft. She walked around the place while I sat on the carpet against the wall and plowed into my bagel, with lox and the entire works. I gave grace and bit into the mother of all bagels. It took me ten minutes to work that first bite down my throat.

Funny, I was going to have this very same breakfast on the fly bridge of the *Oh Happy Day* the morning I woke up freezing in the middle of the ocean.

I daydreamed how fast my other life went away and how fast this new one approached. I was uncertain how this was going to work out, but maybe I didn't need to know. I wondered if my pursuing the failed Pentagon bid was motivated by a subtle misguided streak of revenge. Was I just out to clear my name? That would have been more ego driven than truth driven. Was I out to save my ego by showing I was not to blame? Should I walk away from that whole thing entirely? Should I just let it go?

In the distance, I watched Claire walk in and out of rooms, analyzing her canvas. She measured the important spaces, windows, and walls. I sat alone in the quiet emptiness of the open space soon to be my living room, and suddenly I remembered the old family den with all that human ruckus. As I sat there eating my bagel in the quiet happiness, I was humbled by it all.

I was grateful that I had a bed of my own again. It really didn't change the scheme of life, because I reminded myself that not even the Son of Man had a place to put his head. Yet, knowing there was a place where my head would fall asleep provided a sense of security, albeit a false, artificial, and temporary sense of security. Maybe I was just blowing things out of proportion, but that's okay right now because I was in this new place I call home. And I was not going to judge my thoughts and feelings.

After a few minutes of walking around, Claire started getting ideas. As she toured the empty kitchen, I reminded her, "You have to start from nothing and turn it into something." When she came back into the living room, I asked, "What do you think?"

"It has great potential," she said enthusiastically.

I told her, "I'm going to put my desk in the loft. What do you think?"

"Good idea. That would be my choice. What kind of desk do you want?"

I hadn't given it a thought, so I shrugged my shoulders and said, "I have no preconceived ideas. Whatever we see, whatever we like." I opened a bag and showed her $25,000 in cash. Confidently, I assured her, "I'm sure we'll never spend all of this." And we were out the door on a bona fide shopping spree.

We started shopping for large-piece items first, and worked our way down in size. It seemed after several hours and several stores, all we did was point, walk, and buy. Point, walk, and buy. We were always doing one of these three things.

It was another day of imitating an ATM machine.

As we went from store to store, Claire organized the scheduling of the delivery of everything: washer, dryer, two sofas, stove, tables, bed, dressers, home theatre units, etc. I liked how Claire already knew my style and taste, having worked with me for many years.

Exiting Saks Fifth Avenue, with our arms stuffed with several bags, we walked to the car to drop them off. And who knew it was noon already?

Claire suggested we take that load to the apartment, get some lunch, and then resume our shopping. We dropped a load off at the apartment, and during lunch I asked her, "Claire, I'm wondering if there might be a FedEx record of a package going out the last week of December? Would you mind looking into seeing when the bid was shipped? I'd be interested to know. Do you think you could do that?"

"Sure, I can probably find it online," she said.

After lunch we resumed our day of walking, pointing, and buying. At the end of the day, the bank was down to a mere thousand dollars. I spent twenty-four thousand dollars. In one day! I had only one thousand left in my wallet. I was a little shocked. How could I have been so cavalier? And then I remembered I once spent almost ten times that much on a ruby necklace.

Holy cow, all money is relative.

At the end of the day, I drove Claire back to her house. While parked at the curb, I pulled out the last thousand dollars to give her. I held it out for her to take.

"Michael, are you kidding me? I thought we talked about this already. I'm not taking your money, end of story."

I knew she didn't earn that much at BriMar. So I stood my ground by telling her, "Thank you, it's nice of you, but I'm not going to let you do this without some form of exchange, and *that* is not negotiable."

I told her, "I would have given this to someone else to do the same thing you did for me today." I stuffed the money in her coat pocket.

"It's not about the money, Michael. You were the best boss I ever had. Don't forget your first delivery is tomorrow at 2 p.m. from Sears. Good night," she said. And then she closed the door.

I shouted so she could hear me through the closed windows. "Thank you, Claire!"

I went home to Ralph's, tired and exhausted. I must have walked fifteen miles that day and carried a ton. After a brief prayer of gratitude and asking God for His blessings upon my friends, my head sank into my pillow.

The next morning I woke up to find Ralph and the family getting ready to go to church. Holy cow, it was Sunday already. Ralph asked, "Do you want to go with us?"

I bowed out, saying, "Maybe another day." Maybe never, I thought to myself. At least not back to *that* church. But I did need to find a new church, a sanctuary other than God's ocean and mountains.

I quickly got back to my new apartment to start emptying the ton of bags of things I had purchased. I was energized to put the stuff away.

When I got back from lunch, I saw some papers at my front door. While I was gone, Claire had dropped off a printed schedule with contact numbers of when the furniture would be arriving. I thought she might come up with something like this. I'd have to call her and thank her. And sure enough, the 2 p.m. delivery arrived on time.

The following day, Monday, July 31st, found me back at the apartment early to receive the first arrival of the day at 8:30 a.m. The morning flew by as I continued to organize, put away, and then throw away. The amount of packaging overwhelmed the garbage bins.

Late that afternoon, I got a call from Larry. His friend at the Pentagon had located the bid that morning and was sending him a copy. It would be there in a couple of days. I thanked him for making the call.

Internally, I reckoned that the conversation I had with myself yesterday as to whether or not I should proceed down that road may not matter after all. If things are in motion, then let them ride.

Over dinner at Ralph's house, I told them how much I appreciated being treated like family, and that they were welcome to crash at my place anytime.

Early the next morning, Tuesday, August 1st, I awakened to the inner rumblings from God waking me up to pray. I took a deep breath and remembered that tonight I'd be sleeping in my own bed. I smiled and got up to address God properly and gave Him my focus and attention, my adoration and appreciation, my sense of awe and more appreciation.

After a half hour of praying, sometimes in whispers, I got up and showered. I gathered my things, including the perfect photo. I rolled out my twenty-one thousand dollar vault of cash on tiny wheels, and I walked past the family getting ready for the day. We said our good-byes and I invited them over to see the apartment.

On the drive there, I pondered my cash situation. I calculated that $21,000 translated to $1,200 to spend each week until I got my money in November. Without paying for a single thing but food, gasoline, and cell phone, I would have to work hard at spending this amount of money every week. And remember, after returning the fifty thousand to Ralph I would be left with only two and a half million dollars come November. Again, I'll be very okay with that.

While organizing my apartment, my new home, I thought about work and wondered what kind of job God was going to bless my life with. I remembered the promise He made to me at The Tea Gardens. And yet, I also wanted to make sure that I had no expectations of the Almighty. I couldn't forget this vital lesson: never make expectations of The Almighty. I knew this lesson better than anyone.

Throughout the day, delivery trucks continued bringing furniture. I snuck out for lunch and to buy a computer and necessary attachments. I brought it all home and assembled it. It took me hours and then the day was gone.

I spent the night hooking up the various electronic attachments to my new TV set. And then suddenly it was midnight. The hours had flown by so fast that I began to suspect cosmic trickery.

I prepared for bed and as I walked around the apartment locking the doors and windows, I stopped to look at all this stuff. I took a moment to absorb this new atmosphere. I thought to myself, God did this. He put all of this here, and He can take it all away.

I took a deep breath, closed my eyes, and fused this powerful thought with my focus, prayer, and emotion. Everything we see and touch was first a thought in someone's mind. And in that moment, I was thinking great things. And in my mind, I saw the best was yet to come.

I turned out the lights and went to bed. In between the freshly washed sheets, I stared into the tranquil darkness of the room. And in that peaceful void, I fell asleep.

Friday brought a call from Larry, wanting me to meet him for lunch. At Rusty's Pizza, in the back booth, Larry pulled out the bid from a large brown business folder and handed it to me. I held it in my hand and smiled.

"I'm going to have to go through this very methodically," I said.

Larry said disappointedly, "I asked him for the original, and he told me it wouldn't be a problem, but he sent us a copy. That sucks."

I put the bid back in the envelope and replied, "I don't see the fact that it's only a copy as a problem."

He suggested, "Start with the big numbers first and then work your way back." I agreed with his approach.

My cell phone rang. Claire asked if I could meet her between 5:30 and 6:00 p.m. at the same coffee shop where we met before. I agreed and we hung up.

I passed the afternoon waiting for the cable man. Who knew daytime television was so bad? No wonder the world dislikes us. They think that's how we act, and that we're all adulterers and homicidal maniacs.

I got to the coffee shop on time and placed an order. I picked up the newspaper and waited for Claire. I had finished my first cup when she arrived. I noticed she had her backpack still with her. She ordered something and joined me at the table. She discreetly handed me a large brown manila envelope. Inside it was a color printout of the bid from my computer. I noticed another item. Claire said, "It's the printout of the FedEx record showing the package was dropped off at the Atlas Station at 3:58 p.m. and shipped out that same day on December 26th."

I invited her to dinner, but she regretted that she had made other plans. I thanked her again. After ten minutes of laughing, she dashed off, saying, "Call me, Michael, oh, and thanks again for the money."

I told her, "You need to come see the place." With a broad smile, she walked out the door.

Driving home, I thought about my approach to comparing the two bids. How funny they should both come to me the same day. I was looking for the point of origin from where everything else changed around it. I'd probably see a lot of different dollar amounts. But there was a core dollar amount which everything else revolved around. I had to find that figure.

When I got home, I prepared myself for a long night of homework. I settled at my desk and laid the two bids side by side. One was in black and white, the other was in color. Of course, I was expecting this comparative analysis to take me days. I would start a notebook in Excel and use the comments in the cells to reference other related alterations.

I reminded myself to go for the big numbers first. And with that clue I went to the grand total amounts and saw the discrepancies. Within a half hour I calculated first dollar amount difference.

Holy cow, I thought to myself, could the wrong bid have just been sent by mistake? No. We never made mistakes like that. I went up the column of numbers and noted each one that was different from the version in color, which Claire gave me.

I noted every abnormality on the spreadsheet. In time, dozens of cells had many comments.

Around midnight, I surfaced for air. I asked myself, who might have done this? Who would have deliberately raised the bidding price so high they would jeopardize everything?

Every time I ran through the short list of potential suspects, only one name remained after a process of elimination: Charles McGraw. But I didn't yet have enough evidence to point fingers. I had to focus on the evidence. I was charting it right in front of me, but I was burnt out and called it a day.

The next morning, I picked it up where I left off. And the morning quickly became afternoon. The grand total of the difference came to $137,000,000.00, resulting in an additional $47 million profit.

The late afternoon brought unexpected company. I found Adam at my door and invited him inside. He handed me a printout of the entries and exits as logged by the security system during Christmas vacation week between December 23rd and January 3rd. It showed the janitorial crew coming and going on January 2nd. On the day after Christmas, Charles McGraw entered through the front door at 9:37 a.m. and left at 3:40 p.m. that same afternoon. He was in there for six hours reconfiguring this bid. "It took him eighteen minutes," I said out loud. From 3:40 to 3:58, it took him eighteen minutes to get to the Atlas FedEx station.

Holy cow, without intentionally setting out to do so, I had reconstructed his day.

That evening, in the privacy of Ralph's home office, I spelled everything out to my four friends. We all knew that the only true way of knowing whether or not Charles did this was to get into his computer. If there was still a version of this altered bid in his computer, then we ought to be able to get to it. "But how, and is it legal?" I asked.

Ralph said, "The only ethical and legal way to do this is to get Henry Beck to pull Charles's computer."

Adam suggested, "And it's got to be done without Charles having a single second to delete any files."

"Good point, Adam," I said. I looked at Ralph and asked, "About Henry Beck, how do we get to him?"

"He's a member of the Montecito Country Club."

"Oh, that's right, I forgot," I said.

"I can deliver Mr. Beck, no problem."

"Thanks, the sooner the better," I said to him.

Ralph replied, "I guess it should be just you and I, no need to break protocol by involving Adam and Larry. And you can lay it out for him like you did for us."

"Do you think he'll see it?" I asked.

"Depends on how good of a salesman you still are."

"Not the answer I was looking for, but the point is well taken," I said. Still, I had confidence in the elements I'd put together to have an intelligent conversation pointing in a particular direction. Will he bite? Who knows?

CHAPTER ELEVEN

EXPOSED

Several morning's later at around eight o'clock Ralph called to recap how he bumped into Mr. Beck just a little while ago at the Montecito Country Club. Apparently, Ralph slipped a valet $50 to call him the minute he saw Mr. Beck pull up. Ralph continued, "After that, it was all catch up. I proposed a meeting with the three of us, and he said he would listen to you."

"Where?"

"It's not so much where, but when. He says he'll meet with you at 4:00 this afternoon at Denny's in Carpinteria."

"Today?" I stammered. I cleared my throat and said, "Well, I'm ready. Let's go to Denny's."

I quickly got ready for the day. I still had to make duplicate copies of the two separate bids. Over the next few hours I organized a strategy in my head and printed my evidence out of Excel workbooks and burned the files onto a CD. I assumed he'd take anything I offered him to review. What should I put them in, a brown manila envelope? No, a manila envelope won't do for a man like Mr. Beck. After all, his package will be close to six hundred pages.

I went looking for a handsome pouch. At a stationery store I bought an elegant, well-crafted leather pouch with a sturdy zipper.

Ralph picked me up that afternoon. On the way south to Carpinteria, Ralph surmised, "It's obvious he chose this place because he can't be seen at his usual places having this conversation."

"That's good. That's a sign that he's taking me seriously—well, so far."

We got to the diner, and the hostess walked us to the back of the restaurant where Mr. Beck sat waiting for us. He greeted me with an uneasy handshake. We started the conversation on the subject of the weather. Well, we had to start somewhere, I thought to myself. We humans are so funny. There's an elephant in the room and we could be talking about the wallpaper. And the elephant at the moment was under my arm.

But in no time Mr. Beck asked, "What do you have?" I started on how I first had my suspicions when this all started to happen. I told him that all roads led to Charles McGraw. And then I went into the high points, including the key entry data and the FedEx waybill.

After fifteen minutes, Mr. Beck asked me, "Is that all you have?" There was doubt in his tone.

I delved into details of the difference between the two copies of the bid. Not wanting to burn out his fuse with complexities, I explained the discrepancies between equations in the most suspenseful way I knew how in order to make the numbers sound intriguing.

Mr. Beck asked me, "Is that all you have?"

There was that tone again. But there was a little voice in my head telling me he was hooked because what came out of his mouth may not have been what was going through his head.

"No, certainly there's more. Plenty more," I replied. And with a nod of his head he gestured like he was ready for me to give it to him.

"But I don't have it," I said.

"Where is it?" he asked. I wasn't sure if he was being sincere or cynical.

"It's in Charles's computer," I answered.

He scratched his head and said, "I see. Are you guessing, or is it in his computer?"

"I can't be certain of anything, having been away from it all," I told him.

He offered, "So are you suggesting I yank Charles's computer out from under him?"

"Yes, I am. But you cannot give him a second's worth of notice, otherwise he'll start destroying files," I warned him.

He nodded and said, "Okay, give me a little time to think about all of this. I'm not saying I'm going to do anything. I'm just absorbing information. Is there any place else I should look other than Charles's computer?"

I unzipped the leather pouch and showed him the two different colored bids. "No, to answer your question, I think you might find the gold version in his computer. And if you do, then that will be concrete proof. The yellow version is what was supposed to be sent, but the gold one is what they got."

"This is a tall order. I don't generally like whistle-blowers, Michael. I figured this meeting would warrant my attention for at least fifteen minutes." He looked at his watch and said, "And look, it's gone on for almost an hour."

Remembering how much money I brought into BriMar, I said to him, "Yes, and this hour has only cost BriMar one hundred and thirty-seven million dollars." I saw the pang on his face, which only authenticated that the truth really does hurt.

We left on a cordial note and vague follow-up plans. I dropped it in his lap, and if he does anything with it, it'll be his business. If he doesn't, then he can watch BriMar continue to sink into a sub B class stock.

When I got back to my apartment, I fell onto the couch. It was a day full of surprises. What did I think Beck would do with the information? I was sure he'd take a look at it. He didn't get where he is being in denial after having so much evidence. I also think that it's all circumstantial evidence without Charles's computer.

Straight from Denny's, Mr. Beck went home to his mansion in Montecito. He went upstairs to his luxurious office, got on his phone, and called his most trusted accountant, who came right over.

From out of the pouch, Mr. Beck pulled out both bids and a dozen printed pages in Excel. Both men went straight to the Excel printouts and examined the numbers and the comments. They uploaded the accompanying CDs on two separate computers. Hour after hour, they calculated numbers and equations, building a case of suspicion. Anger fueled Mr. Beck's adrenaline and that kept him up late. At around four in the morning, the accountant crashed in one of the bedrooms.

But Mr. Beck was too angry to sleep. He kept playing with the numbers and thought he recreated what must have gone through Charles's mind when he sold himself to the devil. He looked at the clock and realized that in another half hour he'd have been awake for twenty-four hours. Reluctantly, he crashed.

A couple hours after the sun rose, Mr. Beck got up, showered, dressed himself in some gorgeous Italian suit, and called his security service on his cell phone. He directed the person on the other line to have two body guards waiting for him in the parking lot at BriMar at 10:00 a.m. and not to enter until he arrived. He went downstairs to where his service staff had already prepared his breakfast.

When Mr. Beck arrived on time in BriMar's parking lot, he found his two bodyguards ready for duty. He instructed them, "The objective here is to remove a computer. I'll tell you which one. Take it out and place it gently on the back seat of your car. I'll call you with an address of where to take it. Who's got a knife?" They looked at each other; neither one of them had a knife. Mr. Beck handed them an elegant, black Swiss Army Knife and said, "Cut the computer lines if you have to. Better if you don't, but use it if you have to. And be sure I get that back." He turned and walked towards the front door.

In the front lobby, Mr. Beck told the receptionist to summon two BriMar security guards. When they arrived less than a minute later, Mr. Beck told them of his plans and proceeded to the executive suites. He entered to everyone's pleasant surprise. But their pleasantry quickly faded to confusion. Mr. Beck and his heavy-handed entourage made their way towards Charles's office.

Mr. Beck politely greeted Charles's secretary, Eveleen, as he walked right past her to rap on Charles's closed door. Flustered, Eveleen tried to intercom Charles to announce Mr. Beck, but he went flying through the door.

Completely taken by surprise, Charles declared, "Henry, what a surprise, come on in. Were you in the neighborhood?" And then Charles noticed the four horsemen from his own apocalypse in tow behind Mr. Beck.

Mr. Beck ordered the last man inside to "Close the door." Mr. Beck turned to Charles and said, "I'm sorry to barge in on you like this, but I have reason to believe things didn't turn out right because of something that may have been done in this office."

"What are you talking about, Henry?" Charles asked.

Mr. Beck continued, "Would you please step over here to this side and away from your computer?"

Charles went from confusion to panic in a split second. Suddenly the blood rushed to his head and it overflowed with memories of damaging files throughout his computer. He had to stop this invasion immediately. He could not let this happen.

Charles stood defiantly against anyone who came around his desk.

Mr. Beck addressed his first BriMar security guard: "Take his computer."

Determined, the first guard replied, "Yes, sir" and walked around to get past Charles. But Charles pushed him away. The guard tried again until Charles shoved him up against the wall. The two other guards instantly jumped on Charles while dodging his punches and elbows. But now and again in the scuffle, Charles laid a solid punch on each of them. Finally, one of the consultants hit him so hard it knocked the wind out of him.

Mr. Beck shouted at the top of his lungs, "Stop, Charles, don't be a fool!"

From outside the doors, a dozen staff members heard sounds of furniture crashing , men hollering, and bodies hitting the floor.

Three guards restrained Charles on the floor while the fourth cut the connections to the computer tower. Mr. Beck stopped the guard. "No, shut it down properly. Close each program and then unplug it."

Finally, one BriMar guard slapped a pair of handcuffs on Charles, now subdued on the carpet by his desk. Mr. Beck looked down at him. "It didn't have to be like this, Charles. What were you thinking?"

"Drop dead, Henry!" Charles yelled at him.

"In due time, Charles, but not today, and not before I get to the bottom of this accusation, which you seem to be substantiating by your bizarre behavior."

"What accusation?"

In his rage, Mr. Beck slammed his arms on the desk and in one swipe of anger, threw everything on Charles's desk across the room.

Mr. Beck screamed at Charles, "We're going to get to the bottom of this and find the truth, I promise you that!"

"Drop dead! Get these off me!" Charles demanded of the handcuffs.

Mr. Beck replied, "Not until that computer is out of the building."

Mr. Beck told the two BriMar security guards to wait five minutes and then escort Charles to his car and to be sure to take his keys and security clearance.

Outside the office, the crowd was staring at the door, when it opened abruptly. The first thing they noticed was Charles's bloody nose and torn jacket as he was escorted out in handcuffs.

Eveleen slumped in her chair, bewildered at the sight of her boss.

The two private guards took the computer tower, along with all the connections, out the door to their car.

In the parking lot, Mr. Beck walked very deliberately to his car. In the privacy of his car, he called the security company and instructed them where to take the computer.

For the rest of the day and into the night, Mr. Beck waited anxiously for a phone call. Finally, at 10:30 that night, it came.

Randy, the computer technician on the other end, detailed his file-reconstituting process to Mr. Beck's confusion.

Mr. Beck yelled at him, "Just give it to me in English!"

"I was able to recover the file," he said.

Mr. Beck was suddenly weighed down with extreme disappointment.

Randy continued, "And I can see that it was deleted on December 26 last year. Would you like me to see if it was transferred to another drive? It probably was. That might take me a bit longer."

Mr. Beck realized that any further details would be pointless and said, "No, don't bother. Can you extract the file?"

Randy replied, "Yes."

"Can you print it out for me?"

"Yes, I can even email it to you."

"Of course you can. Go ahead and email it to me now and I'll have someone pick up a hard copy in the morning. Thank you and *good night," Mr. Beck said, sighing with resignation. He slumped in his sadness.*

When the hard copy was delivered the next morning on Mr. Beck's desk, he opened it to the page he was looking for and saw that the over-inflated grand totals were identical to the gold copy that went to the Pentagon.

It was Charles, beyond all shadow of doubt, Mr. Beck thought to himself. But the motive, other than greed, eluded him.

With one phone call to the phone company, Mr. Beck organized a conference call for BriMar's board of directors at 11:30 a.m. When the conference call took place, he told them what he knew. He started from the time Michael approached him a few days ago to his phone call last night with Randy. When Mr. Beck finished explaining his findings, the secretary of the board called for parliamentary procedures. With enough members on the call to sustain a quorum, Mr. Beck's motion for removing Charles from his title and the company entirely was seconded by another member. The board then voted unanimously for Mr. Beck's motion.

I started the following morning with breakfast and a prayer. I was sincerely happy for a new day and decided that I was going to take the day off. It wasn't like I had a job, but I was taking the day off from any responsibilities and maybe read a book under an umbrella on the beach. I packed a lunch, newspapers, a couple books, and other essentials.

I was out the door by 9:30, and minutes later I was walking on the sand. I camped near the water's edge and settled in under my shade. After reading a couple *Wall Street Journals*, I couldn't believe two hours had passed.

It was all too perfect, and so of course my cell phone had to ring. Oh, no, civilization was calling. Ralph called to tell me that he got a call from Mr. Beck, who wants to meet me for lunch at The Patio Restaurant in the Biltmore at one o'clock. Yes, today. And he wants me to go alone. I sat up. Oh, no, I thought to myself. He didn't "get it," and now he wants to let me down by myself. That made perfect sense; he doesn't want to embarrass me in front of Ralph. Oh, well. But don't jump to conclusions, I warned myself.

I rushed home, showered, changed clothes, and altered my cavalier disposition. Should I take a copy of the bids, just in case he wants to talk about it? I'll leave it in the car. He didn't mention it. And why does he not want Ralph to come along? I guessed I should expect the worst.

I pulled into the hotel on schedule and entered the lobby. I announced myself to the hostess, who escorted me through The Patio Restaurant and walked me to the far side of the outside patio. Adjacent to the stairs that lead down to the sandy beach, Mr. Beck sat with his back to the ocean, giving me the preferred view as I sat across from him. This subtle choice on his part only reflected his upper class upbringing.

He stood to greet me. His demeanor was friendly and complimentary. I ordered an iced tea with lemon, and Mr. Beck followed suit. As the hostess handed us menus, Mr. Beck said, "I hope you're hungry, Michael."

I could only come up with one answer: "Yes, I am indeed."

"That's good," he said. We ordered lunch and delved into conversation headfirst. "I don't know what you've heard, but I went into Charles's office yesterday and took his computer out from under him. Just like you said to do. When he reacted like a maniac, I knew you were right. When he became violent, I knew it beyond all doubt." He took a deep breath. "I sent the computer to an expert and he recovered the file you claimed would be there. And you were right, it was there. He sent the erroneous bid. He sent it and it cost us years."

I was sad that Charles would risk our livelihoods to feed his greed. For a second, I actually felt pity for him.

He continued, "When Charles reported the Pentagon bid failure to the board last January, he wanted you out of there as fast as possible. I thought to myself, this is unlike Charles, but given a few other factors he threw in, true or not, he convinced the board to allow him to fire you. So we relented and granted him his wish."

Then the pity vanished. I remembered Charles telling me that it was he who tried to save my job. And now I was hearing a completely different side. But I kept that other part to myself, as I didn't want to interrupt Mr. Beck.

He continued, "But now, I can see the entire situation differently. I want you to know that I fired Charles yesterday, and I'm offering you his job today. Would you be interested?"

I squirmed in my chair, a bit lost for words. Maybe he said, if I heard him right, I could have my old job back.

All I could manage was a high-pitched "Pardon me?" I chastised myself mentally for making him repeat himself.

Mr. Beck repeated, "Michael, I'm here to offer you Charles's job. It was insane that you were fired in the first place, but now I understand that Charles had to remove the person who would have been able to catch his miscalculations. Do you accept the position?"

I answered his question with a question. "How much does it pay?" Mr. Beck leaned forward and in a dignified, low voice said, "$750,000 a year salary, and stock options worth one and a half million. Bonuses, depending on performance, can quadruple your salary."

As he started telling me this, I looked towards the ocean and down to the bottom of the stairs. Just on the right side of it, one morning a long time ago, I fell asleep on the sand at the foot of these stairs. I remembered that old woman hitting me with her umbrella. "Oh, go get a job" is what she bellowed at me. That scene took place a mere eighty feet from me, but a lifetime ago. I was a wretched mess then, and look at me now. In that second, I was lost in the time-space continuum as I remembered standing up from the sand and looking this way, to see if anyone was looking. And now, I was looking back. I was looking back at myself, saying and telling that man, "Don't give up." I looked back across time to say to myself, "I'm here, and I'm looking back at you, and I'm saying have faith, and don't give up on God."

For a second, I was paralyzed in the memory of that morning when I woke up to my first day of being totally homeless. And now, eighty feet from that point of realization, God was truly and radically changing my life.

I snapped to the sound of Mr. Beck's voice asking, "What's the matter? All right, I know the salary is lacking. All right, I'll raise it to $980,000. In two years, when things get back to normal, we'll make it $1,600,000 a year. Say something."

"I think your offer is just fine, Mr. Beck. I'm honored by your confidence and I hope I won't let you down. Can I start today?"

"Sure, the day's half over, but absolutely. That's what I expected from you, Michael, hunger," Mr. Beck replied. He had no idea.

I sat relishing this delicious moment. Mr. Beck went on how he dissected the bids with the help of my Excel printout. I told him, "Mr. Beck, whenever I wondered what I would do if I ran the company, I decided I would diversify our client listing. I mean, let's break into other markets apart from just the Pentagon. What do you think?"

To my surprise he said, "I've had the same idea, and that's why I hated watching Charles sit there doing nothing about it for half a year. When that bid didn't come through, I said to myself, 'There's a sign if I ever saw one that told me it was time to spread to other markets.'" The satisfaction of the moment drew a silence to ponder the coincidence of having the same objectives for BriMar.

After lunch, we drove separately to BriMar and met up in the parking lot. I opened the front doors for him and asked the receptionist to have Adam, Larry, and Claire meet us in the Executive Suite. I followed Mr. Beck as he led me to the Executive Offices. People actually stopped and stared at the sight of us walking down the hall. We walked through the Executive Suite bullpen and proceeded to the office reserved for the president of the company. We all greeted Eveleen as we walked to the open doorway. Inside, there was no sign of Charles. It was completely barren except for the vacant desk, chair, and empty cabinets.

Mr. Beck turned to me and said, "It's your office now, Michael." I was dumbfounded. I heard the words over lunch, but as I walked into my new office, it really sank in. I was back. I turned around and saw everybody huddled in the doorway to watch.

Larry, Adam, and Claire walked up as Mr. Beck announced to everyone within ear shot, "Folks, let me reintroduce you to the new president of BriMar Industries, Michael Whiley."

They applauded. I was embarrassed, but you couldn't tell by my ear-to-ear grin. "Thank you," I said to them. I was taken up by the euphoria that swept the room, especially between my friends.

Mr. Beck excused himself, saying, "I'll call Ralph and start the paperwork. Welcome back."

Out of respect, I walked Mr. Beck back to the front door. I shook his hand again and said, "Mr. Beck, the best is yet to come."

"I believe you, Michael," he said before he walked out the front door.

I walked back to my office and found my three friends waiting for me. Someone closed the door behind me and then we all gave such a loud whoop we practically shook the walls. We could not stop laughing, hugging, and celebrating the moment.

"Welcome back," Claire said with a hug.

Larry asked, "Congratulations! How did you do it?"

"He found it in Charles's computer," I replied.

Adam piped in, "You always had a hunch, and look how it turned out."

"I gave him the clues where to look," I said.

Happy to have me back, Larry and Adam left to return to their offices. On her way towards the door, Claire asked, "Want to catch some dinner tonight?"

I said, "Sure, I'll call you." And then she left.

Eveleen walked in and I could see she was feeling uncomfortable. She said, "I just want you to know that I'm here to help until you decide on someone to hire, or have Claire come back to work for you."

Her question threw me for a loop, so I suggested, "Sure, we'll proceed as you suggest, Eveleen, and when I get things clear in my head, then we can take that step when we get there."

I sat in the chair. I felt strange sitting in it, remembering that Charles had destroyed my life while sitting in this very chair. I'd have to get rid of it along with the desk. I wanted to start everything clean.

Eveleen returned with pads to write notes. "I have to start with my own desk, phone, chair, everything."

Out of respect for her twelve years working for Charles, I didn't say anything demeaning about him. "If you could order the essentials, I'll look for furniture later today," I told her.

Over the next hour, she and I both filled page after page with my to do list, my to buy list, my to meet with list, my call list, and finally my to read list that included financial statements for the first two quarters, plus other reports, months of press releases, and so forth.

When the phone rang, she answered it. She looked at me, smiled, and said, "Michael Whiley's office." She listened to the other person and put them on hold. "Would you pardon me? May I take this call at my desk? I'll be right back."

"Of course," I replied.

She left and closed the door behind her. I could hear her words, "Michael Whiley's office," still bouncing through my head.

I was once again in awe of the rocket speed God had taken to give me back this life that I once knew. Well, almost. I went to lock the door.

I pulled the chair forward and rested my elbows on the desk to fold my hands in prayer. "You did this. You did all of this, and from this very chair and space he destroyed my life, and look where You have brought me, oh Lord." Addressing God out loud, I said, "How can words describe my humility knowing that You, oh Lord, maker of everything, reached down into this world and made this happen?"

Without having to search my memory, God reminded me of that time I prayed for Charles and the board when I got home the day I got fired. And from the power of praying for those who genuinely betray and hurt us, I gave God the license to get involved, always remembering and never forgetting "Vengeance is mine says the Lord."

There was a knock on the door, startling me out of prayer. Then the phone buzzed. It was Eveleen calling me on the intercom announcing Ralph was calling.

I picked up the phone and Ralph screamed in my ear, "Well done, congratulations! I can't believe it, but you did it!" We laughed hard. I busted my gut laughing at so many absurd things in my life. My laughter was uncontrollable as I pounded my fist on Charles's desk. Finally, when my throat became raspy, I caught my breath and settled down.

He told me to drop by later that day or the next so we could talk about the details of my new arrangement with BriMar.

When our conversation was over, I got up to go home. I told Eveleen that I would return the next day. And then I just laughed at myself some more.

After a fun dinner with Claire, I drove home and reflected how this day started, and who knew it was going to turn out like this? Throughout the night, I paced the apartment as I was bursting with immeasurable hope. I turned on my laptop and started writing notes, as I had my very own brainstorm. When the rush wore thin, and my body begged for sleep, I crashed in bed, curled up to my new laptop.

The next morning, before anything else, I was aware of a bliss running through my veins. The floor felt three feet below me as I made my way to get ready for what might be the happiest day of my life this year.

I paused to think that if it weren't for God's protection, we would all be merciless victims of unimaginable powers of evil.

But God overwhelmed me with His blessings beyond all my expectations. He orchestrated this whole affair, and today He's chosen me to run this company.

Being president, I could go into the office anytime I want to. Right? I slowly pulled myself together, and as I was ready to start walking towards the door, I stopped and sat on my new sofa.

I basked in the moment and realized the immenseness of this amazing opportunity. I contemplated just how a little more than a month and a half ago this day would have seemed like mockery in my daydreams. In prayer, I asked God for His guidance in this new job. I'd never been president of anything before. I thanked Him for His magical and mysterious ways in bringing my life around. And every day, I shall thank Him for revealing Himself to me. I know many people wait their entire life for God to show Himself, and yet He took time out of running the universe to reveal Himself to me.

My first meeting that morning was with Eveleen. I assured her that her job was secure and I would very much like for her to stay if she would have me for a boss. Eveleen was agreeable to stay, but her concern went to Claire.

"I'll handle Claire, and everything will be fine," I told her.

The day was filled with meetings, more financial reports, phone calls, and more financial reports. If we were going to revive this company, then we were going to have to look at each division and give it a diagnostic test for survivability.

At the end of the first day, I called Claire and asked her to dinner. It was casual, and she was excited to hear about my day. Over dinner she brought up the subject of her wanting her old job back. But I explained to her that there would not be a place for Eveleen if it weren't for this position. I explained, "Without this, she would be terminated, and at her age I'd rather not do that. I hope you would stay where you are."

She thought for a moment and then sighed, "I was just really hoping things could go back to the way they used to be."

How odd that things could never ever be like they used to be, I thought to myself. If there's one place that's gone for good, the past really shows us that's it's gone forever.

Claire snapped out of it, sat up, and said, "But I'm happy for Eveleen. I know she fits perfectly where she is. I do not see any need to disrupt her life."

They were words I would expect from someone who is mature enough to look beyond herself and genuinely wish for someone else's well being. Isn't that the essence of God's teachings? Putting yourself second, even third, or fourth?

We both got a little quieter. Truthfully, I'd thought of her and having fun with her too often. But I would never say such a thing like that to her. But I also really enjoyed sitting in silence with her.

Dropping her off at her house, I told her, "This doesn't mean we still can't have dinners or lunches together, or even catch a movie."

She smiled and said, "Of course. Good night, I'll see you tomorrow."

For the next three weeks I threw myself into learning the job. I met with every department head and their directors. I already knew almost everyone and their work objectives. I had come to appreciate the art of listening. I consciously trained my mind to be without any prejudgment.

After all, since I got my second chance I really did want to do things differently than before. What's the point of getting a second chance if you're going to waste it by doing the same things the same way, time and again? What's the point if you're going to approach people the same way, with the same old attitude, after you've had a wake-up call from the grips of death?

Second chances are about moving the rudder of your life with a different approach. In the split-second time I had to react, I hoped I would choose an approach that reflects the best choices He would make.

A different approach would be to daily give that person a new blank page, one without prejudgments, without fault or blame. That's what He would do, and does, daily. Just look at me.

And this time around, I wanted to infuse my life with compassion. Let compassion be the invisible board member in the room as we consider possible cutbacks. Let compassion find its way into the equation as it relates to our staff and our product, and our shareholders. Is it possible? Can compassion find a seat in the boardrooms of corporate America?

And too quickly it was Labor Day weekend. I thought I would pass on this holiday, as I had no labor to celebrate. I sure as heck didn't feel the need to go camping. I just wanted to work through the long weekend and get a grip on the past quarter reports.

September flew by as I started creating plans to move the company from being primarily a one-customer company to branching out to Europe and Asian markets.

Over the next weeks, I went to several churches in hopes of finding one that resonated with my spirit. I could always go back to my old church. "Why would I want to do that?" I asked myself. I guess

I'll one day think about going back to my old church. One day in the distant future, I may think about it.

As we plowed into October, I marveled at how fast the days raced by. I was freaked about how it seemed like every four days it was Friday again.

When I woke up one morning, I was haunted by the beautiful memories of Rachel, since today would have been her seventeenth birthday. One year ago today, October 8th, for her sweet sixteenth, we surprised her with a huge beach party at the yacht club. We had the local favorite rock band along with her closest seventy friends on a perfect Saturday afternoon.

It's odd, I thought to myself, that I didn't even remember John's birthday back in May. Perhaps it was because I was so miserable, I didn't want to exacerbate my pain. And so I just kept it out of my head.

But today it was time to visit my kids. I left the office shortly after four o'clock, picked up five bouquets of flowers, and drove to the Santa Barbara Cemetery. I parked and walked up the slope to our family plot. My walking slowed down as memories flashed through my head. From A to Z, the memories raced across my mind in fast forward. But I kept walking.

When I arrived at our family plot, I laid the flowers on each grave. And then one by one I prayed for each of my children. Sometime, while praying for Edwin, I got the feeling that my children and God had their time together.

And with that acceptance, a wave of comfort washed over me, telling me everything was going to be okay. I pondered the weight of their sacrifice getting pulled in by God's drama. Were they still together? Or had they gone their own separate ways in God's heaven? It mattered not. I sat on the grass and floated back to my complete life with my wonderful children. I daydreamed what they would look like at their graduations. A couple hours later, it was time to leave.

When Sunday came around I drove across town to try a Southern Baptist church. On my way there, I thought to myself that I had to address my resolve with Pastor Ryan. Or did I have to? I prayed out loud, "Dear God, give me wisdom." I realized that Pastor Ryan took his role in God's play and could not have returned any of God's money back to me.

In my desperation, I had forgotten the enormity of his spiritual guidance for so many people. Oh, no, there I did it again. I opened that box emitting a sliver of forgiveness....a tiny sliver.

I thought of my friends, whom I hadn't seen in weeks, and impulsively I turned the car and headed to my old church. I planned to walk in late and sit in the back pew, just like old times.

Everything went according to plan. I listened with my mind and heart at what Pastor Ryan was saying, and I found bits of pearls inside his sermon. I noticed that when he saw me and we made eye-to-eye contact, he lost his place and stumbled in his train of thought. He took a deep breath and picked up where he left off.

When his sermon was over, Pastor Ryan walked down the aisle and took his place by the front door to greet his exiting flock. As I stood to leave, I was unexpectedly swamped by a crowd welcoming me back. I was overwhelmed by so many people who were genuinely happy to see me. And I was happy to see the many kind faces I had not seen in a long time.

Claire waved at me from a distance. I gave her the universal hand sign to call me.

There were more people gathered around me to say hello than there were making their way to leave.

Over the next twenty minutes I unintentionally held court in the foyer, laughing and shaking people's hands and getting a few hugs. My children's friends were eager to say hi and give me a smile. I looked over at Pastor Ryan, alone by the door.

As I was listening to the fifteenth person to catch me up on their life over the past year, I excused myself and walked over Pastor Ryan with my hand outstretched to greet him properly.

He shook my hand and welcomed me, "Back to the flock."

Thinking I'm not "back," I felt I should tell him. I started to say, "I'm still looking..." when he interrupted me.

"Let me show you the youth center."

I asked, "Oh, you have a new model of it?"

"Sure, we have a new model of it," he replied.

He led me around the corner of the church building, and hidden from the street was the new, full-blown, already built, youth center. I looked for a name, but it was just called Youth Center. Hey, imagine that!

I was awed by what came of that donation.

"It came in at one million two hundred thousand dollars. But without your half a million we would not have secured those matching donations. What would you like to call it?" he asked me.

"You want me to name it?" I asked.

Pastor replied, "Absolutely, whatever you want to call it."

We walked inside. Large enough to fit a full-size indoor basketball court, it was also designed to function as a second speaking hall and theater. I was amazed.

I looked around and could feel that it was filled with happiness, hope, and youthful inspiration.

I thought about a name. I offered, "How about Gabe's Youth Center? And the plaque under it will read, 'Because it's in the fire that gold is purified.'"

I remembered how challenging adolescence can be on anyone going through it. I hoped this place would serve as a haven for teens, where confusion is shut out and ignorant peer pressure is held in check at the door.

I shook his hand and in true habit I said, "See you next Sunday, Pastor."

From the hidden well of his guilt, Pastor Ryan got tears in his eyes and said, "Michael, I'm sorry for not being a better pastor for you. I'm sorry I wasn't a better friend and that I wasn't a better human being to you. I have waited and waited, prayed and prayed for this day. Prayed that I would someday ask you to forgive me for treating you with such low regard." He broke down when he continued, "With every major step forward in building this place, I always remembered it was because you made it possible, and as this place got bigger, so did my guilt. I'm so appreciative that God gave me this chance to say this to you in person, and not carry it the rest of my life. You've no idea how many times I thought that I not only let you down, but that I also let God down."

As I went to hug him, I realized he just played his part in God's drama. I reassured him, "Pastor, it's all in the past. I totally forgive you, and I'm sorry, too."

And with that, I found closure to what was a bitter and hurtful situation. And who would I blame? The situation came with a secret design and a hidden purpose we weren't aware of while we were in it. I was glad it was over.

I found more freedom by forgiving Pastor Ryan. Forgiveness allowed me to stop thinking about that hurtful time. So yes, I guess forgiveness also heals our emotional bodies.

And forgiveness brings the freedom to create new beginnings.

CHAPTER TWELVE

ALL BECAUSE OF YOU

At BriMar I created a new position, title, and budget for Claire, primarily to research the feasibility of penetrating foreign markets and to report on necessary steps to move our product through Asia and Europe.

Separately, I instructed Larry to investigate buying a helicopter company that might be interested in selling. I liked the idea of instead of just building and selling the airframe and aeronautical computer software, build and sell the whole helicopter and go from there.

In the coming weeks, with Larry's report, I submitted to the board a motion to start considering the possibility of buying another company. Although we were challenged fiscally, even a wounded lion must search out ways to kill in order to reinvigorate itself.

Truthfully, it was the only way we were going to save thirty-plus jobs, and I had to go into the red to do this. But it was worth it because at the other end we'll be a new dynamic company with more product to sell. This was long-term thinking, and I hoped the members of the board of directors would see it my way.

When Claire submitted a report to me, I told her that she needed to get to Asia and start shaking hands by the end of October. "How many meetings do you think you can set up for yourself in Asia?" I asked.

Opening her report to a specific page, she said, "Twenty."

I laughed. "I would be happy with half of that. Remember, you're not just selling our product, you're selling the entire company."

A week later, I sent Claire and Adam off to Asia. Over the course of two weeks, I got regular email updates from them, working their dog and pony show through ten major cities. Although this was just a meet and greet, it was all about first impressions. Apparently, Claire was good at it.

I heard Larry's report privately to make sure he had found a potential company to buy before I made any calls for a board meeting. We strategized for hours on how to sell it to them. I was flabbergasted at Larry's research.

During the board meeting, I delivered our completed feasibility study on purchasing another company. With his keen statistical mind, Larry was with me as back-up.

Larry reported, "There are fewer than fifty helicopter manufacturers, and only a fraction that would be feasible in our financial ballpark. We found a potential candidate in Phoenix, Arizona. Having been awarded a defense contract last January, the company was stretched to capacity and was not staying on the delivery schedule."

Mr. Beck asked, "What's the name of the company?"

Here's the best part.

Larry answered, "Rabill Corporation. The company that was awarded *our* Pentagon contract last January. Well, apparently it's overstretched and quite vulnerable to a buyout."

I thought that if we bought this company, it would be a perfect circle. It's like a tiger whose dinner was stolen by a hyena and the tiger not only retrieving his stolen dinner, but devouring the hyena as well. Haa! I'm now committed to making this happen, whatever it takes as long as it gets approved by the board of directors.

November arrived like a huge, ringing bell announcing the end of my divorce. I was staring at one week left of my broken marriage. I considered not attending. I wouldn't need to go as long as I had Ralph there. Why would I want to see Joanne? I didn't. No need. Why open old wounds that still seemed as fresh as yesterday's killing? No, I wouldn't go if I didn't have to. Besides, I was sure she wouldn't be there.

But over lunch, and with only a few days to go, I shared my apprehensions about going to the divorce proceedings with Ralph. I explained, "There's no point for me to go. That's why I have you."

Ralph offered that it may help my closure.

I replied, "Closure? I had closure with her when I stood on the sidewalks outside of La Trattoria begging for change. I had closure with her when I shivered under a cardboard box in the middle of the night under pouring rain when it was forty-one degrees outside. I had closure when I couldn't afford to pay to see a doctor. Believe me when I say I've closed the chapter on the subject of my future ex-wife."

"Well then, will you do me a favor?" Ralph asked.

"What?" I replied with a little tone.

"Will you just pray about it?"

I nodded. He continued, "But you have to pray with a sincere heart, all right?" he said, demanding.

"Granted, always pray with a sincere heart," I said, reaffirming his condition.

When I got home, I considered my feelings about seeing Joanne. I prayed to God for His wisdom, and naturally God reminded me of my resolution to practice infinite forgiveness. Of course He would! He showed me that this principle is not limited to the depth of whom I choose to forgive, and that I cannot exclude anyone outside of the infinite. The *infinite* includes everyone known and unknown. What was I thinking?

I weighed the good points against the bad. I should walk away and not look back. Another voice beckoned to go say good-bye to the mother of my children and the woman who helped create a home and a family for most of my adult life.

I considered how getting out of one relationship affects how we open the next. If I got out of this marriage angry and hostile, would it infect my next relationship? This was my theory. But it does raise the question, "Will I ever *have* another relationship?"

So, with God and Ralph prodding, I did an about face and decided to go to the divorce proceedings.

The night before was torturous. Images and memories of Joanne crashed down on me every time I came close to falling asleep.

She gave me her best, and then she gave me her worst.

Finally, November 7th arrived. The most dreaded and anticipated day of my entire life. Yet another milestone day in my life as I was getting my small fortune back.

In the limousine ride to the Beverly Hills Courthouse, Ralph and I analyzed my financial books as they were kept up to this time by a court appointed trustee. Ralph pointed out that my personal wealth increased by fifteen percent in funds and stocks in the last four months. I reflected to four months ago and knew that it was in August that God paid me a visit and made me a promise. How funny.

In June, I was to come into $2.6 million but now it was closer to $3.1 million. Besides my salary and newly acquired stock assets, my wealth was now closer to $3.7 million.

I was amazed and yet not surprised. I mean, I have lived my life in a perpetual state of surprise. And this was just more evidence of God keeping His promise. I just hoped to keep up my end of the deal. And the fact that I was sitting in this car going to release Joanne of her guilt showed that I was also keeping my promise to Him.

Our limo dropped us at the front entrance of the courthouse on Burton Way. Inside, Ralph and I took our seats in the courtroom and waited for the judge to arrive. A group of lawyers settled in at the opposite table as Joanne sat down with them.

Joanne and I looked at each other. Once we locked eyes, I swear I thought I saw hers say, "I'm sorry."

I had so many feelings in those couple minutes: anger, betrayal, love, memories, sadness, confusion, and even compassion.

There was an empty canyon in my gut. But I knew that *time* is like a train with an engine that won't slow down for me, for her, and not even for the earth.

And *time*, I believe, will heal the gaping hurt I carried in my heart.

I thought I was going to be more ambivalent, because I wasn't prepared to have these wounds opened and have questions staring me in my face. Of course, I played my poker face and showed nothing of the silent screams raging in my mind.

After the judge entered and walked up to her bench, Ralph proceeded with the fifty-fifty split proposition. And because of the thorough preparation on his part, the whole process took about an hour. Ralph handed me some papers to sign.

A lousy, stinking one hour and the final nails were hammered into the courthouse records. My life as I once knew it will only live in my memory and on these documents. Then it was over.

Ralph and I moved to the exit and proceeded down the hall to the elevator. Joanne caught up to me as I waited for the elevator. She motioned to me to step towards her. I excused myself to have a private conversation. I was dreading to actually have to talk to her, but I felt obligated to give her the moment.

Joanne confessed, "Michael, I just want you to know that I'm sorry I left you, but I was scared. Michael, only death and destruction followed you. I was scared for my life. Was I going to be next?"

I believed she was scared. But I never imagined that she was scared for her life. But looking back on it, her fear may have saved her.

Regardless, I said, "Okay, I'll give you that one, but taking all our money and leaving me penniless? Why would you ever do that to me? I remember the day we wed...until death do us part...we both said it. I meant it. I would rather have died for you than ever leave you, Joanne. You let me down."

She replied, "Michael, I had to make sacrifices, too. I had to choose between being with you or being dead. I've missed you every living day of my life. But with this over, I'm sure we'll pick up our lives."

Her words were like arrows of truth shooting through me. I now had a deeper understanding of how Joanne played her role in God's drama, a role she nothing to say about. She was an actress in God's three-act play He called my life.

I didn't want to admit to her that I missed her, too. "I guess there's nothing left to say..." I said. But what came out of my mouth wasn't what was going through my mind. Silently, I wished that we could spend an hour, a day, a week, a month talking about things we once knew; talking about a place we once shared; talking about a grief no one else could understand. And from my heart I said, "I forgive you, Joanne. I would never have denied you fifty percent of anything."

"I know," she said tearfully. And with that she and her pack of lawyers stepped into the elevator. Realizing this was our last moment together, I looked at her for the last time. I tried to smile, but my half smile could only register sadness.

And with a wave of her hand, she sent me her last kiss.

All I could hear were Gabe's words: "God is your only soul mate."

During the quiet ride home on the 101 north, I recalled driving this highway coming back from Bel Air when I went looking for her. I recycled the confusion and pain that filled me that day, and there it was again – that infinite forgiveness He branded in my heart.

But today was today, and the cold metal spear of abandonment that was lunged through my heart on that distant dark day was forever buried.

In this world of so much pain and terror we inflict on one another, how can we ever find a trickle of love to forgive each other of huge crimes committed against us? Only in God can you find enough love. Or, perhaps with *time*, when the spinning wheel of the earth grinds at your petty hate and your petty anger just a little bit every day, you'll find the freedom you've longed for.

Later, back at Ralph's office, we started the process of money transfers and changing the certificates into my name.

Ten days later, I was once again a multi-millionaire with personal assets of $3,650,000. It seemed all so very strange and artificial. I returned Ralph's $50,000 in the very same suitcase he had given me. I rolled it up to his house, and when he unzipped it he found it full of 20s, 50s and 100s. I had printed out on legal size paper the words "In God We Trust." I laid the paper across the neat piles of cash inside the luggage.

A week later, with the approval from the board to buy Rabill, the staff moved into a higher gear as we began to reshape the company to help it capture a bigger market share.

I knew we couldn't fail. Because of His promise in the Tea Gardens, I had an ocean of faith that He was going to blow things up out of proportion. I had to give God the whole world as His net to fill with His abundance.

One Sunday afternoon after church, Claire and I went hiking up the water falls behind Montecito. It was a good hike and a perfect day. When we stood above the falls, I stepped closer to Claire for her safety. But as our arms brush by each other, I was struck by the realization that I'd been unconsciously flirting with her the whole afternoon. Holy cow, I slid into this frame of mind totally unaware of an attraction I'd developed to her. Keeping in mind that she worked for me, I had to drive such thoughts away.

At the office, Eveleen brought up the subject of Thanksgiving, and it got me thinking about what I wanted to do for that occasion. I decided to book a large private dining room for ten adults and about eight kids at the Four Seasons.

From out of nowhere, I called Claire and asked her if she had plans for Thanksgiving. She said "yes," but then "no."

I invited her to join my gang of friends and their families for dinner. I even offered to drive.

When Thanksgiving Day arrived, I found myself waiting in the car for her in front of her house. She appeared at the door and I could see that she had put a considerable amount of effort into making herself look really nice. *Really* nice.

Holy cow, this is not a date, I thought to myself. But out of nowhere, I bolted out of the car and went around to open the door for her. I didn't know where this impulse came from, but I suddenly found myself holding the door open for her as if this were a date.

"Thank you, Michael, I hope I'm not overly dressed," she said sheepishly.

"Not at all, you look...really nice," I said.

After I got back in the car she asked, "Why did you open the door for me?"

"I don't know, it was just an impulse when I saw how beauti...nice you look," I replied. But I also noticed how uneasy I'd become. I shook it off and pulled into traffic.

Her perfume wafted through the car like a fragrance mixed by angels. From where I'd been, I'd smelled too many garbage bins than I'd like to admit.

We arrived at the seasonally decorated private dining room and found everyone cheerfully celebrating.

I had arranged for Claire to sit next to me. And through dinner, we all laughed and spoke of things we were grateful for. I didn't know exactly when, but at some point through dinner, I think I fell for her. Hearing her laughter and the way she conversed with the others, I stumbled into that weird and funny feeling of infatuation. And it seemed the perfect thing to do, in this perfect time, in this perfect room.

Afterwards I drove her home. I opened the car door for her and extended my hand to help her out. When she stood up, she was close to me. In a flash, I asked myself, if not now, when? So I impulsively kissed her on her lips. It was a clumsy kiss, full of hesitation and self-doubt. Realizing how poorly I just handled myself, I said, "Oh, no." And I knew I had to kiss her again to make up for the first disaster.

So I leaned in to her, closed my eyes, and as we both fell into a lingering kiss I thought of what I was doing and said, "Oh, no" again.

She abruptly pulled back and asked, "What's wrong now?"

I said, "What's wrong? There are too many things going wrong right now to list them all."

She shook her head and contradicted me. "But haven't you heard that if you get just a couple of the wrongs together, then it turns into a right? Just relax because you don't have to live your entire life in this moment, right now."

Hearing her advice, I cared not for logic or rationales. We both leaned in to kiss again, but she pulled back and said, "I should go. I can't do this if you're my boss."

I looked at her in disbelief and asked, "But what did you just say about enough wrongs can make a right?"

Confusion overtook her face. "Uh, aah...but I work for you," she stammered.

I thought to myself, there's only one thing to do and that is to fire her. "Fine, you're fired," I said to her. I caught myself and said, "Gee, I've never said those words to anyone before."

She looked me in the eye and asked, "What? What was I thinking? You're my boss."

"Not anymore, I just fired you. You're fired," I reminded her.

Bewildered, Claire asked, "You're going to fire me just so you can kiss me again?"

Sheepishly, I looked down and asked, "Was that what I was thinking? Yes!"

She pulled back and gave me a terse "Good night." She started walking up the grassy slope to her front door.

"Good night," I replied, slapping my hand against my forehead. I thought to myself, "Oh, man, what was I thinking? What have I done? I've ruined my friendship with Claire."

Halfway up the grassy knoll she turned around and ran towards me. She ran down the slope so fast she slammed into me, and my back bent backwards into the car. She wrapped her arms around me, kissed me, and said, "Did you really fire me?"

I replied, "Sure, why not? If that's what you want?"

"Let me get back to you on that."

And then she turned around again and walked back up the lawn to her front door. Just like a woman. They're professionals at keeping men on hold.

"Wow, what was that?" I asked myself. I got in the car and drove home. How many spinning plates could I possibly have in the air at once? What was I thinking? Okay, I don't want to get ahead of myself.

I was more than relieved to have the divorce behind me. It was tough enough knowing there was a final date to my marriage. And after it was over, I was never the same. I was better.

It was the first of December and there's that thing they call the Christmas Season. I was not ready for Christmas, yet. It carried too many powerful memories.

I called Claire on her cell phone. By now, we figured that if I called her on the regular hard line, it was business. But if I called her on her cell phone then it was not business. I asked her out again and I was not surprised when she said yes.

Over the first couple weeks in December, Claire and I built a friendship that brought out parts of me that I thought were dead and gone. She was inquisitive and nurturing. There's a secret we men have. Sometimes when we happen to quietly catch a woman brushing her hair, or doing something womanly, it strikes a spark in us men and we silently go, wow. Those moments don't happen often. Unbeknownst to her, she had done that to me a couple times lately.

Claire and I spent many evenings together until about ten o'clock and then we'd go our separate ways. And yes, it was starting to become apparent to too many people.

As Christmas approached, I decided to do something very un-Christmas-like and maybe get out of town. I was neither ready nor interested in going through that ceremonious indulgence in so much material exchange. The happiness that I lived last Christmas was still fresh in my heart and too tender to rekindle, and I felt I had to escape their memories. I had to get out of town. Go someplace where I could get away from all this Christmas.

I invited Claire to go skiing with me in Aspen. She passed on her Christmas visit with her family in Reno to spend it with me.

I reserved two rooms at the Jerome for eight days. It'd been a long time since I had gone skiing. We rented some equipment and hit the slopes. It is remarkably awesome how we can play in God's rain turned to snow, packed gingerly high up on His mountaintops, and slide down them on these little planks called skis.

Claire made me feel bigger than life. And just as she pulled away from me to ski down the hill, I thought to myself, "I think I could love this woman."

A true test of any blossoming or long-term relationship is, do they make you feel like you could conquer the world? Or do they make you feel under it? And Claire always made me feel like I could do anything. This true ultimate test can be applied to whatever relationship, whenever or wherever.

One afternoon while Claire was reading a book by the fireplace, I took a walk down a street and found myself turning into a jewelry shop. I hadn't been in one of these shops in a long time. With Joanne's thirst for gems and jewels, I learned to appreciate expert craftsmanship in fine jewelry. I meandered into and out of shops for the next few hours.

That evening, I took Claire to an outdoor lounge called 39 Degrees Lounge inside the Sky Hotel. Under a perfect starry night, next to a blazing fire reflecting off the pool, I whispered to Claire, "I knew I was falling for you when you first appeared at your door on Thanksgiving. Do you remember saying you would do anything for me? I need you to do just one more thing."

With hardly anyone nearby, I got down on one knee and pulled out a little black velvet box. Her shock bounced wildly through her mind and she shouted, "Oh, NO!" And I hadn't even opened the box yet.

Still in shock, she repeated, "Oh, no."

I burst out laughing because that's the funniest thing I had heard all my life. I fell off balance and my butt landed on the pavement and I rolled over laughing. I laughed because it was the last answer I was ever expecting.

"Yes! I said yes!" she screamed at me.

She fell on top of me, making sure I heard her repeating, "Yes."

"Yes what. I haven't even asked you anything!"

As I looked up at her, she leaned down to kiss me. Then she lifted her face to look down at me. The tears in her eyes made them twinkle just like the stars dazzling across the galaxy behind her.

After reconfirming for the sixth time that she would marry me, I let her open the box to reveal two carats of Aspens' best.

I asked, "Will you marry me?"

"Yes."

I slid her engagement ring on her finger. She was awestruck and so was I. It was a safe guess that she was going to like the two-carat, princess cut, solitaire diamond mounted on white gold.

A couple days later, on the morning of December 31st I woke up feeling sad. It was one year ago when my life spun out of control.

I spent the day with Claire, and I knew she could see the shift in my demeanor. I had flashes of memories that I was not sure if I wanted to welcome or chase away. Confusion only made my sadness worse.

I confessed that I had no party in me to go out and celebrate the new year. I told her, "I just want to spend it alone in my room, and pass it very low key."

Tenderly, she glided her hands through my hair and said, "I completely understand. You don't have to explain anything."

So that evening I kept to my room and refrained from watching anything about New Year's Eve on TV. I did try to lose myself in a movie, but the movie wasn't enough to distract me from the memory of my life one year ago that night.

I turned the TV off and sat on the floor against the wall. And in the silence, I looked back across the year and saw that my life ran the gamut of human conditions to the very extreme. I remembered times when I was certain I was going to die. Pondering who I was, I asked, Was that me? Yes, that was me. And whoever that was will always be with me.

I started noticing the clock, as though I was tracking in my head our movements to the minute one year ago.

I dared to stare into the abyss. And the abyss stared back at me with an empty hollowness that suffocated me, as if I were drowning from a lack of peace.

I folded my hands in prayer. "God, please fill this vacuum. Take my anger, take my confusion, and above all, take my sadness." In my head I asked what could be the most important thing I could ask of God, and without any prodding or imagination, these words came up from my heart: That He may never lose sight of me. I know that as long as He knows where I am, it's all going to be okay.

I considered that He is the wind that rushes by me and that's how He knows where I am. He is the sunlight shining everywhere, every day, on everything I do. I have absorbed the truth that there could be no sunlight nor ocean without Him *being* the sunlight and the ocean.

We must stop separating God from that which we see with our eyes.

I prayed for my children. I prayed for Joanne and asked God to fill her life with His happiness and drown her in His love.

I had no doubt that Joanne, wherever she may be that very evening, was taking a look at her life one year ago this night. I felt sad that I couldn't reach out to her for a hug. She's the only other person on earth who might understand my pain. And through my tears I chuckled when I recalled her sizzling diva persona that night. She was beauty with its many prisms. She was illuminated with life and she dazzled everyone with her touch. Tears came at the memory of such happiness.

And then the storm hit. It could have been known as the perfect storm that involved another trio of forces: God, Satan, and of course the pawn, me.

I asked myself about a resolution for the new year. But I thought I would pass, as I was still working on last year's resolution.

One month later, on January 30th, at forty-three years of age, I married Claire by the shores of Lake Tahoe. The entire battalion of friends and coworkers were summoned away for a three-day weekend and flown to Lake Tahoe to witness our union in matrimony. I hired experts to arrange the details for securing planes, luxury buses, hotel floors, limousines, and for Pastor Ryan to perform the ceremony. The crowning part of this extravagant event was the estate we rented for the week. It sat on the water and had its own pier, boats, and staff.

With Claire's family attending from nearby Reno, we filled the makeshift chapel by the water's edge. Under a blue sky and snow capped mountains, we exchanged our vows in front of over two hundred guests. And as we spoke our vows, I believed that God will this time do His part to help us keep these vows.

Within a month of getting married, Claire got pregnant. That summer we purchased an oceanfront house in Summerland. Our house sat right on the water with full beach view. Living at the ocean, I know I walked by this very house on those long walks contemplating my woes. Who knew that time and space conspired to laugh at us?

September brought the arrival of our first son, Andrew. He came healthy and with a smile. Claire took maternity leave and decided to make her leave permanent. Who could blame her? I would be happy, too, if I could hang out by the ocean all day with a child who does nothing but love me. That would be all right with me.

Over the weeks and months, when I found myself at crossroads, I asked myself how much of that "other" life I would allow to rule me, and how much would I discard. I didn't want to go looking for answers in the past. They were not there.

I learned valuable lessons during that time. I couldn't let that sacrifice on my part go to waste by doing things just like everyone else, just because everyone else was thinking or doing something a certain way. I had to be okay when I didn't always fit in.

I had to accept being different, because He expects me to be different.

And so, I went back to the Tea Gardens in my mind. I believed in time I will have all the answers revealed to me. Isn't that His promise, that He will give us all the answers to all the questions we could ever ask?

And I continued to be aware of my opportunities to tithe.

A year after Andrew was born, Claire delivered a baby girl, Brittany, into our world. What a happy day it was when we brought her home to meet her older brother. It was an odd feeling, as if I had lived this day once before, bringing a baby girl home to meet her older brother for the first time.

The year flew by as I once again tried to balance work commitment with my family obligations. And of course, work always came in second. Well, not always. My investments continued showing profits as my assets reached almost five million dollars. And that year's resolution was "infinite patience." I hoped to practice it with my children and in everything I do.

During a very intense negotiation phase with a European customer in Hamburg, Germany, we were not making any progress and I left feeling like the deal was going to crash and burn. I got on the next plane home and while in the air at 35,000 feet I silently asked God for His help to resolve this dilemma. From outside of me I heard the words, "I made the universe, don't you think I can make this happen?"

I knew it was Him. Besides actually answering me, He was reminding me that He can even hear my thoughts. It was another one of those moments when He showed me how close He really is and that He is not afraid to reveal Himself, once He's out of the box.

It was hard to believe that just after turning forty-five, Claire got pregnant again. I knew she was already a bit overwhelmed with the two kids, so we hired a nanny and a housekeeper.

Two years and two months after we were married, Claire delivered a second son. It took us three days to come up with a name for him, but I gave in to Claire when she wanted to call him James. I liked it.

Although I still donated money to my local church weekly, I took my tithing global. God put it in my heart to address healing people in rural America and third world countries. It was in other ways that I came to understand the dynamics of giving. Drinking water was a scarce commodity in many parts of the world, and I put a bit of focus there.

Over the next two years, BriMar's investment in Asia and Europe started showing contracts and potential deals worth nearly half a billion dollars. I found myself intentionally not doing things a certain way just because I had done them that way in the past. With this attitude, I was able to redefine myself and allow that second chance to come through my life in a revitalized way. A couple times a day I'd consciously take a second and ask myself, "How do I want to handle this? Like the old way? Or is this a chance to take a different approach?" And I did this from work to every relationship I had.

All parents share a special moment when we walk through the front door at the end of the day. I kept a secret to myself; sometimes when I came home, as I entered the door, for a split second I had the same feelings like I felt in my past life. I smiled at the sight of Andrew wobbling towards me to give me a hug. I had flashes of John doing the same thing.

The contracts paid out, and my company stocks and bonuses propelled my financial worth to seven million dollars before my forty-eighth birthday.

Over the next four years we tripled our orders, sending the company profits skyward. Of course, I knew it was God. God was behind it all.

We tithed half a million dollars to our same church (who knew I would ever do *that* again) and another million dollars around the world.

I'll never forget a dream I had one night that year. In it I was driving down a multi-lane freeway like the ones in Los Angeles. I was going along with traffic at 65 miles an hour, but I just happened to be doing it in reverse. As I calmly changed lanes, I could see the other drivers facing me, since my back was to the forward movement of traffic. It was all so natural and composed.

The next morning as I got in my car I remembered the dream and asked myself what the significance was of the car going forward, yet in reverse? Was my life going backwards? The answer came from outside of me as I heard the words, "A son of God does not need his eyes to see."

I was stupefied by the answer and awed that I heard it. I really heard a voice say those very words. This was never anything I could have come up with on my own. Nor, could my imagination ever come up with an answer so bold.

Several years later at fifty-two, my salary, stocks, and bonuses sent my net worth upwards of twenty million dollars. Claire and I financed the building of five hospitals deep in various poverty stricken areas around the world.

The next four years passed in a speeding blur. Although I was fifty-six, I felt more like forty—okay, forty-five. My net worth climbed to thirty million dollars. My hair was showing gray, but I fought it. Maybe one day I'd relent and let it be its natural color, but not as long as money can buy color.

Sometime that winter, Mr. Beck passed away. Unbeknownst to me until the reading of his will, he left me personally five million dollars, and one million shares of stocks from his vast holdings to start a charity. Not a million dollars, a million *shares*, which were currently valued at sixty-five million dollars. And it was only one half of his entire financial portfolio. I was dumbfounded, humbled, and speechless. I was so profoundly moved by this honor, I could hardly articulate words and barely spoke to anyone throughout the day and night.

Claire and I started a world-wide charity foundation with the sixty-five million dollars. I thought perhaps my friend Mr. Beck left me this gargantuan mountain of money because he knew I would handle it responsibly, and that I would likely put his name on it. Because as we all knew, I surely didn't want my name on it.

With Mr. Beck's donation, our foundation worked with a motor home manufacturer and built one hundred medical clinics that traveled throughout the country all year long. This mobile medical outreach program reached thousands of poor people in large cities, and people who couldn't get medical attention because of living in isolated parts of rural America.

About three years later, still feeling young at fifty-nine, I was talking with my friend Terry, now a Santa Barbara real estate mogul, when he mentioned that the three story French Chateau that we so admired in Montecito was for sale. Terry said, "The asking price is $22 million, but I think they'd be willing to go down to twenty."

I threw in my fake insult, laughed, and put in a bid at fourteen million. Offering eight million in cash up front, I was able to squeeze them down to a final price of sixteen million dollars.

And the best part was, I surprised Claire and the kids. The day I took the keys, I got the family in the car and drove there. I parked off the pavement in front of the mansion and asked, "Honey, how much do you think that mansion is worth?"

I was just remembering a moment in my life that made its way around the wheels of space and time, and found birth in this new world.

"I don't know, why?" she asked.

"I just thought I'd ask," I answered.

Confused, she asked, "You got us all in the car and drove us over here to ask me that?" I put the car in gear and drove up to the gate. "What are you doing?" she asked.

I looked at her while holding the remote to the gate and said, "Honey, kids, Abracadabra." I pointed the remote at the gate and it opened.

The kids went, "Wow."

I drove up the driveway to the massive front doors. Claire bellowed, "What are you doing?"

I turned the car off and said, "Welcome home, everybody! It's your new home, kids." The kids rushed out and started yelling and running around the yard.

"You rented this?" Claire asked.

Suddenly, I was really nervous. I managed to stumble, "Uh, no, I, we bought it."

"Oh, no, you did not buy this house without talking to me about it first!" she yelled.

"Yeah, I sort of did, because you would have said that we couldn't afford it, and I didn't want that *doubt* floating in space, so I just stole it for sixteen million dollars! Yee haw!"

I got out of the car and ran to the kids, shouting, "Think of the fun times we're going to have!" Spontaneously, the kids and I started dancing like little happy fools. "They came down from $22 million! We stole it right out from under them! I could sell it tomorrow for twenty million and make a four million profit, but who would want to do that?"

She continued yelling, "Sixteen million dollars?" The kids and I formed a circle of happy, dancing feet.

I looked at Andrew, Brittany, and James, and realized that they were about the same age John, Rachel, and Edwin were when we had that conversation in another life. That other world seemed like it was just yesterday. This milestone day was another weird and wonderful cog that turned the wheels of time, and I relished living in His timing.

Claire got out of the car and walked to the front door. She tried her best to be mad but her happiness broke out at the same time. I jumped to get the front door for her. As my hand was on the doorknob, the moment got very solemn. The kids lined up behind their mom. Naturally, in my heart I knew we didn't steal anything. This was a gift from God, saying, "Hey, I remember you."

"Your new chateau, Mrs. Whiley," I said to Claire as I opened the door for her for the first time. She and the kids stood frozen.

Again, I was yanked back in time to when we drove by this house that Sunday morning on the way to church. My three kids were asking about this place. Not in any corner of my existence at that time did I believe that one day I would be moving into this place. If you had told me back then, I would have responded with doubt. And doubt would have kept me from having it.

This was a milestone moment of our life as indicated by the dropped jaws and stunned silence. Jovially, I tried imitating Dick Van Dyke in *Mary Poppins,* and in my best cockney accent I said, "Well, let's go on in, don't be daft."

Slowly, they walked in and stood frozen in the three-story rotunda foyer.

As I looked at all this grandeur, for a second I thought that the house was just for royalty and folks way higher up in the social order than we were. But I stopped and remembered that having gone the miles I had traveled inside my heart and soul, maybe that's why I knew that this mansion fit *me* just fine. This house just might be big enough to fit my character.

With its eight bedrooms and twelve bathrooms, it came with its own projection theater and helicopter pad in the backyard. Who knew it had a helicopter pad? It was never visible from the street.

The beautiful fifteen-foot wide marble staircase is from Carrara in northern Italy. It's the same marble Michelangelo used to sculpt his *David*. The polished marble wound up all the way to the third floor.

As a kind of a joke, the house has an oval-shaped office that overlooks a real rose garden off the first floor.

This mansion will outlive everyone I know. It will be here for centuries, so I promise to give it a run for its money. Or, my money...uh, try God's money?

"When did you buy this?" Claire asked me.

"Yesterday," I replied. I watched Claire and the kids discover the house. This day will live in our memories for the rest of our lives.

All of that past experience prepared me to fill this space with wisdom, personality, and above all, love.

Over the years, we decorated it with souvenirs from our many trips around the world.

We hosted fundraisers on the lawns, far too many to count.

The years and the prosperity churned like engines that no one could stop. At sixty-one, I never thought that they would turn so quickly. It was the same year I purchased my first super-yacht. A 121' yacht with a mast longer than the entire length of the *Oh Happy Day.* We christened it *24 Karat* as a salute to the profound conversation I once had with a stranger named Gabe.

At that time, his words were like boulders of wisdom that helped me get through those horrid days of trials. *24 Karat* is a sleek, black yacht that can sail around the world in about a month's time. I had it painted black with gold font and gold trim. I later remembered that those were my high school colors. This just showed me that we are still influenced by every phase of our lives, even subconsciously.

Through the years I asked myself what God meant when He said that I was now a son to Him. One day while driving my car, I pondered the thought and finally realized that the answer might be in *who* I am. Not what I am, or what I do, but rather who I am.

I noticed at times I was overcome with waves and phases where I wanted to give away everything to anyone in need. My compassion screamed, "Please, let me help you." And in those quiet realizations I found it was Him molding me to live as a son.

And then there were times during significant events that I would just sit idly by, and it took all my energy and wisdom to do absolutely nothing. But then to see the most optimum results come about when I did not do a thing just showed me He was at work, even when I was not.

As Andrew entered college, I was about to turn sixty-three. Our family finances increased to forty million dollars.

That year I had one of the most awesome and inexplicable experiences I ever had in my life. On Saturday, March 21st, at around

4:30 p.m., while bicycling on the bike path along the ocean, I glanced over at the sun and I saw two suns. The second sun was to the right of the real sun and only slightly less intense. Initially, I thought I had double vision. Wanting to slap myself back to reality, I slammed my brakes and nearly fell off the bike in hopes of shocking myself out of this hallucination. But it continued. This was not double vision. Another bicyclist rode by, breaking my eye contact with it, yet it continued. The second sun started moving towards the first and they were both so bright that I could only look in the middle of them. The second sun continued moving towards the first until it actually moved into it. And I thought, wow. And then it was over. Or, so I thought.

But then the second sun moved out of the sun on the left side of it. It continued moving out away and then it stopped. It then moved back toward the first sun and went into it again. And then it was over. I was humbled, honored, and clueless as to what I had just experienced. Not a week went by in my life that I didn't think about that cosmic show that I believed was just for me. Let's be real, I didn't hear news reports of masses of people seeing two suns that week.

The kids grew up so fast. We watched Brittany and James graduate from college far too quickly, it seemed. Over the next couple years, we buried both of Claire's parents .

When I was sixty-seven, Andrew had his first child, making me a grandfather. It was a supremely joyful occasion, except for anyone pretending to still be young. Because when I heard that "g" word called by the toddlers, it was time to stop thinking I was still young. Heck, I think I just admitted that I might be middle-aged.

What a thrill I felt when I gave Brittany's hand away in marriage. As I sat listening to the wedding service, I watched God's love permeate the many members of my family.

Over the next few years, I watched my children start their own families. And often they came to me for advice and guidance on how I did it...twice. I never kept my other life from my children. When they were old enough to understand, I told them what happened to me and to my first family.

Mr. Beck's foundation has in the past ten years dispensed forty million dollars and is currently valued at seventy million dollars.

In his late sixties, my friend Larry passed away. He will surely be missed by a great many friends and family.

I decided to take an early retirement at seventy-six with a cash and stock buyout worth over eighteen million dollars. And this was in addition to the thirty-eight million dollars the family was already worth. We estimated the total value of our portfolio closer to fifty-six million dollars.

During those late years in our seventies, I buried my brothers, Terry and Adam. Sadly, we hadn't spent much time with one another in the last couple years, since we were hardly around.

Late one night, God awoke me as I was asleep in bed. He came as a floating ball of invisible energy. I could see through it, but it slightly distorted the background shapes. He came up my side of the bed, stopped to my left, and telepathically said, "Come with Me." And in the time it takes to change from one thought to another thought, I was instantly floating in the dark void of space looking at galaxies dotting God's black canvas. God was to my immediate left. The nearest galaxy was the size of my hand if I were to stretch my arm and spread my fingers. It was a dazzling spiral galaxy with hues of bright pink that filled out from the center. With just a thought, God said, "That's where you live."

I was gazing at the Milky Way. I froze the moment in my soul that I should never ever forget for all eternity.

And then I was instantly back in my body and completely awake. I realized my consciousness had made this quick trip with God and left my body in bed. But I was fully awake. Having had this real experience literally shocked me out of sleep. It was not a dream since I was fully awake from the second God showed up in my bedroom.

I got up out of bed and had to walk it off. I walked to the kitchen and kept taking deep breaths. I sat down and replayed it over and over again in my head. I know God can't be contained in a ball of see through material, but it was just a speck of a speck, of a speck of Him.

I "got" the idea that "a son of God doesn't need his eyes to see".

I spent my retirement traveling the oceans and distant lands with the kids and friends. Of course, I had a full-time crew of experts who oversaw everything. While sailing the Indian Ocean, at eighty-one, word came that my best friend, Ralph, passed away the night before. There was a time when hardly a day passed that I didn't speak with Ralph. I spent fifty years of my blessed life comforted, knowing I could get Ralph on the phone. Sadness overtook me when I heard the news. I returned by plane to bury him in the Santa Barbara Cemetery. My sadness lasted for weeks. Eventually, many months later, I finally learned to suppress that impulse to call him.

I watched my grandchildren have children. My, how great-grandkids can become a handful when you're eighty-eight. But those grandkids threw themselves at me like I was in my fifties. Since there are eighty-eight keys on the keyboard of a piano, I amused myself by taking piano lessons. I played an excellent air-piano by turning on the piano computer and moving my hands over the keys, pretending like I was playing the song.

And through all of this, I knew that God had watched over me every day of my life, as I kept my compass set on Him who is all things. I taught my kids about the mystery and ultimate wisdom He has for our lives. However bad times may get, we must always be patient with God to reveal understanding.

When we celebrated Claire's seventy-seventh birthday, I beamed at the perfect mother and wife she had been across the decades. She aged with grace, and our love for each other had no limits. She was a great inspiration to our large, and getting larger, family. And never for one day had she let me down.

Over the past thirty years we'd gone around the world too many times to count. We'd watched sunrises from the foothills of Kilimanjaro in Africa to the peaks of Haleakala in Maui, Hawaii; we climbed the pyramids and traveled throughout Europe with the entire family. I thought back to the days when we raced *24-Karat* from Newport to Ensenada, Mexico. I took the whole family and we worked as a team, only to come in third place. But they were now first-rate memories.

I spent my mid-nineties taking the kids' kids out on cruises across oceans and trips to the local parks. I tried to get out as often as I could. When I was home, I spent hours a day in prayer in my office. My office was right next to the elevator, so I didn't have to bother the staff much.

On my hundredth birthday, I woke up before dawn, as I wanted to be on my rooftop patio to watch the sunrise. Alone, I sat overlooking the ocean and the town in the predawn glow. As I looked at the sun, I became cognizant of my intuition telling me that this was not the year I was going to pass away.

In the early morning golden light, I looked through my telescope and I could see the Tea Gardens. It looked so close, it was as if I could touch it with my reach.

I spent this milestone birthday on the *24 Karat* out at sea, knowing the kids were planning a party at the house that evening. It was supposed to be a surprise, but I knew they were up to something. And I suspected they had invited several hundred of our closest friends.

As my driver pulled the car through the gates, I saw that they had turned the estate into a huge open circus. Holy cow, there was a giraffe and a Ferris wheel on my front lawn. There were more livestock on my lawn than at the Santa Barbara Zoo.

The year flew by, and a great deal of money was given away. One of the greatest and most fulfilling aspects of my life was being put in a position that enabled God's blessings to flow through me to help so many people in financial need.

I woke up on my hundred and first birthday and asked myself, "Am I done here? Maybe, I'm done here." And with a sweet, peaceful resolve I prayed that if He chose to take me home that year, that would be okay by me. I thanked Him for his blessings that continued to grow and prosper. Six months before, the entire family's financial wealth grew to sixty-five million dollars on top of the three million we spent keeping the family in shoes every year. And then I thought to myself, "I haven't given away enough money!"

So I went on a giving spree. And it seemed I gave to anyone and everyone who even shared a time zone with me. Over the next year, I gave away more than ninety-five million dollars, which included Beck's monies. It seemed that for as much as I gave away, my overall investments returned an astounding twenty percent of what went out to charity.

On my hundred and second birthday I woke up with a smile in my heart. I reached over and rang the bell indicating to the staff and anyone in hearing distance that I was awake. Shortly, my nurse made his appearance and greeted me warmly. In my wheelchair, I took the elevator with him to the rooftop patio for breakfast, a newspaper, and a good-morning kiss from Claire. Still full of life and love at ninety-one, she didn't look a day over eighty. I smiled up at her and kissed her hand. She greeted me with "Happy birthday" and told me the kids were planning a party in the late afternoon. I always loved seeing them.

I had always had a last will and testament since I was forty-four. My will leaves my great grandkids and everyone in between forty to forty-five million dollars. Andrew was now a grandfather himself at sixty-four. Even as old as I was, God never put me in a place where I had to bury another child, grandchild, or great-grandchild. I never had to replay that pain that suffered me gravely, burying my first three kids.

As I looked around the vista of the ocean, town, and the mountains, I reflected back on my life and in particular that year of my trials and tribulations when I was in my forties.

I don't so much remember the pain, as I do the rewards.

Because there was no greater reward on earth for me than knowing that He knows who I am.

But now I just wanted to go back to my bed and sleep some more. As I was being wheeled back to my room, I thought, if I know just one thing in this world, I know that the Infinite, He who lives in the core of the sun, knows my name. He, who so masterfully put the North Star in its perfect place, knows my name.

As Claire and my nurse helped me back under the covers, I sensed a part of me falling backwards, as if the bed didn't catch me. I saw Claire holding my hand and smiling at me.

Suddenly, I saw tiny gold sparkles. They appeared everywhere in the room. I closed my eyes and I could still see them. I opened my eyes and I could still see zillions of tiny, gold, sparkling explosions filling my sight. Everywhere I turned to look I could see them.

And then I heard Him. I could hear Him calling me. He was calling my name.

I looked up at Claire, who also calling my name and tapping my hand.

The gold particles came together to form a single pulsating, kidney-shaped light. It got bigger and bigger. It got so large, it eventually obscured everything behind it.

I closed my eyes and I could still see it. I felt a bliss I had never felt before. All the while, His voice kept calling my name, pulling me farther into the light.

But Claire, holding my lifeless hand, knew I was no longer with her.

Deep inside the light, I saw a door. It came to me.

It was trimmed in gold. I reached for the knob and slowly opened it. I saw an aisle that ran up the middle of a plane. I stepped inside and as I started walking up the aisle, I saw Him walking towards me. When He reached me, He gave me a hug.

After we broke from the hug, He gestured to me to have a seat in the overstuffed white booth. I slid in, looked out the window at the view of earth from 70,000 feet, and then turned to Him.

We smiled as I waited to hear what plans He has for me next.

Two weeks later when Claire passed away, I made sure that I was waiting for her when she stepped into Heaven.

The End.